ANNIE TA

This book is a work of fict... organisations, places, events and incidents are either products of the author's imagination or are used fictitiously.

Sample of reader's reviews for previous books in this series

<u>Book One - Things will never be the same:</u>

I could not put this book down a great read Michelle 28/8/2015. Four Stars

A good read kept me in suspense and a dramatic ending. Beverley Taylor. 6/9/2015. Four Stars

Excellent Read. Now reading Sad Man equally as gripping. Love the continuity of the characters. Andy 27/09/2015 Five Stars

<u>Book Two - Sad Man:</u>

Love the series and could not wait to get started on Sad Man and I was not disappointed. Amazon Customer October 2015. Five Stars

Another brilliant read. Maria Heath 2/2/2016. Four Stars

Fabulous could not put it down.... I can't wait to read the next one. Mrs D A Heaton 29/1/2016 Five Stars

Book Three - Joy Follows Sorrow:

Great read from a great author David Misell Mellor 27/11/2015. Five Stars

Wow fantastic third book in the John Gammon series MandoK 1/11/2015. Five Stars

Another good read can't wait for the next one Michelle 28/02/2016. Five Stars

Book Four - Never Cry On A Bluebell:

I have just finished reading this book it was equally as good as the other three. Bring on book five I am addicted.JHL 26/2/2016 Five Stars

Loved all four books, brilliant can't wait for book five. Amazon Customer 21/3/2016 Five Stars

ANNIE TANNEY

John Gammon's life hung like a silk thread blowing in the wind of destiny. Angelina sat waiting. Thirty minutes had gone by which felt like thirty hours. The white standard hospital clock seemed to be stuck in time. Angelina knew she had to stop watching it, the consequences of John dying meant she couldn't bare it. How was her relationship going to be the same ever again with Saron her best friend, when she knew she had feelings for John?

A duty nurse asked if she would like a coffee. She couldn't understand what she said, it was like she was in a cotton wool world and everything was in slow motion. If the soldiers had been a few minutes later they would both have been dead, of that there would have been no doubt.

Minutes turned into hours it was 2.00am, Angelina's phone rang it was Saron. "I am trying to get a flight back from Ireland. Mum is coming back with Aunty Annie.

ANNIE TANNEY

When I told Annie, she said she had to come she said John is waiting for her!!" said Saron. "Does she know John then Saron?" "No" replied Saron, "She's never met him but she asked me for picture and I had one taken at Lord Cote-Heaths shoot with me. I had it framed. I never told him, you know how funny he gets about being tied down. For some reason I brought it over with me. Annie Tanney said nothing will happen to him until she holds his hand. I asked what she meant she just smiled at me".

"What's happening Angelina?" asked Saron. Angelina replied, "John is in surgery, it isn't good Saron, the paramedic gave him at best a 15% chance". The phone went quiet. Angelina continued "I'm sorry Saron, I just don't want to build your hopes up". Angelina could hear Saron breaking down. Then Annie came on the phone, "We will be with you soon my dear". The phone went dead how strange she thought, but somehow she felt positive after Annie spoke to her although it was short and sweet.

Angelina was feeling totally drained, she felt very alone, her head everywhere. Her thoughts and feelings were wrong. Saron was her best friend, but it was Angelina who was sat alone waiting to hear the all the sad news.

It was 6.00am and still no sign of any news from anyone, she asked the duty nurse and all she would say was "Mr Gammon was in the best possible hands". As she walked back to the plastic seat in the corridor Sandra Scooper and Carl Milton had arrived they all hugged each other, any animosities didn't seem to matter. Sandra was concerned, both she and Carl had seen one ex work colleague murdered, and now the chances are that their boss was now in a similar dire situation.

Angelina explained what had happened with Lund and what the paramedic had said. At that point Carl had to console Sandra. "This is awful. Nurse, nurse, do we have any updates on Mr Gammon?". The nurse answered cautiously, "Are any of you three relatives?". "No, he doesn't have a family. We are his work colleagues and friends". "If you would like to step into this side office please" said the nurse, "I will get the surgeon to come and speak to you".

Angelina, Sandra and Carl entered the small office after five minutes the surgeon came in. "My name is Mr Preston, I am the head surgeon that has been operating on Mr Gammon. The good news is he is still with us and fighting for his life. We have removed one bullet which created other problems, not insurmountable, but still problems which my colleagues are working on now. The second bullet is very close to the spinal nerve if we operate there is a very likely chance Mr Gammon will never walk again. Obviously this is a decision Mr Gammon cannot take and in these circumstances a family member would normally decide". Angelina answered him, "Saron, his girlfriend, is flying in from Ireland, she will be here in a couple of hours can you wait that long". Mr Preston replied, "Yes we can wait, we are still working on the first problem. The final problem is that when he fell back off the chair, it created a small blood clot on his brain. We have to operate very shortly or this will kill him. The downside to this procedure is that we will not know if this will render him speechless, which is very common in these procedures, but we have no choice. If there is any consolation in these circumstances, Mr Gammon is a fighter. He really should not have survived these multiple traumas. I can assure you he is in the very best hands and we will do our very best for John. When his girlfriend arrives, please let the nurse know and insist that she lets me know straight away. I wish I had better news for you, but thank you" and Mr Preston left.

All three of them sat staring into space. Carl was thinking of that awful night when his beloved Beth passed away. Sandra's heart was breaking she knew she loved the man. Angelina felt guilt and remorse.

Almost two hours and fifteen minutes had passed when Saron arrived, with her was the lady whom Angelina assumed was Annie Tanney.

Annie was a diminutive lady with dark green eyes, she had slight curvature of the spine and appeared to be in her late seventies. Angelina told quickly and quietly told Saron what the surgeon had said. Saron spoke to Angelina, "Angelina, John has an uncle I think, somewhere in Sheffield. Should we let him know so he can make the decision?"

ANNIE TANNEY

"Does anyone have his number?". The problem with John was that everything was played so close to his chest and it wasn't his uncle but his father. Angelina said "I'm sorry, we don't have the time Saron". Saron signed the necessary papers and the nurse hurried to the Operating Theatre. Then Annie spoke up. "John Gammon will not die. I am here now". Everyone looked at Annie as if she was some kind of fruit loop and wasn't to be believed. Saron asked Angelina to go with her to the coffee machine.

Saron explained to Angelina, "Annie Tanney is renowned in Maam, a little village in Galway, Ireland. The people she has cured you would not believe. As a little girl she tells the story that when she was seven years of age and playing with her friend Beatrice Connor, they both saw a vision of a lady dressed in blue with a white linen headscarf. The lady held little Annie Tanney's hand and turned to her friend

Beatrice and said. "This day you are witnessing a great thing. Do not be afraid Annie I have given you the power of healing. Take this with you in life do not use the gift I give you for gain only to cure the sick". Annie's friend said there was a red glow appeared all round Annie then it turned a brilliant white and the lady had gone. The girls never discussed what had happened until they were in their early teens. Her friend's father had come back from the war and he was in a wheelchair. The girls were playing at her friend's house upstairs when they heard Mr Connor weeping downstairs. They rushed down to him. "What's a matter da?" asked Beatrice, he hadn't heard the girl's come downstairs. "Nothing Beatrice go and play". Annie looked at Mr Connor and said "you want to walk again don't you Mr Connor?" "Be off with you both, go and play". Beatrice continued, "Annie can help you da", but Mr Conner replied "Nobody can help me

Beatrice". Undaunted Beatrice continued, "Let her try da, stop being silly". Annie approached Mr Connor and lay her hands on his legs. Mr Connor later said the heat was intense and his mind wandered as if he was in a trance this lasted five minutes and then Annie stopped. "Stand up Mr Connor" Annie told him. "I can't walk girl you know that". "You can now Mr Connor", she said and she helped him up, took away his chair and he stood there. After a tentative few seconds he took his first steps in many a year. There was much rejoicing but Annie told him he could not say she had done it and made him promise. True to his words it was never spoken of again".

"Is this true Saron or just some made up Irish blarney?" asked Angelina. Saron replied, "Annie went on to cure many people, I only know because one of my mum's friends witnessed many of her healings. Me and mum were at her friend's house when you called and I was very upset, Annie Tanney was there and took control of the situation and that's why I brought her here Angelina. I have nothing to lose but everything to gain". They got their coffees and returned, Saron very anxious and Angelina confused.

It was 10.21am when Mr Preston ushered everyone into the little office. "Please, sit down. We have stopped the loss of blood from the first wound and that seems to have been successful. The small blood clot on the brain has been removed and if John was to ever recover I don't know if that will affect his speech. The bullet lodged near his spinal cord was a different story we have removed it but should he pull through he will never walk again".

Saron put her head in her hands and cried uncontrollably. "Why do you keep saying if he survives?" she asked. Mr Preston continued "Well this is the final part I have to tell you. Because of the injuries he sustained and the trauma his body has gone through we are helping him with his fight, he is now on a life support machine".

The devastating news affected everyone in the tiny room. Even Carl could not hold back the tears.

Mr Preston spoke again. "All I can say is, I hope and pray for John. He is an incredible fighter, at one point we lost him but managed to get him back that was at around was 2.00pm. It was if he was waiting for someone". "That's when you phoned Saron", said Angelina. Saron looked at Annie Tanney and Annie whispered, "I told you he would wait".

"Obviously it is critical he gets plenty of rest. No more than two people will be allowed into his room once he is back from the operating theatre" said the surgeon. "Mr Preston thank you and your team for everything you have done for John". "We are in God's hands now, we have done all we, as human beings, can do and he left the office".

They all sat there in silence. Eventually unfazed by what had just happened, Annie stood up and said "You all need to leave now. I will be staying with Mr Gammon". Sandra looked at Carl and not being slow at coming forward she said "I think that is Saron's decision". Saron answered "Sandra you don't understand, but I will explain one day".

They all left. Angelina gave Saron a cuddle and said she would phone tonight. Annie turned to Saron's Mum, "You and Saron need to leave, I will be with John until the Lord decides if I can save him". Saron's Mum kissed Annie and thanked her. "Come on Saron" she said to her daughter. "Can't I stay with you and John, Aunty Annie?" "No my dear" replied Annie "Myself and my

Guardian Angel will be the only people allowed to stay". Saron's Mum beckoned Saron to leave. "Saron turned and said, "I will come and visit every day and sit outside". "That is your choice dear", replied Annie.

Milton and Scooper had gone back to work. Di Trimble was on the desk. A meeting was to take place at 11.00am, Robinson had called for it to be in the incident room.

"So sorry to hear about Chief inspector Gammon" Di said to them both, "My prayers are with him". "Thanks Di" was the reply.

It was almost 11.00am everyone was assembled in the incident room when Robinson strode in like a preening Peacock. He started by saying that Brian Lund was on the run and that he had escaped custody. "Bloody typical ineptitude", shouted Smarty. "I won't have any more of that talk Smarty", said Robinson. The room went quiet. He continued, "Right, well we will all have heard that former Sergeant Hanney was killed yesterday, while it looks like he was trying to save Gammon's life. I have no doubt Gammon, being the Maverick he was, would have caused this situation". The whole room went deathly silent. Smarty again stood up. "You are an arrogant prick and not fit to lace the boots of John Gammon and I am not listening to this shit anymore" Smarty walked out. Robinson shouted "Get back here or I will suspend you". Bancock and Lee stood up, as did Milton, Scooper and the rest of the staff. "Suspend him and you can suspend the rest of us".

Robinson was left on his own. Robinsons phone rang it was Lund. "Robinson you have to get this sorted. The only people who saw my face were Hanney and he is done, Gammon and hopefully he is done, the bird gammon was with, don't know who she is but she is something to do with the Secret Service I think". Robinson questioned Lund, "Where are you Brian?". Lund replied "Do you honestly think I will tell you until you have sorted this out?" "What about you're reporting to the Probation Service?" asked Robinson. "Look the worst thing they can do is put me back inside to finish my sentence. I am sorting my alibi out now, then I will calmly walk into the probation office, apologise and say I needed a holiday" said Lund smugly. "But your tag will say where you have been" suggested Robinson. "That's sorted. The records show I have been in Whitby, the landlady of a certain little guest house owes me a favour. I just need Gammon not to pull through this. His bird I'm not too worried about, it will be her word against mine and you'd better sort that also". Puzzled Robinson asked, "How did you get away?" Lund replied "I hid in the building. They didn't know how many people were in there, so they didn't have a clue". "Look Brian" said Robinson, "I am going to have to go, a lot has happened here and I am the one going to be taking the glory for it". "Remember this Robinson, you are in my pocket. Let me down and you know the consequences. Find that bird and do her in. You hear me? And you ain't got long, the clock is ticking. Text yes to me in one week and that's your lot". Lund hung up. Robinson felt physically sick at the thought but he knew he had no choice.

Robinson went to speak to Sergeant Milton. "Who is in charge of security at the hospital where Gammon is?" "Manchester Police Sir". "Right, I want the names of whoever has been with Gammon on the night he was admitted and then everyone subsequently since his operation". "I can tell that you Sir" said Milton, "I was there, Scooper was there, his girlfriend Saron, her mother and Annie Tanney from Ireland. Oh and

Angelina. I don't know her surname but she was involved in the fracas when it all kicked off". "So, she was with Chief Inspector Gammon the whole of the time?" asked Robinson. "Why are you asking Sir?" said Milton. Robinson replied, "I want her brought in for questioning". "I don't know where to look said Milton. "Speak with Saron is she at work?" "No Sir, she is too upset". "Well go to her house man and find out who this woman is and where she lives she could be in danger" snapped Robinson.

Milton apologised "I never thought of that Sir!". "Exactly, I am surrounded by flat footed country bumpkins. Just get me her name and address and do it now", snarled Robinson. "Yes Sir". "Oh and Milton don't think I have forgotten what you lot said in there, because I haven't. You have blotted your copy book". Milton said nothing he thought least said soonest mended.

ANNIE TANNEY

Back at Bixton Hospital John Gammon was in a private ward on life support. Annie Tanney had already started her work, she was speaking to John in a very soft, quiet voice and was holding his hands. Every now and again she would say a prayer. Saron and her mother were sat in the corridor. Saron's Mum explained she had to have faith and believe in Annie. Saron nodded in agreement. Saron's phone rang it was Milton. "Where are you Saron?". "Sat in the corridor of Bixton Hospital", said Saron. "Where does your mate Angelina live? The Super thinks she may be in danger". Saron answered, "She is stopping at Up The Steps Maggie's I think". "Does she work Saron?". "Yes, but she is on holiday for a few weeks. She goes all over the world". "Ok Saron thanks. I will try and find her. If you hear from her before me, would you get her to phone my number please Saron?". "Ok Carl".

"Who was that Saron?" asked her mum. "It was Carl from work, the police think Angelina may be in danger because she may have seen the people who did this". Saron tried Angelina's phone, but it kept going to answer phone. Saron sighed, "Mum I don't need this. A friend comes to see me and ends up in this mess. John is critically ill and I am relying on somebody I don't really know to save him. Am I crazy Mum?". Her mum replied, "On the plane Saron, she said to me *"There is light in this world, a healing spirit more powerful than any darkness we may encounter in our lives".* Saron we have nothing to lose. If you want the man back in your life please don't doubt her. She says doubting drains away her healing powers so please stay positive and believe".

Saron got up from where she was sitting and looked into Johns room. There were pipes coming from every orifice. Annie Tanney was holding John's hand. How Saron wanted to do the same. Suddenly her phone rang it was Angelina. "Are you ok Saron?" she asked. "Yes Angelina, no change here. Sergeant Milton just called and said his boss Superintendent Robinson needs to locate you. He fears your life maybe in danger". "Does he now?" said Angelina. "Ok, do you have Milton's number?" "Yes" said Saron and dictated the number. Angelina thanked her and said "I will be over later to sit with you so your Mum can have a break".

Angelina knew why Robinson wanted to locate her. Little did he know about Angelina.

"Sergeant Milton?" she asked. "Yes" was reply. "Angelina Sonjack, how can I help you?". "Oh Miss Sonjack, thank goodness you have phoned. My boss Superintendent Robinson, is concerned for your safety because you are a witness to the killing of Sergeant Hanney and the attempted murder of John Gammon. Could you call into Bixton Police Station?". "Sergeant Milton, I need to speak with you alone. Can you meet me somewhere?". Milton replied "Ok, what about the Sloppy Quiche Café in half an hour?". "That's fine but you must come alone and don't tell anyone, I will explain when I see you" said Angelina.

ANNIE TANNEY

It was 3.30pm when Carl met Angelina at the Sloppy Quiche Café. The place was quiet, so perfect for the meeting. "Good afternoon what can I get you?". Karen Jigley was always the host. "We have the regular menu, plus we have afternoon tea which consists of two jam and cream scone's, two small ginger and toffee slices, four salmon and cucumber triangles, four cheese and sloppy quiche pickle triangles and two handmade chocolates, plus tea for two. We also have The Sloppy Quiche Café Quiche special and a selection of open faced toasties. Would you like a minute to decide?". Angelina asked "Shall we have the afternoon tea Sergeant Milton?" "Fine by me?" replied Milton. "Ok it will be with you shortly" said Karen with a smile.

"Why the cloak and dagger stuff Miss Sonjack?" enquired Sargent Milton. "Call me Angelina please", she replied. "Ok Angelina and I'm Carl". With the formalities over Angelina began her explanations. "Well Carl, this is all going to seem very far-fetched, but this is the truth. I work for the Her Majesty's Government Carl. Only you and John Gammon know this so nothing I tell you can be repeated. The people that saved me in that room were not there by coincidence. My purpose for being in the Peak District is to finally nail Brian Lund. Lund is still very well connected higher up the ladder. The Government don't want a scandal or trust me this would fall like a House of Cards. Superintendent Robinson was placed at Bixton by our team. We know he is bent and we have enough evidence to send him down for a long time, but Lund is a different case. At best we could only get him sent down for maybe ten years, which would mean he could serve just 4 years, that is no good to society this animal needs taking down and the key thrown away. So you see Carl, Robinson wants to find my whereabouts because he can then kill me, which I am sure he will be under instruction to do so from Lund". Carl was shocked to say the least, but if anybody knew about MI5 and MI6 it was Carl, after everything he had been through. Carl agreed to pretend he couldn't find Angelina and they parted knowing that all this could one day blow up.

Almost three weeks had gone by, Saron visited John every day and Sandra called every night after work. There had been no signs of Lund, he hadn't reported into his parole officer, so he was wanted for that offence alone. Angelina knew if Lund got the chance he would have her killed with John on life support she was his only witness.

It seemed that Annie Tanney had not had the effect everyone was hoping for. John had not improved and there was big decision to be made.

Carl had managed to get hold of John's Uncle Graham and he had made arrangements to bring him to the hospital. They all knew this was possibly the end of the road, although Annie hadn't given up. She was still holding his hand and speaking softly to John.

Saturday arrived Sandra Scooper, Saron, Saron's mother, who had not left Saron's side as they had sat in the corridor for three weeks, Carl, John's Uncle Graham, Steve Lineman and Jo were all now at the hospital. Steve had tears streaming down his face, he could not control his feelings, his best mate was about to be despatched to the big man in the sky.

The surgeon called Graham and Saron into the small room at the side of the private ward where John had been for three weeks. "I truly think a decision needs to be made. I am afraid John is only alive because we are keeping him alive and as much as I hate to have to accept defeat this is not a life John Gammon would have wanted. It may be a blessing because almost certainly the blood clot he had, caused some serious damage to his brain". Uncle Graham spoke, "Are you saying turn of the machine?" The surgeon looked at Graham, the expression on his face said it all, he and his team had done the very best they could. Saron broke down, "I can't make that decision Graham".

Graham thought about how he and John were really father and son and how things turn around in your life. John finally knew the truth, yet it was his real father who had to decide on this terrible thing.

Graham pondered for a moment deep in thought, maybe this was God's way of punishing him for sleeping with his brother's wife all those years ago. Graham looked at the surgeon and in a quiet voice said "Ok, switch the machine off".

Just as they got up to leave, the lights in the office started to flicker. The lights then went out and back on again three times. They quickly moved next door to where John was. To everyone's amazement John was sat up with his eyes open talking to Annie Tanney. Shocked Saron said, "I don't believe this!". Within seconds a full team of doctors were at John's bedside, Annie was still holding John's hand, as she had done for three solid weeks. Overjoyed, Saron threw her arms around Annie. Annie, with her beautiful emerald green eyes, just smiled and said "He is yours now. Look after him".

"Where are you going Annie?" said John. "You are in safe hands now John, you don't need me you had the belief". Everybody wanted to shake her hand, but she just asked Saron's mother to take her back to the hall. I will come and see you tomorrow John. John smiled at her and said thank you. She smiled back and left the room.

The doctors cleared the room and began to unhooked John. His heart beat was regular, his breathing was that of a twenty year old man. The doctors could not believe what they had seen. John Gammon was only alive because of a machine and now he was back to his normal self. Who was this woman Annie Tanney?

Steve, Jo and Saron stayed on after the others had left. Bein the first to speak Steve asked John, "How are you feeling mate, you gave us all a massive scare?". "Steve it was really weird. It was as if I was dreaming. I was aware of everything about me, but I couldn't speak or move. Annie kept praying and telling me to come back and that it wasn't my time. It was like I knew her the whole of the time from when she first held my hand. At one point I remember bright lights and then terrible darkness. There were these things, images that floated around and kept grabbing at me. I heard one say "if she let's go of his hand we can take him". You probably think I was hallucinating but in the distant I could see Mum and Adam, but I never saw Dad. Adam said "we are fine John don't worry, go back and find the evil man". Mum never said anything she just waved. She had her favourite blue dress on and when she waved she had a silk handkerchief in her hand that dad had bought her one Christmas. She always joked with him that he was tight and was that the best he could get her".

"Steve I feel fine, they told me not to move for a few days but I walked round the bed last night and feel great" said John. Saron and Jo had gone for coffees. Steve joked, "It was like a bloody Miss World pageant out there a couple of weeks ago! There was Sheba, Sandra, Joni, Saron my Jo and that new bird Angelina. You would have thought it was Brad Pitt or George Clooney that was at death's door". They both started laughing just as the girls arrived back with the coffee. "What's tickling you two?" "Oh nothing just Steve pratting about as usual" said John.

Steve made a move "Anyway we'd best get off and leave you two to get sorted with the hospital". Saron replied, "Thank you so much for your support and prayers you two". "Hey we love him as well you know". John looked at Saron and just smiled at her.

It was a cold crisp night in the Peak District, when Superintendent Matt Robinson finally made his move to attempt to kill Angelina Sonjack outside of Up The Steps Maggie's car park. He very nearly succeeded had it not been for the quick thinking of Dermot McKenna. Dermot was assigned to shadow Angelina, although she had said she thought she would be fine.

McKenna took one shot to drop Robinson dead and that was that. Sadly they still hadn't got Lund, but there was no chance McKenna was taking any risks with Angelina's life. Although Angelina was quite shook up she knew that Lund could not afford to give up on her or John, so she had to be aware of this. Robinsons body was removed and nobody was any the wiser. "That's MI5 for you" thought Angelina.

At the Station, They were told that Robinson had been suffering from depression, hence the mood swings at work, and that he had asked to take early retirement which he did. Robinson had no family so it was easy to explain his disappearance that away.

It was a further four weeks before John was allowed to turn up for work again and boy was he in for a surprise!! The new desk sergeant Ian Yap greeted John like his hero. "Steady on lad", said John, "I only work here". Yapp bumbled on, "It is a pleasure to meet you Sir". "Well thank you?" said John fishing for a name. "Ian, Sir. Ian Yap".

PC Yap was almost six foot five inches tall, he explained to John that he had spent six years in the army and when he came out, he joined the police force. He had heard about the job in the Peak District and said he walking a lot in these parts so he had settled in Swinster. John congratulated him "Well good on you lad, it's a lovely part of the country". "It certainly is Sir", replied Yapp, "Oh by the way Sir, we have a new Superintendent. He said for you to go to his office when you get in". John raised his eyebrows and silently thought "Here we go again another idiot brought in above him".

John climbed the stairs, with a feeling of wellbeing for some reason. He wasn't sure if it was the fact that he had survived his recent ordeal or whether it was Annie Tanney looking over him. He didn't know for sure and couldn't prove why he felt that way, but he was aware that this bubble was probably going to burst the moment he entered the new Superintendents office.

Gammon knocked on his new boss's door. It was an utter shock when he opened it. Sat there in the big leather chair was Angelina. "Where's the new Superintendent?", he asked. "You are looking at me" she said. "But the new lad said he wanted to speak with me" said John. "Yes I know, I didn't want to spoil the surprise". "Does Saron know?" asked John. "I am good at keeping secrets", and she glanced a mischievous smile at John knowing she was playing with fire.

"John, I have called a meeting in the incident room for 9.30 am. Sorry to say we have a murder on our hands. Oh and John be careful, Lund needs us both dead and he is more than capable".

Gammon was just pleased to be back working again and to be alive!!. Gammon knew deep in his heart that one day he and Lund would share the ultimate end and it would either be him or Lund. Gammon no longer cared if Lund went to trial or if he was killed, as long as he was the one dishing out the punishment. As Gammon sat in his office with his dishwater coffee steaming away in front of him, he reflected on what had recently happened in his life. The dreadful way in which he and his brother had not spoken for nine years, all over Lindsay, who really never cared about either of them, yet had caused so much upset in both their lives.

Gammon felt so much guilt about Adam and his girlfriend and that his whole family had been dragged into the sewer by Brian Lund. His hatred for the man had gone beyond anything he had ever felt before and while he knew he had to be professional, he also knew if he had the chance he would take Lund out, of that he was sure.

It was soon 9.30am and the incident room echoed to the sound of his colleagues applauding John back into the fold. "Ok everyone", said Angelina, "I would first of all like to welcome back Chief Inspector Gammon from his holiday!!" Everyone laughed at Angelina's humour. "Seriously though, I personally would like to welcome John back we have many hills to climb here in Bixton and I don't mean the Peaks!! We have unsolved murders on our hands that point solely to Brian Lund. This man has managed to corrupt many police officers and I will say this. If there are any persons left at this station, that have any association with Lund or his crew, speak now, because there will be no second chances with me". Gammon admired how well Angelina was handling the job, she seemed to be a natural.

"To add further to our workload, a young lady by the name of Maria Dooley was found dead near Ackbourne last night, at Bubley. Bubley is only a small village and her body was found by a Mr Wang who has a Chinese restaurant in Ackbourne, but he lives in Bubley. Maria had been hit with a heavy object which forensics are currently trying to decipher exactly if this is the murder weapon. For some reason her left ear was severed. It was not found at the scene. So we can only assume the assailant took this as some macabre trophy". There was a gasp from the officers assembled in the room. Something else found at the scene was a chalk marked drawing on the pavement nearby of a stick man. Don't know if the older ones of you here can remember a TV program The Saint with Roger Moore? But you will see what I draw is very similar but with no halo. My gut feeling on this is that our killer is in his late fifties".

"Myself and John will inform the family. Milton and Smarty, will you do the pubs and clubs in Ackbourne?. Inspector Lee would you interview Mr Wang. Also you will see by looking around the room, we have some new faces and not just mine. Inspector Bancock took promotion and is now in Sunderland, his replacement is Sergeant Thomas Wisey, a local man born in Bixton, who has been in the force nine years working down in Devon. Sergeant Wisey's knowledge of the area will be invaluable to the team. Sergeant Hanney is unfortunately now dead and we all know about that story. He has been replaced by PC Ian Yap. So to recap and close the meeting we have, Sergeant Di Trimble just promoted from a PC so congratulations to Di, Police Constable Ian Yap our new desk clerk, Inspector Lee, Inspector Smarty, Sergeant Milton, Chief Inspector John Gammon and myself. We are a little thin on the ground as a murder team, but I will address this situation at the first opportunity".

Just as the meeting was about to close PC Yap came in with a message for Angelina. "Team, before we go a local vicar from Monkdale found a drawing of the same stick man pinned to the notice board at St Mary Church in the village this morning. We are dealing with a sicko here, team. Wisey can you interview the vicar, get the drawing sent to forensics please? Thank you team, let's re-convene tomorrow same time for an update and before you all go, I have laid on some sandwiches at the Spinning Jenny tonight at 5.00pm, to welcome the new members of the team. If you would like to come along and take the opportunity to get know our new members, that would be much appreciated. Thank you meeting closed".

John turned to Angelina. "That was a nice touch" "Thanks John. Right lets go and see Maria's mother and father. They have already been informed as she had identity on her. I just want to see if she had any boyfriends and the like".

Gammon and Sonjack arrived at a neat little semi-detached bungalow in Ackbourne, the family home of Mr and Mrs Dooley. A young lady answered the door, it was Maria's sister. Gammon and Sonjack were shown into the living room. There were quite a lot of people with Mr and Mrs Dooley, all family members trying to console the poor couple. Gammon asked if they could speak with Mr and Mrs Dooley alone. "May we say how sorry we are for your loss? We can't imagine how this must feel. I am sorry to have to ask you questions now, but time is of the essence. In this sort of case, we must act quickly". Bill Dooley nodded his head to say it was ok, but his poor wife didn't look up.

John continued, "Could you tell me did Maria have any special friends?". Mr Dooley replied, "She had been seeing a guy from Cowdale, called Rupert Bare. He lived at Cowdale Hall. He seemed a nice enough young man. He was very well spoken and very polite. They had met at a horse show. Our Maria loved horses and used to ride at every opportunity". "How long had she been seeing Mr Bare?" asked John. "About three or four months I think. We met him at Christmas. He bought my wife the biggest bouquet of flowers and chocolates when he came for tea, didn't he Shirley?". Mrs

Dooley still didn't look up, or take her head out of her hands.

"Did she speak much about Mr Bare?" asked John. "You would have to ask our other daughter Lexi". Lexi came in the room. "We are very sorry to ask you questions at this most dreadful time for you and your family but……." Lexi butted in. "It's ok. I want this person found. Who has done this?" "So Lexi, your sister was seeing a Mr Rupert Bare from Cowdale?" "Yes". "Were they good together?" asked Gammon "by that I mean did they ever argue?" "Do you think he did this to Maria?" asked Lexi. John replied "I am afraid everyone is a suspect until we know otherwise Lexi". "He was a nice guy although I thought he was a bit of a prat. you know a spoilt child. His family is very wealthy so he was used to getting whatever he wanted all the time". "Did he ever get aggressive with your sister?" Lexi answered, "He was very jealous, he wanted to own her. She had a lot of friends and some of them were guys, so if we were out she would talk with them as friends do. And one night he started a fight with a guy called Jim Dobbin from Monkdale. The problem was that Jim was an amateur boxer, so he made Rupert look quite silly". "When did this happen?" "Only about a week ago in Chicks nightclub in Ackbourne" said Lexi.

"My sister did say after that, she thought maybe Rupert wasn't for her. She was very annoyed with him, she had known Jim for years, they had been at college together so she was a bit embarrassed at Rupert's attitude". "Where does Jim Dobbin live Lexi?" "He lives at Miners Cottage on the Green in Monkdale". John concluded, "Ok, I think we have enough for now. Mr and Mrs Dooley do you need anything else?". Mrs Dooley still didn't look up, so Mr Dooley showed them out. As they were leaving Mr

Dooley said, "Please get this evil bastard". "We will Mr Dooley, take care" and they left the house. As they were walking away, Angelina turned to John, "Right John, lets go and see Jim Dobbin first".

The drive to Monkdale village was delightful. Spring time in the Peak District saw an array of wild flowers of every colour in the fields leading to Monkdale village. "How are you feeling John? Just say if it gets too much for you". "I'm fine, thanks Angelina, I feel really well. I went to see Annie Tanney yesterday with Saron. Saron's dad isn't well so she was staying a while longer. I think Saron's mum wants Annie to stay for good, but I'm not sure that will happen". "She is a remarkable lady John" "Don't I know it", said John "I wouldn't be here today by all accounts if she hadn't have come over from

Ireland". "For sure John. Your life would have ended if it hadn't have been for Annie Tanney".

They arrived at Miners Cottage. Jim Dobbin was hanging out the washing. He greeted them both and appeared on the face of it to be quite a nice level headed young man. They spoke for almost half an hour and Jim explained what had happened. He said he knew how to stop Rupert's aggression without doing him to much harm, although he did say Rupert Bare was noted for throwing his toys out of the pram. He wasn't particularly liked as he always tried to get his own way and most of his friends, that were local, were only hanging round with him because he bought all the drinks and had parties.

Sonjack and Gammon bid their goodbyes to Jim Dobbin and headed for Cowdale Hall. The big sweeping drive leading to Cowdale Hall was very impressive. As they pulled up next to the marble fountain, situated at front of the main entrance, a young man was getting in his BMW Z4.

"Can I help you?" he said quite sternly. They showed their warrant cards and asked for Mr Rupert Bare. He looked briefly at the warrant cards and replied "I'm Rupert, what do you want?" John answered, "A moment of your time Mr Bare". "Well you'll have to be bloody quick, I have a meeting at my accountants in Toad Holes in twenty minutes".

Gammon didn't like his attitude. "Perhaps we would be better doing this down at the station Mr Bare". "Why?" "Well clearly you are struggling for time". Bare replied "Well if you told me what this is about, it might help". "It is with regard to a murder investigation Mr Bare". "What?" he exclaimed. "We believe you were in a relationship with one Maria Dooley, is that correct?". Quite arrogantly Bare replied,

"Well I was seeing her on and off, but then I see a lot of girls. I am quite popular".

Gammon could feel the hairs rising on the back of his neck. What a pretentious dick this guy was. Bare replied, "So what's this about? Is it that trouble in Ackbourne the other night with that boxer friend of hers?" "Shall we go inside Mr Bare" "Just a minute, do I need to call my solicitor?". John answered, "I don't know, do you? We are here to talk to you about your relationship with Maria Dooley who was murdered last night. Her body was found in Bubley". Rupert Bare went quiet for a minute, but didn't appear to show any signs of distress. After a few seconds he said "So what would that have to do with me, pray tell?" "We don't know yet, but your cooperation would go a long way to dismissing you from our investigations Mr Bare". "Well before you pontificate to me Sergeant........". That really stuck in Gammon's throat and he butted in to Bare's comment, "That's Chief Inspector to you son". "Whooo aren't we the special one" said Bare cheekily. "Ok Sir, that's enough. Get in the car. We would like to officially question you at Bixton Police Station". "I want my solicitor" whined Bare. "Speak with him now and tell him we are taking you to Bixton Police Station" snapped John. Angelina could see John wasn't about to take anymore from this obnoxious man so they headed to Bixton and the Police Station. On arrival at the station, John said to PC Yap. "Put Mr Bare in interview room one Ian and give me a shout when his solicitor gets here".

Gammon and Sonjack went up to Sonjack's office. "John calm down" said Angelina. "Calm down? That little gob shite's attitude stinks. The poor parents of that girl are grieving and he wasn't even interested. He may not have any involvement but he deserves a hard time Angelina for his crap attitude. I am sorry but there is no compassion in this world, it just grates on me".

"I understand John, just don't let it cloud your judgement". It was almost 5.00pm when Gammon finished interviewing Bare and he wasn't entirely satisfied with his answers. So Gammon told Bare that they would be holding him overnight while further investigations were carried out.

Angelina offered to drive John to the Spinning Jenny. Saron had gone home earlier with 'flu. The time worrying about John had taken it's toll on the girl. Everyone from the meeting that morning had turned up at the pub. Kev had mentioned to John's friends that Angelina had put on a few sandwiches at the Spinning Jenny. True to form Bob and Cheryl, Jack and Shelly Etchings, Carol Lestar, Sheba Riley, Tony and Rita Sheriff, Steve and Jo and all his work colleagues from the station were there too.

Joni was working the bar, which in some respects was good with Saron not being there. Sheba collared John while he was on his way to the toilets. "So how is my hero Mr Gammon then?" John laughed, "Not sure about the description Sheba, how are you?" "Just to let you know if you get too many drinks down you, my sofa is always available" she smiled cheekily at him flashing her pearly white teeth. John stood there in total amazement. She flicked her long dark hair and walked away.

Scooper hadn't taken her eyes off John all night. Doreen had seen and noted this action. She was the next person to comment to John, "Your admirers are out in force tonight John". John smiled. "Saron is a nice girl, John, she's been through a lot for you John, don't hurt her". "Of course I won't Doreen". John knew deep down that it would probably happen. He was a red blooded male and there appeared to be a lot of low hanging fruit. He wasn't sure if he would ever settle down again. Had the Lindsay thing scarred him?

The turn-out was amazing. Carol Lestar was more than the worse for wear, which meant poor Shelley Etchings and Cheryl were in an even worse state.

It was 10.20pm when John took a call from Saron. Saron was crying. "Just a minute let me get where I can hear you. Whatever is the matter?" Saron sobbed, "John, mum just found dad dead in the bath". John was quick to reply, "Oh no, do you want to come over?" "No John, stay there, the party was mainly put on for you. I am going over to Mum's to stay there tonight, so I will see you tomorrow". "Is Annie with her?" asked John. "Yes, she's good lady John" "I know that Saron. I will pop round before I go into work tomorrow" "John, would you let

Angelina know?" "Of course I will" said John and ended the call. Sad to say, John wasn't very keen on Saron's father. He had made it very uncomfortable for him on Christmas day but it was still a sad time for Saron.

John returned to the party, "Everything alright John?" asked Angelina. "Bad news I am afraid, Saron's father has died" "Oh dear do you think I should go over". John replied "No Saron said Annie was there and Saron is going stay tonight, I'm going to call round in the morning on my way into work". Angelina's face was a picture. She knew what a dreadful situation this was for her friend, but she also knew that this was a great opportunity to see if John was feeling how she was feeling.

The night drew to a close. Scooper was a bit tipsy and Milton offered to drop her off at home. He hadn't been drinking, so took Smarty and some of the others. Angelina turned to John, "Come on John, let's get you home" "Thanks Angelina".

As they drove down to Hittington, Angelina could help herself, she just blurted out, "Shall we sleep together tonight? There I have said it now!!" John's face was a picture. He said "We will have to go to Up The Steps Maggie's". "Not a problem" said Angelina "they give you a key so you can go in via the side door so nobody will know".

As soon as they walked to the room, Angelina, who was dressed in a simple black designer dress, wore a small cross and chain round her neck, her shoes were black patent high heels with red soles, John knew immediately that these were Christian Laboutin's. To complete and complement her dress, she wore a short cropped, white mohair cardigan. John thought she looked stunning. They entered the room Angelina was renting and within seconds she had stripped John. John had done the same to

Angelina. This wasn't going to be any kind of loving encounter. This was going to be raw, unadulterated sex between to consenting adults.

John was wasting no time. Angelina's breathing became more intense as he touched her silky smooth body all over. From her full lips to her inner thighs, he worked his way steadily all over her. Angelina was screaming with ecstasy. John held both her hands as they both reached the fullness of their wanting. They lay silent. Both of them knowing that what they had just experienced, was so very wrong. There was no going back now.

Angelina waited a minute before speaking. "We have a choice here John. We either come clean or this is to be a one off where nobody else knows. That way I still get to keep Saron as my friend. What other choice do I have? Do I tell her, leave the force and the Peak District or I just leave without telling her anything? You need to know something else John" What more surprises?" said John. "Saron has asked me if I want to go into partnership with her" "What doing?" "We are thinking of buying the Tow'd Man" replied Angelina. "Really?" said John surprised at the revelation. Angelina went on. "I've had enough of the police force and the secret service John. We were almost killed the other night and who would have cared?" "Angelina, you said the other night that Lund still had friends in high places, what did you mean? Head of MI5 told me that they had washed their hands of him and that he was fair game now" "I'm afraid John that it is higher than what Claire Singleton knows" "Do you know her?" asked John. "Let's say our paths have crossed" replied Angelina.

"What I will tell you though, is that I have been told, that Lund will be spirited out of the country and given a new identity" "You are kidding me Angelina" "No I'm not John, there will be a report made and handed to the press saying that Lund was shot dead trying to escape near Calais. In reality he will probably end up in Canada or South Africa. I know how much this must hurt John and this one of the reason's I want out" "How come he has that much sway? Who is so frightened of him?" "Again, this is majorly confidential, if he was to release the DVD's we know he has. Then not only the government, but also the monarchy could fall. That's how high reaching this thing is. If he is killed or sent down for a long time, he has told the powers that be, that his instructions are, that the DVD's will be handed over to the media".

"Do you believe the son of a bitch?" "I not only believe him John, I have seen copies of the DVD's and it certainly isn't good".

John lay back in silence for a minute. Finally the anger came out. "This stinks. I lose my family, all those poor girls murdered and he gets away Scott free, it can't be right?" "I didn't know until we arrested Robinson. I was pulled aside by a very high ranking Government Official. He showed me the DVD copies and I had to sign the Official Secrets Act. So now you know everything. Lund's death will be announced within the next few days" "Why did he accept the short sentence he has just done?" John asked. "Well, that way it was a trade-off. He knew he would not do the full fourteen months and he could run his operation from inside he was supplied with a mobile phone. It was a small price considering the ramifications John".

John jumped up. "What are you doing?" asked Angelina. "Getting dressed" replied John, "I have cheated on my girlfriend and I have just been told that the man, I personally would have done time for, will be free as a bird and there is sod all I can do about it. So trust me, Angelina, I am very pissed to say the least. I will see you around". With the sentence barely out of his mouth, John left and walked the 2.5 miles back to Hittington.

Angelina lay all alone, knowing there was no other way she could have dressed up the news to John. Subconsciously she had made up her mind to take the pub with Saron and get out of the cess pit she had been working in for the last fifteen years.

When John arrived at Saron's cottage, he felt even worse. The girl who had quite possibly saved his life and whose father had just died. He had just cheated on with her best friend. What kind of person was he? He looked again at the bottle of Jameson whisky sat on the side, but he knew if opened the bottle he would not stop until he had emptied it and that wasn't good for anyone.

John really hadn't slept well. When the alarm went off at 7.30am he showered, got dressed and headed for Saron's mother's house.

The grandeur of the place never failed to impress John. The butler answered his knock on the big oak door. "Welcome Mr Gammon, please come in, I will fetch Miss Saron". John nodded. Saron came down the stairs, she looked dreadful, she hadn't slept a wink all night.

"Thanks for coming John" "I'm very sorry for you and your Mum's loss Saron" "Come through, Mum is with Annie Tanney in the drawing room". Annie's face lit up when she saw John, he wasn't sure if it was her remembering what she had done for him or the fact she genuinely liked him. He was sure that that last fact would have changed if she knew what he had done last night.

John stayed for half an hour and then left for work. He told Saron that Angelina had mentioned about the pub and their potential partnership. Saron explained that she thought it was a good business opportunity for them both. John agreed but was still feeling angry with himself over his selfish behaviour.

"If you decide to move Saron, I will take the cottage on if you wish" offered John. "That seems like a good idea John. I'm seeing Denis and Clara tomorrow so will know more then" "Ok will you be home tonight?" "Yes, Mum will be fine. Annie will be here so shouldn't be any problems". John turned to

Saron, "I'm sorry to ask, but what did your fatehr die of Saron?" "The Doctor's certificates said "Ischemic heart disease", basically a coronary heart disease. Strangely mum said he had never complained of chest pains or anything like it, unless he was hiding it. He could be very stubborn". "Ok. Well I'd best get back to work I will see you tonight" "Call me when you have left John?" "Ok bye". John left and drove to Bixton. His mind was wandering everywhere. He was fighting guilt. He had a feeling that his career had stalled while he had been in the Peak District, and he wondered if he had lost his drive. On arrival at Bixton Police Station he was met by Rupert Bare's solicitor.

"Are you going to be charging my client Chief Inspector or will you be releasing him?" John looked over at PC Yap. "Release Mr Bare please Yap, I have finished questioning him for now, but I may need to question him as the investigation progresses". "You kept my client here out of spite Mr Gammon" said the solicitor. "No comment" said John and Gammon walked away leaving Bare's solicitor shaking his head.

Angelina met John on the stairs as he made his way to the office. "Morning John". "Morning Ma'am". Angelina threw him a look that said "Don't be childish" but Gammon couldn't help himself. "We have a meeting in the incident room at 9.30am John" said Angelina. John replied "I'll be there".

Gammon entered the incident room, all the staff were present. Angelina strode in. "Ok, listen up, I have just had it confirmed Brian Lund was found attempting to board a ferry from Dover to Calais. During the attempt to apprehend Mr Lund, he was shot and fatally wounded he died at the scene". The team all cheered. Gammon had to look away. Angelina could sense his annoyance, but she had no choice and he should have realised that. "So what does that mean to our ongoing murder investigations?" she continued, "I have been told by The Crown Prosecution Service that cases are all to be closed now". Everyone was aware of how much this meant to John Gammon, but he outwardly didn't seem in the least bit pleased.

"Ok, we have spent enough time and resources on Lund, let's get down to the job in hand and that being finding Maria Dooley's killer. What have we got team? Forensics maybe you can start" "We are pretty sure that the object used to kill Miss Dooley was a builder's lump hammer. Approximately a 2lb hammer we believe. She was sexually assaulted but no semen was found. The stickman drawing left at Monkdale Church hasn't brought up any DNA I'm afraid".

"Ok Milton what have you got for us?". "DI Smarty and I visited all the pubs in Ackbourne and the two late night clubs. Maria was seen on CCTV in two of the pubs and one of the night clubs. In both pubs she is seen talking to a blonde haired male, approximately twenty eight years old, believed to be one Andrew Bilkin from Rowksley. We have sent a squad car to pick him up for questioning". "Good work you two" said Angelina "DI Lee what did Mr Wang have to say for himself?"

Lee began. "I have to say he was bit difficult to understand. He has lived here for thirty odd years in Monkdale, but still struggles with the language. He said he knew Maria. Quite often she and her boyfriend Danny Stevo would have a take away on a Saturday night. He said they were a nice couple seemed very much in love" "But we were led to believe she was seeing Rupert Bare?" replied John. "I did question that Sir and he said she was always with Danny Stevo. He said he found her body at 2.00am precisely. He knew that because the church bell was chiming when he stumbled across the body by the gates of the church. He said he immediately called for an ambulance and the police from his mobile. We have checked the time of the calls and they all check out. We also have Mr Stevo coming in this morning for questioning" Angelina issued her instructions. "Ok John you sit in with Milton and Smarty and I will sit in with DI Lee. Scooper take DI Trimble and collate a list of all local builders within a five mile radius. I want each one questioning and anyone without an alibi that can't be verified I want them bringing in for questioning. Do I make myself clear? Right well let's get on with it then".

Gammon, Milton and Smarty entered Interview Room One. Andrew Bilkin was already in there with his solicitor, Bernard Hargreaves. Gammon knew him well he mainly dealt with the scumbag cases. Milton set the tape up.

"Good morning Mr Bilkin. Are you fully aware of why you are here today?". In a thick Derbyshire accent he replied. "Yes, because Maria is dead". "Ok, thank you. You don't mind if I call you Andrew do you?" "No, that is ok". Gammon thought that this guy clearly wasn't a full shilling. "Where do you work Andrew?" "For the Duke Sir" replied Bilkin. "The Duke of Devonshire Andrew?" asked Gammon, "Yes,

I look after his bananas. Did you know Joseph Paxton got them from Mauritius in eighteen hundred and something. They are the most famous banana in the world". Andrew was clearly passionate about his work. "So Andrew who told you Maria was dead?" asked Gammon. "Can't remember" he replied. "Try a little harder Andrew" "It was Tony Lacey. He works with me but he said not to tell anyone. He was washing his tee shirt in work time. Duke don't like that. Not paid to wash own clothes, paid to look after greenhouses" "Sure he is Andrew. How well did you know Maria?" went on John. "She used to speak to me when her boyfriend went to get drinks but when he came back she would turn her back on me and pretend we weren't friends" "Did that annoy you Andrew?" "A little bit" he said. "Did you ever get angry with Maria?" "I threw some flowers at her last Valentine's Day" "Why was that Andrew?" "Because I waited for that boyfriend to go to the barm, then I took my flowers to her, she got really mad" "What did she say?" "She called me backward, then said I was Forest Gump. I don't know who he is but he must be funny because everyone was laughing". Gammon glanced at Smarty. "The other night when you were seen talking to her in two different pubs were you still mad at her Andrew?" "I wasn't mad at her. I loved her and she loved me, I know she did" "Do you like drawing Andrew?" "Yes I draw a lot".

Gammon pushed a pen and paper towards Andrew. Let me see you draw the first thing that comes into your mind.

Andrew started scribbling he drew a sun then what looked like an angel. Then he drew a couple of stick men and said this is me and Maria when we get wed. "Did you tell Maria you wanted to marry her Andrew?" "Yes of course I did". "What did she say to that?" "She was with her friends and she said 'go away Forest' and laughed, which meant she was happy. I know because I told Tony at work and he said she must really fancy me. Tony has loads of girlfriends so he would know Sir".

"The shoes you are wearing Andrew, did you go out in them last night?" "Yes, my Nana bought them for me for Christmas. She said they were designer one's. I love my Nana". "Could you take them off for me and give them to Inspector Smarty? We will get our Forensic team to look at them". "Does he like designer shoes like mine?" "I believe so Andrew".

Gammon passed the shoes to Smarty and he hurried down to forensics with them to see if there were any matches against the evidence found at the crime scene.

John carried on with the questioning. "How did you get to know Maria?" "She works at the hairdressers and my Mum took me. She was very kind. She asked me if I wanted a cup of tea and a biscuit while I waited for my Mum. I knew then she liked me, Tony said I was in there".

"Would you like a drink Andrew while we take a break?" "Can I have some Ribena, my Mum always buys me Ribena?" "I'll see what I can do. What about you Mr Hargreaves?" Hargreaves declined, he knew Gammon was using this as a delaying tactic while Forensics were looking at Andrews shoes.

The results from Forensics, were not what Gammon wanted there was nothing linking Andrew to the murder of Maria Dooley. Gammon had no choice but to let Bilkin go. He then spoke with Ian Yap on the desk. "Send a squad car to Chatsworth. I want a Tony Lacey picking up for questioning. When he arrives give me a call and put him in Interview Room Three please Ian" "No problem Sir".

Gammon met Angelina on the stairs, he was still fuming over the Brian Lund decision and he knew she could feel the atmosphere. "Just to let you know, poor Danny Stevo was clearly unaware that Maria was seeing Rupert Bare. He said that he had bought an engagement ring and was going to ask her to marry him on the night she was murdered but she had phoned to say she was going out with some mates and she would see him the following night. I think he is telling the truth John. We can always bringing him back in if we have too" she said.

Angelina turned to John. "Listen can you hold the fort? I'm meeting with Saron up at the Tow'd Man, we are having the "two bob tour" and then would like to have a couple of hours this afternoon to discuss what we think, so we are going on to The Wobbly Man for a late lunch. No point in coming back unless something massive turns up, so

I will see you tomorrow". John decided Angelina wasn't at fault so he wished her all the best then carried onto his office.

Little did Gammon know, but Angelina had virtually decided to leave the force. Just before she arrived at the Tow'd Man, she would give Gammon a call and ask him to get a file out of her locked desk that she needed for her meeting with Denis and Clara. This was all going to prove to be a scam. She had purposely left the file, because in the locked draw was also the address where Lund was staying prior to his new life in Canada. Angelina knew John would have to act on this information. She also knew that he would realise that if Lund was murdered, the authorities would not look too hard for anyone responsible. They had already reported him dead. The important part of the deal for his new life in Canada, was the handing over of all the information contained on the Dvd's about the Government and the Royal Family, so there was no chance now of a scandal. It appeared everyone had won except Gammon and she knew what Lund had done to him. Now she was leaving the force and the secret service, she thought what the hell.

Gammons phone rang. "Hi John, can you do me a favour? I have left the pub details in a file in my drawer. Would you grab them and drop them off at the Tow'd Man for me please? The keys are in the metal cupboard, at the back, in a small grey envelope". Gammon wasn't to chuffed, "I'm not her servant" he thought but he agreed anyway. He got the keys and unlocked the drawer. He reached in and grabbed the Tow'd Man file. It was then, to his surprise, he saw a file marked "Brian Lund - Highly Confidential". His curiosity got the better of him.

Gammon began flicking through the file and read that Brian Lund was staying at Maple Cottage in Chesterfield. He was to be there for another three days before he would assume his new life in Canada as Brian Webster. Gammon sat for a moment deliberating. He quickly wrote down the address, grabbed the file for Angelina and locked the draw once again. He put the note in his pocket, put the key back in the grey envelope and placed it back in the metal cupboard. He left the office and headed off out. "I won't be long Ian, I just need to pop out" he said to the sergeant as he passed by. "Ok Sir", said Yap.

Gammon left Bixton Police Station knowing everything he was thinking was against absolutely everything he stood for, honesty, professionalism and above all else the law. His mind was in a whirl, he now had the opportunity to avenge his family and all the victims of this evil bastard, Lund, before he loses the chance forever.

Gammon arrived at the Tow'd Man and handed Angelina the file she'd asked for. Saron gave him a quick kiss. Angelina smiled at John. He could feel that she knew the enormity of what she had done for him.

John left and returned to the station whilst to decide his next move. A few hours had slipped away when the phone rang, it was Saron. She was extremely excited. "Guess what John? We have agreed a price so I think I am going to hand in my notice". John replied, "I'm very pleased for you both, I'm sure you will make it a great success", Saron continued "Denis and Clara are lovely people and you can rest assured whatever their books say they will be spot on. Denis is as straight as a die. I am so excited we are going to celebrate, are you going to some and meet us?" "Can do, where are you going to be?" "Well we are still in the Wobbly Man at the moment, so come here John" "Ok Saron, I'll be with you in about twenty minutes".

Gammon knew he only had three days to make a decision as to what he was going to do. He nipped down to forensics and grabbed a white bunny suit, a mask and over shoes. He put them in a bag and returned to his office. No one had seen him, so he was safe. Turning the office light off, he threw his coat over the bag he was carrying, went downstairs and said goodnight to Yap. "Goodnight Sir, I'm off in ten minutes myself. There's a big game on tonight, we play Arsenal in the FA Cup". Gammon didn't want to get into too much of a conversation in case his parcel was spotted, so he just wished Ian good luck with the match and carried onto his car.

John knew he would need an alibi. So he called his real father, his Uncle Graham. Graham was taken more than aback. "Hello

John, how are you?" "I'm good thanks Uncle Graham" said John "I see that Brian Lund chap has been killed, couldn't have happened to a better chap after what he did to our family, hey John?" "Yeah you are so right Uncle Graham. Listen, I need a favour. I doubt this will happen, but if anyone asks, can you say that I was with you at yours tomorrow night?" "Why lad, have you got women trouble?" "Something like that Uncle Graham". "Yes lad, no problem I'll do that for you. When are you going to come up to Sheffeild and see me? I'm not getting any younger you know, John" "As soon as the weather turns, I will pop up" "Ok lad. You are ok aren't you?" "Never been better, Uncle Graham. I'll speak soon".

John was more than happy he now had an alibi in place and with a bit of luck Saron would be working at the Tow'd Man tomorrow night It was darts night, so if he could get away reasonably easy, he could sort Lund out and be back before anybody knew.

John arrived at the Wobbly Man. It was quiet, just a few holiday makers eating. Saron and Angelina were sat by the fire, both looked a little tipsy and clearly in a good mood. "Hi girls, what are you drinking?" "Can we have another bottle of Lady Blonde?" "No problem, whatever that is" said John. "It's a sparkling wine and we are putting some Chambord in it as well".

John walked over to the bar. "Hello Rick, long time no see. I heard you were selling" "I was John, but it fell through. I wish Joni would come back I'm really struggling at the minute" John sympathised "Sorry mate I can't help you there, I have no influence over Joni". "I understand John but if you get chance put me a word in please. Right what are you drinking?" "I'll have a pint of Winking Wilson please Rick". "We've sold loads of that John, it's from Mycocks brewery. You know the local lad who set up the micro-brewery. The locals love it" "Can I also have a bottle of Lady Blonde?" asked John. "Blimey mate, those two can drink, that's their second bottle in an hour" "They're celebrating Rick, they've just agreed to buy the Tow'd Man" Rick sighed, "I heard Denis and Clara wanted to retire lucky buggars".

John returned with the drinks. Both girls looked stunning Saron in a tan coloured lamb leather jacket, with a cream coloured mohair, cropped jumper, a small tan leather skirt and boots. Angelina was dressed in a more formal black business suit with a crisp white blouse.

"So what do you think John?" asked Saron. "Well I think I am about to lose my best forensic member and my boss all in one day. But joking apart I'm very pleased for the both of you. I'm sure it will be a massive success". Saron babbled on excitedly "We are going to do B & B. The barns at the back are crying out to be converted. What is the name of the architect/project manager you are using John?" John replied, "Her name is Jayne Thornley-Coil, she is excellent, very professional and her eye for detail is superb" "Who is doing the building work John" "Pete Barrington" he replied. "How much longer will your place be before they are finished" "I'm honestly not sure Saron, to be honest, but Jayne said about six weeks when I spoke with her last week" "Do you think she would be interested in doing our work, John?" "I can ask, do you want me to call her now?" he said. "Brilliant if you don't mind" said Saron.

John called Thornley-Coil. "Hello? Jayne? John Gammon here. I'm sat with Saron and Angelina Sonjack and they were wondering if you would be interested in doing a job for them? They have just agreed the purchase of the Tow'd Man pub". "Lucky you rang today, I have a big job coming up so if they want me to look at this one it will have to be this month John" said Jayne. John answered, "Let me hand the phone to the girls and they can sort the details out with you". The conversation lasted a good half hour by which time John was ready for another drink. He left the girls discussing with Jayne on his phone.

"Same again John?" "Please Rick". A voice could be heard from the other side of the bar saying, "and mine's a double Bacardi and coke". John spoke to the owner of the voice, "Hey Sheba, how are you?" "Good, thanks John. I've just popped in to deliver a lamb for Rick's freezer". John laughed, "Well for somebody delivering dead animals, you certainly scrub up well". "Why thank you kind Sir" Sheba replied "What are you doing just sat with Saron and Angelina" John said, "They are celebrating" with a smile Sheba said, "Not got her pregnant have you Mister Gammon" "No Sheba, not at all they have agreed to buy the Tow'd Man off Denis and Clara" "Oh wow, how great for them. Perhaps you will have some time off the lead now to take me out!" and she laughed her threw back her head and her silky long black hair revealed her stunning eyes. They sparkled like Tiffany diamonds. "Are you going to joins us Sheba?" "Why not, John" was the reply.

John walked back to the girls and took Sheba with him. "Look who I found loitering at the bar" "Hey Sheba, come and sit down with us. What are you doing out on your own?" "I've just been delivering a lamb for Rick's freezer" "What dressed like that?" said Angelina. John was quick to reply, "That's what I said Angelina, she's the best dressed meat delivery girl I know". Angelina laughed "I knew the fashion guru would notice Saron" said Angelina nodding her head towards John. "Yeah old Gok over there" and they all laughed.

"So have you sorted anything out with Jayne Thornley-Coil girls?" enquired John. "Yeah we are meeting her Saturday" said Saron. "What are you going to have done to the Tow'd Man then ladies? Asked Sheba. Saron too up the conversation, "Well it needs a new kitchen, we want to do more food, not particularly fancy food, more aimed at the holiday trade. Then there is a lovely set of barns we want to turn into holiday accommodation. The field we would like to turn over for caravan and camping. It's got so much potential Sheba". Sheba nodded in agreement, "It's all very exciting, what about your jobs?" "Well" said Saron, "I'm handing my notice in to Angelina in the morning and she is doing the same to her boss too". Sheba looked a John cheekily, winked at him and seductively said, "Looks like you will be on your own John" "That's normal for me Sheba" he replied. Angelina had seen the exchange between the two but said nothing.

It was 11.45pm when they finished at the Wobbly Man. Sheba had left half an hour early taking Angelina home. John looked at Saron, "Come on Saron", he said. Saron threw her arms round John and kissed him. Rick shouted across the bar, "Put him down you don't know where he's been" Saron retorted "No, but I know where he is going though" turning to John she said "Come on lover take me home to bed". Rick winked at John as they left.

John put Saron to bed. She was pretty much wasted and so he sat with a glass of Jameson's whisky and his thoughts. His mind was on the killer. Why was he or she leaving drawing of Simon Templar type characters on churches and at the scenes of the crimes? What was the significance? Was it that the Simon Templar character was called the Saint and so this was to become some kind of sick joke? It was almost 3.00am when John climbed the stairs to bed and snuggled up to next Saron.

John's sleep was disturbed by his phone ringing. He sat up in bed and could see it was the station. "Sir, sorry to bother you, Di Trimble here. Another body has been found along with the same drawings as last time but in Rowksley woods" "At this time of night, Di?" asked John. Di said, "Apparently the gamekeeper, Mr Lockwood, found it Sir". By this time John was half out of bed, "Ok I'm on my way Trimble. Get Lee, Scooper and Milton in work and I will see them there".

John dressed and ran down stairs. Saron was still fast asleep so he left a message for her on the kitchen table. It read, "Had to go into work usual crap".

Gammon arrived at Bixton Police Station. Scooper, Lee and Milton were already there. Immediately John said, "Right bring me up to speed". "Forensic are at the scene Sir. Apparently the body is that of a lady who looks to be in her mid-twenties. A gamekeeper called Albert Lockwood found the body at approximately 3.50am this morning. The lady in question had been quite severely beaten around the facial area". "Ok, I've heard enough. Scooper you drive, let's go and see for ourselves" and off the two went.

ANNIE TANNEY

Rowksley had quite a large forest area. It had been owned by the Marchant family but was given to the people of Rowksley in 1963. A volunteer group had worked very hard to make beautiful pathways for the local community to enjoy. A retired game keeper had looked after the pheasants, so twice a year they held shoots which generated money for the volunteer group. It was a wood often used by courting couples. This made John think. Was there a chance someone may have seen something?.

Whey arrived at the scene, the Forensic team had already erected the white tent. John spoke with Bill Ludlam. "What have we got Bill?" asked John. Bill relayed the details so far. "Female about thirty five years old, sexual assaulted and then battered to death. I would say approximately at 12.20am tonight. I will, of course, need to get the body back to the lab to determine all the details". "I need DNA Bill". Bill tapped the side of this noise and indicated, "I knew you would say that John, just give me time and I will get you as many answers as I can". Thanks Bill. Let me have a look at the body" "It's not a pretty sight John".

Bill pulled back the white cotton sheet. The woman's face was a collection of deep lacerations, her nose was visibly broken, her lip was split and her whole face was black and blue. Her left ear had been removed. Whoever did this was in a frenzy John thought. "Ok Bill, I've seen enough. We're going back to the station now let me know as soon as you have identified the body". "Oh and by the way John, there's a drawing of a stick-man in chalk on that tree" said Bill point to the tree concerned. "Can you get me something off that Bill please?" asked John. "We will do our very best John, said Bill.

Gammon, Scooper, Lee and Milton all arrived back at Bixton. "Do you want a coffee Sir?" asked Scooper, "Yes please Sandra".

It was now 7.30am, so the officers stayed and carried on with the day to day work. By 11.00am forensics called Gammon to the lab. "What have you got Bill?" "No DNA John, but we do have a name for the poor wretch on this slab. Her name is Poppy Chi. With all the bruising and lacerations it was difficult to see that she was Chinese. Her dental records show she visited the dentist about a month ago, so it was quite easy to get a match. She had been violently, sexual assaulted and as you can see attacked in a very vicious manner. We have found no semen anywhere" "But I thought she was sexually violated?" asked John. "She was John but not by a male organ. We found nothing on the chalk drawing".

"Scooper had some other news Sir, another drawing has been found at Rowksley church, a stick man again!" John questioned "I wonder what the hell does this all mean?. Ok, thanks for the quick response Bill". "Is Saron not well John?" John answered, "No she wasn't, but I left early this morning has she not arrived?" "No" was the reply. "Ok Bill, I will give her a call".

John rung Saron, she was a few seconds answering the call. "Hello" she said. "Saron are you not in work today?"asked John. "I'm at Mum's, we think she may have had a stroke the doctors are here now. Can you tell Bill I won't be in today nor possibly tomorrow too. I have left the key in the usual place John, I will stop at Mum's tonight". John was sympathetic, "Blimey Saron it seems to be one thing after another at the moment". "Annie is with us and she has been really good, she told me Mum will be fine" said Saron. "Well if Annie has said that then, speaking from personal experience she will be. Listen Saron, I will call you tonight after work" "Ok John thanks".

John called a meeting for 9am in the incident room. With the information board filling up, Gammon got down to the facts. "Right everyone I have no doubt in my mind we have a serial killer on our hands. This person is collecting the victims' left ear as some kind of trophy and leaving these drawings in chalk at the scene of the crime and then a paper drawing of the same stick man at a church".

John began to breakdown the information. "Victim Number One. What do we know, Scooper?" Scooper spoke, "She was a white female, her name was Maria Dooley she came from a normal family. The only thing tarnishing her slightly is that she was in a long time relationship with a lad called Danny Stevo, but it seems her family thought Rupert Bare was her boyfriend. Other than that she seems clean". "Ok thank you Sandra, Inspector Lee carried on, "The assailant used a 2llb lump hammer, the same type a builder would use. We have interviewed fourteen local builders all have concrete alibi's for the night of the murder". John nodded. "Ok thank you Inspector. So we have what appears to be normal girl, maybe in the wrong place at the wrong time. The current suspects Andrew Bilkin, Tony Lacey, Rupert Bare and Danny Stevo have all been interviewed but with nothing coming from the interviews that casts any suspicions on these people. I might add that that is other than Tony Lacey, the gardener at Chatsworth, who appears to take great pleasure in winding up Andrew Bilkin, who clearly is not quite the full shilling. Also Lacey washed a tee shirt he had been wearing at work. This might not sound much but let's get a bit of history on Mr Lacey please Milton. Check his bank accounts, credit cards, does he have a police record etc etc, then bring any information to me please Carl".

Moving on John said, "Victim Number Two, Poppy Chi. Scooper?" Scooper recounted, "Her body was found last night by a retired game keeper in Rowksley Woods. She had been sexually assaulted and viciously beaten and her left ear had been cut off too. As yet Sir we haven't had chance to investigate much further". Gammon went on, "Inspector, you and I will go and break the bad news to the family straight after this meeting. The one thing we do know is we have a tie here. Mr Wang found the first victim and Poppy Chi was Mr Wang's niece, so we have a common thread here. Inspector Lee and Sergeant Wisey could you get looking at Mr Wang's bank accounts, credit cards, police record etc etc? Let's see if we are missing something here".

"Ok" said John, "Let's get on with it". A voice came from the back of the room. "Before you all disperse, I would like you to know I will be leaving the force from today. My immediate replacement has yet to be decided, but Chief Inspector Gammon will be running the show until further notice. I know you haven't known me long, but I would like to thank you all for your support and I wish you all the very best for the future. I am having a bit of a party Saturday night at the Spinning Jenny everyone is welcome. Please feel free to bring along your partners and friends. I am sure I will see some of you again, as I will be becoming part owner of the Tow'd Man public house from next week. Thanks". Angelina then left the interview room. The staff chatted quietly in groups about the announcement. John spoke up "Ok you lot, let's get focused on the task in hand. Scooper, bring the car round".

ANNIE TANNEY

ANNIE TANNEY

Mr and Mrs Chi lived on the outskirts of Monkdale, in a small hamlet called Ibley. There were only five houses in the hamlet, all of which had been farms in years back. Mr Chi had been the Ambassador for the Peoples Republic of China, so he was a very high ranking official. He and his wife had chosen to live in the UK after he had retired in 2012. His wife wanted to be near her brother Mr Wang. This was quite unusual situation but was duly granted by the British Government.

The Chi house was a beautifully restored Jacobean farmhouse. As Gammon and Scooper walked up the little path to the front door, either side of the path was swayed in lavender and smelt beautiful. The gardens were immaculate. Scooper knocked on the old oak door. A lady answered. She looked about forty years old and very well dressed. Gammon and Scooper showed their warrant cards. John asked "May we come in Mrs Chi?" "What is this all about?" asked Mrs Chi. "It may be better if we could step inside to discuss the reason for our visit" said John.

Mrs Chi showed Gammon and Scooper into the neat sitting room. In one corner was a magnificent Grandfather clock with a beautifully ornate face. In another corner was a baby grand piano. Photographs of the family adorned the top of the piano. "Please take a seat" said Mrs Chi, and she showed them over to the leather settee. "Is your husband here Mrs Chi" asked John. "Yes", she answered, "let me shout him. Xian two policemen are here to see us". "Just a moment" the voice came back. Mr Chi was about five feet six, slightly balding and looked quite a bit older than Mrs Chi. He came over and shook hands with Scooper and Gammon bowing as is the custom.

Mr Chi asked, "How can we help you?" "Please sit down", John replied. Both Mr and Mrs Chi sat down. "There is no easy way for me to tell you this, but I am afraid your daughter was murdered last night". Mr Chi was very angry. "You come into my home and upset my wife and I. Our daughter is in New Zealand, how dare you make such a mistake like this?" John apologised, "I am very sorry if this information is incorrect Mr Chi, but I would like you come with us and identify the body. The person we have in the mortuary is one Poppy Chi. She has recently had dental work done on her teeth". Mr Chi was now very angry. "I have friends in your government and you and the people that tell you these lies will lose their jobs".

Gammon stuck with his line on enquiry and insisted that Chi had to come to the mortuary. Gammon's mind was racing. What if they had got it wrong? Of all the people to upset Mr Chi was not that person. The Chi's got in the car and didn't speak again on the way to Bixton. As they walked down to the mortuary Gammon could feel his heart racing he could not contemplate if Mr Chi was right and he was wrong. They entered the mortuary and Bill Ludlam was waiting. "Mr Chi, Mrs Chi you may find this very distressing". Mr Chi just glared at Gammon, Scooper stood behind them holding her breath. The consequences were not worth contemplating if they had got it wrong.

Gammon nodded to Ludlam and he removed the cotton sheet to reveal the girls face. Mrs Chi fainted. Scooper just managed to save her before she hit the floor. Mr Chi looked straight ahead tears rolling down his cheek. He finally looked at Gammon and said "That is Poppy". Gammon thanked Bill Ludlam and instructed Scooper to take the Chi's to the meeting room. He instructed her to get them two coffees with plenty of sugar in for the shock. Gammon felt relief and sadness at the same time.

They all sat in the meeting room. John began the interview. "I am very sorry for your loss but I do need to ask you some questions Mr Chi". Mr Chi nodded in agreement. "Did Poppy have a boyfriend?" said John "No, she was a good girl" "You said she was in New Zealand Mr Chi?". Mr Chi answered, "We believed she was Mr Gammon. We gave her £15,000 six weeks ago. She has called us every week from New Zealand and said she was enjoying it!! We also have a son Chen, but Poppy was adopted. She was the daughter of Mai Luu who was our cleaner in China. She died very young and her husband could not look after her so we adopted her" "Did Poppy know she was adopted?" asked John. "Yes we told her about a year ago" replied Mr Chi. "Did you see any difference in her behaviour after you told her?" "No, she was a lovely girl", said Mr Chi. "She had been to University in Leeds and left this year with a Masters' Degree in Business Studies. We were so pleased with her and the trip was a present for doing so well". "Did she say who she was going on the trip with?" asked John. Mr Chi answered, "She said her friend from university Maggie Williams was to go with her". John wen ton, "Do you have an address or any contact details for Maggie?" "No Mr Gammon, but we do still have Poppies laptop. She said she wasn't going to taking it with her travelling in case it was stolen. So maybe she will be on there" "Could we have the laptop please, Mr Chi?" "Why do you think she lied to us Mr

Gammon?" John considered his answer carefully, "I am afraid the kids of today are like that Mr Chi. Her brother Chen, where is he?". Mr Chi looked down. "I don't know. We haven't had any contact from Chi for over three years" "Is Chen adopted too?" "No Mr Gammon. He got into some bad company and in the Chinese New Year three years ago we fell out. It was making my wife poorly, he is a naughty boy". "When you say naughty, what do you mean? Mr Chi". Chi replied "He was dealing drugs and things and stealing from us, it had to stop" "So you have no clue where Chen is?" asked John. "No, and I don't want to know. He has shamed his mother and I" said Mr Chi sadly. "Well look Mr Chi, thank you for your co-operation. Sandra will take you home. Would you like a grief councillor to stay with you?" John suggested. "No thank you Mr Gammon. We must be strong and face this ourselves". "If you could give Inspector Scooper a recent picture of Poppy along her laptop please, that would help with our investigations". Mr Chi spoke softly, "Thank you Mr Gammon and I am sorry for my earlier outburst. You have been very kind".

Gammon was distracted, he was thinking about what he had to do with Lund tonight. He was feeling like the guy Mr Chi was portraying.

Scooper took the Chi's home and Gammon went back to his office. It was 3.30pm when Scooper arrived back at the station with the picture of Poppy and her laptop. Gammon locked the laptop away and told Scooper he would look at it in the morning. It was almost time for Gammon to do what he never thought he would have to do, being a serving police officer.

Gammon set off for Maple Cottage in Chesterfield, he needed to get there in the light to work out how he could get inside. By the time John arrived at the small cottage, one set in a row of three, the weather had changed. It was raining heavily and very windy. John noticed a small lane at the side of the cottage so he drove down it. He managed to hide the car behind a big wall, a perfect hiding spot. John quickly changed into his forensic bunny suit with the hood and put the overshoes on.

He got back into the car and waited. He just had to wait for it to go dark. By 7.40pm it was dark enough. He left the car and quickly ran round to the house. When he got to the back door he tried the handle and the door opened. To John's surprise, tied to a chair in the kitchen was Lund. He had been tortured and stabbed repeatedly and was already dead. John's heart was pounding and he knew he had to get out of there and quick. The job had been done already.

He made it back to the car and once inside ripped off the protective suit and overshoes.

John threw them on the back seat and his hiding place behind the wall. On the way out he almost hit an old Vauxhall Nova with a young couple in it. "Damn" he thought. Luckily the weather was so bad it was doubtful that they would have seen him or the number plates.

Once on his way back, his heart was beating like crazy. He phoned Saron. "How's your Mum Saron?" "She is a lot better John. Are you out running? You sound very out of breath" "No, just left work had a heavy day" "Listen John, if you don't mind I am going to stay with Mum and Annie. She's been brilliant John, she held Mum's hand the whole time. We are so lucky to have her here" said Saron. "Don't I know?" said John "Ok Saron, I will call you tomorrow. I think I will nip for a quick pint and something to eat. Speak to you tomorrow" and John cancelled the call. He decided to go to the Spinning Jenny for some food.

When he arrived at the Spinning Jenny, Doreen informed him they had a darts presentation going on, so they weren't doing food. John had almost finished his pint when Sheba Riley came in. John remarked, "Delivering lamb again Sheba?" "Ha Ha very funny Mr Smoothy. I actually called in for some food" "You're out of luck Sheba, they're not doing meals tonight, so I'm going to Up The Steps Maggie's for something" "Do you mind if I tag along Mr Smoothy?". John was thinking "How could he refuse such a beauty?".

"No Sheba, that's fine. I'm going now do you want a lift?" Sheba replied, "No I'll meet you there". "Goodnight Doreen tell Kev I said Hi" said John. "I will John", said Doreen, "goodnight Sheba".

They each got to their own cars. John remembered that he still had the bunny suit and cover shoes on the back seat and he needed to get them put in the boot. So he waited until Sheba had set off and then quickly hid them in the boot.

They arrived virtually at the same time in the pub car park. "What kept you?" laughed Sheba. "Sorry, I Just got a call from work" said John. "Oh really? I thought you were hiding something from me!". "If only she knew" thought John.

John was pleased. Lund was dead and he hadn't had to do anything.

Maggie's was quite busy they had a new chef on duty. John and Sheba sat in the corner. A young girl came across with the menus.

"What would you like to drink Sheba?" "I'll have a double rum and coke please, John" "Ah, sailing with the captain tonight hey Sheba?" Sheba just gave him the dusky maiden look. "I'm going to have a pint of Strawberry Blonde I think. I'll fetch the drinks while you decided on your food" "Strawberry Blonde? So you don't like dark hair then Mr Gammon?" "Give over with the teasing Sheba". She laughed and threw back her dark hair revealing sparkling eyes.

"Right what are we having?" The young girl returned to take their order. "I'll have the slow cooked pork terrine with pickled baby carrots and hazelnuts and for my mains I will have the Ackbourne pork plate with horseradish mash, spiced red cabbage and pork spiced jus" said Sheba. "and for you sir?" asked the waitress. "I will have the Scallops with red lentil Dahl and cumin carrot coriander, followed by the Venison with bitter chocolate with the infused mustard bubble and squeak, asparagus tips lightly battered". "Would you like any wine Sheba?" asked John. "Always up for some wine John" she said. "Red or white?" asked John "Red please". "Ok we will have a bottle of the house Merlot please" said John to the waitress. The waitress left with the orders.

"So John, how is the love life? Where Saron tonight?" asked Sheba. "Saron's mum is poorly, so she's staying at the Hall tonight. What about your love life Sheba?". Sheba laughed, "What love life? I'm happy being single to be honest. I have my own place. I love my job and have good friends John. I never get the impression that you are a settling down person John, either in your love life or your working life".

John replied, "To be honest you are right. I've been married before and she hurt me quite bad" "Oh, I didn't know you had been married John" "Yes, but I'm divorced now" "Are you still friends?" "No, not really, she wasn't a particularly nice person Sheba, but that's a long story" "So what's the score with you and Saron?" "Well at the moment we are living together, simply because my cottage was burned down, with Saron now taking the Tow'd Man with her friend Angelina, I think I will rent the Post Office Cottage for myself, until the barns are done down at my parents farm. Where do you live?" Sheba sighed, "I have a tied cottage.

It's owned by Lord Cote-Heath. It's his sheep I look after".

The young girl returned with the starters, placing them neatly in front of John and Sheba. "Enjoy" she said with a smile and she left. "Wow this looks great. How's yours John?" "Superb, thanks Sheba". They finished the starter and then the main course and retired to the bar. John turned to Sheba, "Do you fancy a floater coffee Sheba?" "I'd prefer a good double brandy John" she said. "Ok, brandy it is then".

It was 9.30pm when Shelly and Jack Etchings came in. "Hello you two what are you celebrating?" Shelley and Jack never made comment on the fact that John was with Sheba and not Saron. They were good people who just let other people get on with their lives.

By 10.00pm the drinks were flowing and Sheba was getting slightly tipsy. John nipped to the toilet and Sheba followed. As John went in the gents, Sheba followed him. She grabbed him. Once inside they kissed passionately. "John are you going to stay with me tonight?" drooled Sheba. Once again he was faced with the thought that Saron had done so much for him, but the pull of such a beautiful girl was hard to resist. He agreed and then said "Get out quick in case anyone comes in". Sheba left. They both arrived back about the same time. Jack and Shelley never said anything. "Right you two we're off" said Shelley "Are you going to the races on Saturday with the trip from the Spinning Jenny" "Not booked anything Shelley" said John. "I have" said Sheba. "Well we'll see you Saturday Sheba. You must get booked John there are a few places left. It's a big meeting at Uttoxeter and we've planned to call at the Staffordshire Knot on the way back for a meal. Anyway nice to see you both" said Shelly, and she and Jack left.

John and Sheba had one more drink. John said he would drive to Sheba's cottage and bring her back for her car in the morning. The drive to Sheba's was spectacular. The night sky was a carpet of bright twinkling star's, the little country lanes were dotted with wildlife at every turn. He saw two foxes, a badger and several rabbits. Sheba had her head on John's shoulder and had snuggled up to him.

They arrived her cottage, with it's small leaded windows and beautiful oak door, John was impressed. He got Sheba out of the car and she was pretty much done for, so he took her straight upstairs, gently undressed her leaving her underwear on to cover her modesty and slipped her into bed she wasn't aware of anything. John made his way down stairs and slept on the settee. Not quite the night he had expected after the toilet incident but that's life.

John was awake early so he made some toast and waited for Sheba to surface it was 8.0 am and still no sign her, so John left a note on the kitchen table with his phone number, saying "Call me when you need picking up to fetch your car". John climbed into his car and nipped back to Saron's for a quick shower and change of clothes. He had left his phone in the car and had fourteen missed calls. All from Angelina, so he called her back immediately.

"Hi Angelina sorry, I had left my phone in the car" said John. "Well, have I got some good news for you John. Brian Lund is no more. His body was found by officers today. Whilst it's no longer anything to do with me, I still have contacts who have told me know. It appears he was tortured, a young couple saw a Freelander leaving the scene in an erratic manner. They didn't get the registration number of the vehicle, so I guess that was lucky for whoever did the deed. There won't be a follow up because he was officially dead as part of his cover, so this is a win, win situation. I thought I would let you know".

Gammon could tell that she thought he had done it, but it didn't matter. The evil bastard was finished and that's all that mattered. "Ok, thanks Angelina I will see you soon". Once changed Gammon set off for Bixton.

"Good morning Sir" "Good morning Yap. Any incidents I need to be aware of from last night?" replied Gammon. "Nothing reported Sir" confirmed Yapp.

John Gammon climbed the stairs and on his way grabbed a cup of the dishwater coloured coffee from the machine. He sat looking at his pile of paperwork. Scoopers head appeared round the office door, "Morning Sir" she said. "Morning Sandra", replied John. "Sorry to hear about Saron's mum John" "They think she will be ok" he continued, "She has had a lot of stress on lately". "Will you give her my best wishes when you see her?" she asked. "Yes Sandra, thanks, I will"

Gammon carried on with his paperwork. In the pile there was a letter for him from the Chief Constable of Derbyshire advising him that he was in charge at Bixton Station until further notice.

"Sir, I have a Jayne Thornley-Coil on line one for you" "Ok Ian thanks, put her through".

"Hello Jayne, how can I help you?" he asked. "Nothing really John, just an update for you, I am expecting the your project to be completed in the next two weeks, earlier than quoted, so obviously cheaper as well.

So that will mean I will be able to get straight on to your friends pub quicker than I thought" Obviously pleased John said, "That's great news Jayne, I will let them know and thanks for the big effort getting this project done ahead of schedule" "Not a problem John, it's what I do best. Speak soon".

Gammon finished the rest of his paperwork. He took Poppy Chi's laptop from where he'd put it. He opened it up and strangely he didn't need a password, he was straight in. Gammon headed for the in box for her e-mails. One of the last emails she received, before telling her parents she was going travelling in New Zealand, was from her brother Chan. It appeared there had been about twenty emails back and forth between her and Chan. The first one made reference to her drug habit which, she denied. He insisted he was right and he knew this to be fact because he was the one running the streets of Ackbourne and Bixton.

Gammon had never heard of this man's name before, which concerned him somewhat if, what he was saying, was true.

By the tenth e-mail Chan's tone was getting quite vitriolic. Chan said "You are a stupid little bitch, your mother was a whore cleaner. My mother is too good for you"

Poppy didn't replied to that e mail for a few days, then she emailed back. "How dare you call my mother when it's you who has brought disgrace on our family? You have always hated me and the feeling is now mutual. You are jealous because I am now in Mother and Fathers affections and you are out of their lives. I will inherit everything and you will get nothing".

The emails continued in equal amounts of nastiness, but the final email was the chilling one. Chan wrote, "You daughter of a

Chinese Whore, I am going to kill you and cut you up. They will never find you and therefore you will get nothing. Keeping looking over your shoulder Poppy". He signed the email off with a picture of a smiley face and a knife. The emails at that point dried up.

Gammon looked further back and found she had a friend called, Rosie Wilson, who she had been at college with. She had arranged to meet with Rosie for a coffee and a catch up, two months before she had left on this fantasy trip to New Zealand. John looked in Poppy's address and book sure enough there was Rosie Wilson. Her address was listed as 76, Churchtown Road, Dilley Dale and a mobile phone number.

Gammon called the number listed for Rosie. A quietly spoken lady answered. Hello? Is that Rosie Wilson a friend of Poppy Chi?", asked John. "Yes who is this?" was the reply. "I'm Chief Inspector John Gammon of

Bixton Police" "How can I help you?" she asked. "I wondered if we could have an informal chat Miss Watson?". "I'm not sure" she said. "Miss Watson, I am a police officer and I could ask you to come to the station" explained John. "Ok, I understand. Can we meet at Starbucks in Dilley Dale at say 2.00pm?". "That will be fine Rosie", replied John. "Ok, I will sit in the window. I have long ginger hair" she said giving a brief description of herself. "See you at 2.00pm Rosie" said John.

Gammon called Saron. "How is your Mum?" he asked her. Saron replied "She's a lot better John, thank you. I will be back home tonight and back at work tomorrow. Where did you go last night?" "I went to the Spinning Jenny, but they weren't doing food, so I ended up at Up The Steps Maggie's, they have a new chef. I bumped into Sheba Filey, so I sat and had a meal with her". Saron went very quiet and then said "You do know she fancies you don't you?" "Don't be daft Saron, we only had a meal together" he said. "Sorry John, the green eyed monster was surfacing there", she said apologetically. "Don't worry Saron, we are fine" "Ok, forget I said that. What time will you be back tonight?" "Not sure, but hopefully not too late why?" Saron answered, "It's just that I have invited Angelina for dinner and I was doing to do a coconut chicken curry" John replied, "I'll do my best, say 6.00pm. No change that to 6.30pm, so that I have time to have a shower" "Ok, before you go John, will you pick up a cheesecake for desert? I can't be bothered making anything". "Ok Saron, see you later".

Gammon arrived at Starbucks and Rosie Wilson was sat in the window just as she said she would be. John grabbed a coffee and sat down with Rosie. He showed her his warrant card. "What is this all about Mr Gammon?" asked Rosie. "I'm afraid your friend from college, Poppy Chi, was found murdered. During our investigations your name came up as a friend in her emails". Rosie looked shocked. "I'm sorry Rosie did you not know?" "No Mr Gammon" she said shakily. "Can you just try and give me some background on Poppy, please Rosie".

Rosie began, "Well we were at University together and were friends from day one. Poppy was a bubbly character, but by our third year she had changed" "What do you mean changed?" asked John. "Well, she had started hanging out with some unsavoury characters" said Rosie. John asked, "Can you expand on what you mean Rosie?" "Well she had started seeing a guy called Billy Holland. He……", Rosie stopped and then continued, "Mr Gammon, I feel bad talking about Poppy like this. She was such a lovely girl until she got with Billy" John tried to put Rosie at ease. "Rosie you may have the clue to her murder, so please don't think you are being disloyal to Poppy".

Poppy took a deep breath and started again. "She met Billy at a gig we had gone to see, The Who. Poppy's father bought us the tickets for her birthday. We were singing along and dancing, like you do, when this guy started dancing with Poppy.

He was older than us, I would have said he was in his mid-thirties, but a good looking guy. He had quite long black hair and the features similar to those of Johnny Depp's character, Jack Sparrow. I always used to joke with him in the early days, asking him where is parrot was and things like that. He seemed a really nice guy. I had stayed in one night and Poppy had gone out with Billy. When she came back it was clear she was on something. She started saying she could see pink elephants with diamonds for eyes, it was all very weird Mr Gammon. Two days after the incident I asked her about it and she got really angry, saying it was none of my business. She did apologise sometime later, but she admitted to me that she had taken Heroin. I was shocked Mr Gammon. Things just went from bad to worse after that. She became hooked. She told me once that she was so desperate for a fix, Billy had told her that she had to sleep with a client of his and then he would give her the fix she wanted".

Rosie went on "How the hell she passed out with such good results is beyond me as she was high as a kite all the time. She said that she and Billy were going to live together. He had told her to tell her parents that she was going to go travelling and that she would need about £10,000. Which I know they gave to her, and I know she gave it all to Billy, so he would keep her supplied with heroin. A couple of weeks ago she told me her brother Chan, had contacted her. He had found out about Billy and the heroin and he had threatened to kill her, saying his parents didn't deserve this. I know she was worried, because the last time we spoke, she said she was going to get clean, but it was going to be hard because she said Billy liked her on the heroin. It was such a mess, but that's about all I know Mr Gammon"
"Do you have an address for Billy or Chan?"

"Poppy said she wasn't allowed to give me her address with Billy, because he wouldn't like it and that he could get violent if she didn't do as she was told Mr Gammon".

John said, "Rosie, thank you for your help. This is my card, if anything else comes to mind, please give me a call day or night" and he handed her his card. "Ok Mr Gammon". Rosie put her coat on, her extra-long scarf and her gloves and she left the coffee shop. Gammon finished his coffee and headed back to the station.

Di Trimble was on duty when Gammon arrived back. "Good afternoon Di. Can you get me Inspector Scooper and Sergeant Milton to my office please?" "Will do Sir" she said.

Gammon climbed the stairs and grabbed a coffee. As he walked past the office that had once seen Allen, Griff, Robinson, Sonjack and of course poor Vicky in there, he felt empty. He had loved Vicky and Lund had taken everything that was close to him away. His murder wasn't a consolation for Gammon. Although pleased Lund was no longer around to cause even more misery, he wanted him to suffer and he wanted to be the one to meter the pain to him. What a mixed up person he had become, he thought.

John Gammon sat in his office. First Milton came in and then Scooper. "Ok you two, I have a task for you, I want you to find the whereabouts of Chan Chi and a guy called Billy Holland" "Any idea where they might be?", asked Milton. John replied "I'm guessing Derby for Holland, and Ackbourne for Chan, but I really don't know. I want these men finding and bringing in for questioning as soon as possible". "We'll do our best Sir" said Scooper.

It was almost 5.00pm when Saron knocked on John's door. "John do you mind if I go to

Mum's again tonight? I know I have been neglecting you" "Don't be silly, it's not a problem. I will call at the Spinning Jenny and have a bar meal" he said "You're a star" she said and she kissed him "I have just told Bill I will be leaving at the end of the week. Are you going to come and live with me at the pub John?" John answered carefully, "No. You will have enough on initially. I was told earlier that my holiday cottages are ahead of schedule, so think I will stay at yours until they are done and then take one of them on".

Saron looked a bit down, in her mind she was thinking "here he goes again running from commitment" but she knew that she couldn't say anything or it would drive him away totally. "What's the plan with Annie Tanney?" asked John. Saron replied "I think she's coming to live here with Mum, which I'm really pleased about John" "Well it will certainly be better for your Mum. I must come with you sometime soon, it would be nice to see Annie".

"Ok John, well I'd best get off to Mum's" she said. "Just a quick one, Saron, how did Bill take it about your leaving?" asked John. "I'm not sure, to be honest, you know Bill he plays things close to his chest doesn't he?" "Guess so" said John, "I'll see you tomorrow then Saron". "Bye" she said, and she left.

John decided to have another look through Poppy's laptop to see if he had missed anything. He didn't understand why it wasn't password protected. Gammon started searching word documents on Poppy's laptop. He came across a two page document which appeared to be a letter. The letter was very sad.

"Dear Father,

The past years growing up have been hard for me, my adopted parents have always done their best for me, but I miss you so much and long for the day when I can come and see you again.

I never wanted to tell you this, but I need to share this heavy burden I am carrying and there is only you that will understand.

I met somebody in my last year at University and for the first few months everything was great, but the he introduced me to heroin. I am now just a wretch that can no longer be trusted. I told my adopted parents I wanted to go travelling, so they gave me £10,000 as a present for doing well at University. I realise this is 100,000 in Chinese Yuan and that is worth about two years of work that you would have to do Father, to have that much money. I have been reckless, I have spent the money on heroin. I am so ashamed of myself Father.

You must think of me as a selfish girl who has dishonoured you and my adoptive parents and for that I will be eternally sorry. Chan, who is my adopted brother, left our family home in disgrace. He is a bad man father. Now he has found out about me and he is threatening to kill me and he is more than capable.

I have to go now Father, please don't think too badly of me. I pray you are still alive and that this letter finds you.

Your loving daughter

Poppy"

Gammon sat in his chair thinking how desperate Poppy must have been to open her soul to the one person she trusted and respected in the world. With these thoughts running through his mind, the key to all this was finding Chan and Billy Holland. Gammon left the office.

John pulled up at the Spinning Jenny, the car park was almost empty. "Evening Kev" he said. "Hi John, what do you think to my new red dickie bow? Doreen got it for me, it's got little Springer spaniels on it" "Can I say no comment mate", and John laughed. Kev responded, "No style, that's you John Gammon" "Clearly not, Kev. Is Doreen cooking tonight?" "Yes she is lad, what would you like?" enquired Kev. John replied, "I'll just have the Irish Bangers with Colcannon, red cabbage and Onion gravy. Can you ask Doreen if she will put one of her Stilton Dumplings on as well?". Kev laughed, "She would do anything for you lad, that's a given. What are you drinking?" "A pint of your very best Pedigree mate please".

"When does Saron take on the Tow'd Man John" "Next Monday Kev, I think her and Angelina will do well" "Yes" said Kev "They get a fair few walkers in there, so they should be ok. Denis and Clara haven't really pushed it for the last couple of years and then when the Limping Duck opened up, they must have thought it was time to get out" "How did that affect your business Kev?" Not a lot really" answered Kev. "I think the Sloppy Quiche Café hurts us more when they have their theme nights".

Kev went off to the kitchen with John's order. John sat back and relaxed with his pint, until he got a tap on the shoulder. "Give us a kiss you handsome brute". "So much for my quiet night, Carol" said John. "You can have a quiet night when you are dead and buried" said Carol, "enjoy the flipping moment, that's what I say. You're here for a good time not a long time John". "Very true Carol, what are you having to drink?" "Double Vodka and a full fat coke" she laughed.

"Where are you going to sit for your dinner John?" "Put me by the fire Kev" he said.

John's meal arrived and as usual Doreen had gone over the top for him. It was a really big plate full. Three Irish Bangers, a large portion of Colcannon, a Yorkshire pudding and two stilton dumplings. On the side in separate dishes were cauliflower cheese, carrots, green beans, broccoli and onion rings. "Wow, that smells and looks fabulous Doreen, thank you". "Enjoy lad, I have to look after my favourite son" teased Doreen. "He's everybody's favourite son" piped up Carol. "He sure is Carol. Are you coming to the races on Saturday John?" enquired Doreen. "I'm not sure if Saron will be able to make it Doreen, her Mum hasn't been well and with her taking over the Tow'd Man on Monday it's a bit much". "Well you can still come" she said. "I'll tell you what, I will pay for two tickets" said John, "then if Saron can't come, I'm sure I will get someone else to come". Carol chipped in "With your bloody track record, they will be queuing round the block". "I think you're right Carol" said Doreen. "Oh I know I am Doreen" smirked Carol. "Will you let a man have his dinner?" asked John. Doreen ruffled John's hair We're only winding you up John".

John finished his dinner and had one more beer. It was now 10.30pm and John was ready to leave, when his phone rang. It was Uncle Graham. John never knew what to call Graham, so he stuck with Uncle. "Hi Uncle Graham, are you ok?" "Well sort of John, I need to see you sooner rather than later. Can you come up" he asked. "Are you ok?" asked John. "I will tell you when I see you John" "Ok I will come up Friday night straight after work" "Ok John thank you" said Uncle Graham.

John made to leave. "Thanks Doreen, that was a lovely dinner". "Nice to see you John" said Doreen. "See you Carol" said John. "Goodnight gorgeous" Carol shouted across the bar.

ANNIE TANNEY

It wasn't a particularly nice evening the fog was swirling in the valley as John headed down the road towards Hittington. Hittington church stood majestically, mocking the awful evening weather.

John parked up at the cottage and went inside. He poured himself a Jameson's and tapped Saron's mobile number into his phone. "Hey how are you?" he asked her. "I'm good thanks, sweetheart. Have you had your tea at the Spinning Jenny?" she asked. "Yeah, it was very nice. How's your Mum?" She is good John. She and Annie have had me in stitches reminiscing about the old days. I really am excited about the pub John, and now that Jayne Thornley-Coil says she will be able to start work quicker than we originally thought, we could have it all done for the summer season. What do you think?" "Yeah, it sounds like that's possible. I have booked two tickets for the races on Saturday. There's a bus trip from the Spinning Jenny, then a meal on the way back. Do you fancy it?" Saron sighed, "I can't John, Denis has said we can start moving our stuff in, so I planned to do that on Saturday and Sunday with Angelina. Surely somebody will take the ticket?" "No problem, you have got a lot on at the minute I know. Listen I'm going to get some sleep so I'll speak to you tomorrow" said John "Ok sweetheart, speak tomorrow".

John wasn't too bothered about going to the races, but now he had a ticket, Saron was moving all weekend, so he thought he might as well go.

John was up and showered by 7.30am, so he set off for work early. He called at his favourite greasy spoon, Beryl's Butties, but sadly since she died, the new people weren't making much of a go at it. Something else in his life that had changed.

He arrived at 8.10am at Bixton station. "Good morning Sir" said Yapp. "Good morning Ian", replied John, "any problems from last night?" "Only old Billy Carter, he's drunk in one of the cells. I think the police constable that arrested him, felt sorry for him. At least if he's in here, he gets a roof over his head for the night and breakfast Sir". "Yeah, Billy is more like a resident than a criminal. Make sure he gets a shower and a shave before we let him out Ian" "Will do Sir".

Gammon climbed the stairs and was met by Inspector Scooper. "You're in early Sandra?" he said. "Can't do enough for a good boss Sir" and she smiled that wicked smile. "I think I may have a lead on Chan Chi. An informer I use said he's a nasty piece of work. He traffics girls onto the streets around Derby. He thinks he has stepped into the void left by Brian Lund Sir" "That's all I need, another one of him, Sandra"

"Anyway Sir, I am seeing my informer this morning in a coffee shop just off Hangman's Gate Road, near the market" "Right, give me a shout and I will come with you" said John. "Ok Sir. Oh I forgot to ask, are you going to the races with the Spinning Jenny lot, I didn't see your name down?" John replied "I am, I brought two tickets, but Saron is moving". Sandra asked John, "Could I buy the other ticket from you? Only I didn't really know anyone on the sheet for the bus, so I didn't get a ticket" "Yes of course you can, I don't want paying for it, have it as a thank you for all the hard work you are putting in on this case" he offered. "Thank you Sir. I will let you know when my informer gets in touch".

John got his normal coffee and sat in his office, again he began looking through Poppy's laptop for any clue's that might lead to her killer. He found a reference to a club called "Shoot Up", which she described as being in a cellar in Gun Street. She wrote, "I love this place even though it is dirty, me and Billy score in here. Well I score, Billy doesn't use, very often he is too busy working". Brilliant he thought now we may have a lead. Gammons plan were to go and look at this place after they had met Sandra's informant.

Milton popped his head round the door, "I'm not having much luck with Billy Holland Sir". "Don't worry Carl, I may have found something on Poppy's laptop". Gammon proceeded to tell Carl what he'd found and told him to be ready as he was coming along with him and Scooper.

It was 11.00am when Scooper said the guy rang and agreed be at the café at 11.50am, so they headed off to Derby for the meeting. Gammon managed to park just across the road from where the café was. It was a busy little place. Taxi drivers seemed to be in abundance, drinking coffee and eating. The café looked resembled a throw-back to the sixties. All the tables had plastic checked table clothes and those sugar shakers that always get clogged up, so are of no use to man nor beast.

Inspector Scooper's informant was a guy who looked down on his luck. He hadn't shaved for a few years and wore a parka with a fur hood which had seen far better days. Gammon got him a coffee and they sat down. Scooper explained who Gammon and Milton were and what it was all about.

The informant only gave his name as Jono he said he knew Chan Chi and that he traffics girls from Asia, to work the streets. He said he had always worked the Southside of Derby and Lund ran the North side but when Lund had gone he muscled in and now ran all of Derby. Jono seemed nervy and on edge sharing this information, he was constantly looking round the café.

"How do you know Chan?" asked John. "I drink in the Drovers, always have done, he came in the other week bragging about how it was now his pub and his territory and if anybody didn't agree with him, they were to stand up. Jimmy Steele, who had been one of Lund's men, got up to leave. Chan called him over. Jimmy is a big man all of six feet four against Chan, who is about six feet one. As Jimmy approached him, Chan smashed a pint pot in his face, then all his henchmen were kicking Jimmy, he was in a bad way, they threw him in a wheelie bin in the alleyway. He would have died Mr Gammon, so when I left I phoned for an ambulance. If Chan found out what I had done, he would kill me. Lund was sadistic but this guy is Psychotic".

"Ok Jono, so this bastard drinks in the Drovers?" "No, not all the time he is mainly in Queens Arms in Buckle Street. That's where he runs his business from" "Ok Jono, thank you for your help". Gammon had no sooner got the words out of his mouth and Jono was gone.

"Ok it looks like it's a matter of "the King is dead, long live the King" for the streets of Derby" said John. "We always knew the void would be filled Sir" "You're right Milton, it's just dreadful that these people crawl out of the woodwork, but I guess if we didn't have these people, they wouldn't need us. Right come on, let's see if we can find Billy Holland. If we go to that club there maybe somebody there who knows him. It's on Gyle Street" said John. "Not the Shoot Up club?" asked Milton. "Yes Carl do you know it?" "It's an horrendous place Sir. To get in you are vetted by the staff. We raided it a few times when I was in Rapid Response, but the owners always seemed to be just one step ahead. We never found anything, although there was always a lingering smell of weed". "Well let's try our luck" said John.

They drove down to Gyle Street and just by chance the guy they thought they were looking for was just leaving the club, with two girls. Gammon pulled over, got out the car and walked up to the man. He flashed his warrant card and with that the two girls started to run away. Milton and Scooper chased after them. John spoke to the man, "Are you Billy Holland Sir?". The man replied, "Who's asking?" "Chief Inspector Gammon of Bixton Police" replied John. The man answered, "I could be". John continued, "If you wouldn't mind Sir, we have a few questions we would like to put to you down at the station".

Holland didn't show any signs of resistance. Milton and Scooper had caught up with the runaway girls and had them bundled in the back of the police car. They all ended up in the squashed in the car. Holland, the two girls and Milton in the back with Scooper and Gammon in the front not ideal or legal, but needs must.

Back at Bixton Station, Gammon took Holland into interview room one with Milton. Scooper took the two girls with Inspector Lee into interview room two.

Milton asked Holland if he needed a solicitor, Holland said he was fine, so Milton set up the tape and they started the interview.

"Mr Holland, may I call you Billy?" asked John. "Yes" replied Holland. "Ok Billy, what can you tell us about Poppy Chi?" "I met Poppy at a gig. She seemed like a really nice girl, but it turned out she was a heroin addict" said Holland. John was intrigued, "Are you telling us that Poppy was a heroin addict before you met her?" Yes why?" "Mr Holland, when was the last time you saw Poppy?" "A few weeks back. She was out of control so I avoided her" answered Holland. "You do know she is dead Mr Holland, and that we are investigating a murder?". Holland replied quickly, "No when did she die?" "Are you seriously expecting me to believe you didn't know she had been murdered?" asked John, "You can think what you like Inspector. You asked me to come here, I have nothing to hide" "Mr Holland, we have been reliably informed that you lived with Poppy". Holland got agitated, "That's bullshit. She was sleeping around. I told you she had a drug habit. Why would I want to live with that?". Gammon was a little disturbed, but he had a feeling Billy was telling the truth. "What do you do for a living Billy?" "Oh a bit of this and a bit of that", he replied. John wasn't happy, "Shall we try again Billy? Now what do you do to support yourself?" Holland sneered, "I claim benefits, I don't have a job" "So where do you live Billy?" "Gascoyne Gardens in Ackbourne" he replied "Nice properties Billy. How do you afford one of those?" "I was left family money" "You do know we can check these things don't you Billy?" "Look I haven't murdered Poppy. In fact she had become a liability" "Well can you explain these letters? She told her father back in China that you ran a business and did occasional drugs" "Look she was bloody delusional, I wish I had never met her she was sleeping around, taking drugs and just a total pain in the arse"

John pressed on with his questions. "Well let me tell you what I think Billy. I think you were seeing Poppy, I also think you groomed her into taking drugs to use her for your gains, once she was addicted. I also think you are not telling us everything about how you support yourself. Are you involved with Chan Chi?" "Who's that?" asked Billy. "Try again Billy, because you are testing my patience now" said John. "Ok, yes I have heard of him, Poppy said it was her brother" "What do you know about Chan Chi?" "I know I would be a fool to talk about him to you people" "And why is that Billy" "Because he would cut me up. He run's Derby, I'm not telling you anything you don't already know yourselves".

Again John pressed on. "Ok Billy let me have a little word in your shell like ear. You deal drugs, you got Poppy Chi into heroin and I believe very little of what you have told us. You are a suspect in the murder of Poppy Chi and possibly that of Maria Dooley". "Who the hell is Maria Dooley? I don't know her". "Let me worry about Maria, be very sure that we are watching you every step of the way. You are not allowed to leave the country and if you decide to move anywhere, you must first inform Bixton Police Station of your new address. You are on my radar Billy and that isn't good for you. Interview terminated at 3.05pm Friday the 14th of March. You are free to leave Mr Holland but don't take us for fools. You so much as sneeze in the wrong place and we will nick you. Get him out of my sight Sergeant Milton".

Gammon went back to his office on his way upstairs he called at Scoopers office and informed her that on Monday they would be going to find Chan and bring him in for questioning. He also told her he would need Milton to join them. "Ok Sir, no problem" said Scooper. "How did you get on with the two runaway girls?" asked John. "Not a lot to report really. They had clearly been smoking something and I now think they were high class hookers, but I had no proof, so we let them go Sir" "Are you off now Sir?" "Yes Sandra, I'm going to see my Uncle Graham" "Oh ok, is there any chance you can give me a lift to the Spinning Jenny for the race bus in the morning?" "Blimey I'd forgotten about that, yes of course Scooper" "I think they are all meeting at

10.00am for bacon sandwiches and bucks fizz" she said. "Great, see you about 9.45 am then?"

John left work and drove up to his Uncle Graham's in Sheffield. It was 6.10pm when he arrived at the tidy detached bungalow on the outskirts of Sheffield. This was the first time he had been there since finding out that Uncle Graham was actually his father. John felt a little nervous at the thought of seeing his Uncle. It was going to be a meeting with just them two and he wasn't sure what his Uncle Graham wanted.

Graham answered the door. John thought he didn't look at all well. His skin was a pale grey and he was a little stooped. "Come in lad would you like a cup of tea?" said Uncle Graham "Yes please" replied John. "Go through to the lounge John, while I make the tea". John went into the lounge. In the corner was a display cabinet, filled with Crown Derby. His wife used to collect it. On top of the cabinet were family photos. Pictures John could remember. Adam and John sat on the tractor in their shorts and matching cable knit jumpers their Mum had knitted. Another of Phil and Graham at the seaside, maybe Blackpool, they had "kiss me quick" hats on, a pint in one hand and an ice cream in the other. The one that stuck out from them all was of John, as a baby, with his Mum and Uncle Graham laughing. John picked it up for a closer look. Graham walked in the room with the teas and a plate of rich tea biscuits. John felt a little uncomfortable and placed the picture back on the cabinet. Uncle graham said, "My wife took that John and I know what you are thinking. I tried very hard not to love your mum and she never gave me any reason to believe she wasn't happy with Phil" "Why have you asked me to come

Uncle Graham?" "This is going to come as a bit of a shock John, but I only have weeks to live. I have been suffering with lung cancer for some time now and on my last visit to the hospital, they told me to come home and get my affairs in order".

John was gutted. Why he hadn't tried harder to get to know is biological father?. "I don't know what to say, Uncle Graham, I am finding it hard to call you Dad" "I understand son, but it's no good holding onto past regrets. You need to know that I didn't abandon you or anything, quite the opposite actually, but I couldn't make waves for your Mum and Phil. I want you to know that in my will, my estate is left to you. Hopefully it will make up for how you were treated by Phil in his will" john was shocked, "I don't know what to say" "Say nothing lad. I am very proud of you. I just wish this dammed disease hadn't robbed me of the chance of getting to know you better".

Graham and John talked for three hours. John said he would come up the following week and if need be, he would stop with him overnight. Graham thanked him, and John left for the drive back to Derbyshire.

Tragedy seemed to follow John around, maybe he should make this his last case in Derbyshire and head back to London once the murderer was convicted.

John arrived back and called at the Spinning Jenny. The first person he saw was his mate, Steve Lineman. "Hey top man, how are you?" said Steve cheerily. "Not bad Steve" "What are you drinking John?" "I'll try a pint of Ackbourne Bitter please Steve" "Good choice John" said Kev the landlord, "I've sold loads of this since Wednesday. How are you lad?" "Not bad thanks Kev" said John glumly. "Bloody hell Kev, do we have Mr Happy here tonight Kev? Said Steve. "Leave the lad alone. Had a bad day at work John?" "No Kev, just been to see my Uncle Graham in Sheffield" "How is he John?" "Not good Kev, I'm afraid he has only a matter of weeks to live, he has lung cancer" "Bloody hell lad, I am sorry" "Yeah, he is my last surviving relative Kev". Passing John the pint, he said, "Here have that on me" Steve spoke, "Sorry mate never thought. I was only joking with you" "Steve you weren't to know mate" said John.

Steve changed the subject. "On a better note, I see your name is down for the races. Jo will be pleased her and Saron can have a catch up" "Saron can't make it mate, she's moving her stuff into the Tow'd Man, she takes over on Monday" "Oh is there a spare ticket then?" "No Steve, I've already sold it" "Who too?" asked Steve. "Sandra Scooper", said John. "Bloody hell Gammon, you don't let the grass grow under your feet do you?" "Behave Steve, she's a work colleague" "Yeah and I'm Rod bloody Stewart!" said Steve and he laughed. That got a chuckle from Kev too, his red dickie bow jumping up and down on his Adam's apple.

John called it a night at 10.30pm. "I will see you in the morning lads" "Ok mate don't forget your work colleague!" Steve shouted and he started singing the Rod Stewart song "Do Yah Think I'm Sexy?".

On his way home John phoned Saron, "How are you, sweetheart?" "I'm good John, still packing stuff up", she replied. "Have you eaten?" she asked John. "No, but I'm not really hungry" he replied. "I would like to crack on with the packing if you don't mind. You must have called at the pub for one?" "Yeah I bumped into Steve in the Spinning Jenny".

Before Saron could ask who had taken her ticket for the races, John told her about Uncle Graham. "Oh John I am sorry" said Saron. John told her "He looked dreadful. I said I would go up to Sheffield to see him again next week, they have only given him three weeks" "Oh the poor man. This year hasn't started off too good for either of us John" "I know, I thought last year was bad enough, but here we go again. Listen when I home I'm going to go straight to bed if you are packing" "No problem love, see you in a while" said Saron.

John did has he said, as soon as he got in he went straight to bed. Saron had told him she would be moving from 7.00am, so probably wouldn't see him tomorrow. John was happy with that. He would face the questions about the ticket on Sunday, when he had been to the races with Sandra.

The morning of the races arrived. John had donned his tweed coat, a cream coloured Paul Smith shirt with a bright orange tie, brown moleskin trousers with Kurt Geiger brogue shoes.

Arriving at Sandra's she appeared like a vision. She had a peacock coloured fascinator, complementing her long brown hair. Her dress was blue, with white polka dots and she wore some very high heeled, blue Jimmy Choo shoes.

"Stunning, Miss Scooper" complimented John. "You're not looking to bad yourself Mr Gammon". They both laughed and headed for the Spinning Jenny.

Bob and Cheryl, Steve and Jo were already there. John and Sandra were followed into the bar, by Carol Lestar. Jack and Shelly Etchings, and to John's surprise, Sheba Riley with a guy John didn't know. Doreen was all dressed up in her best dress, as were all the party. This was a big day, the Midland Grand National.

"Ok everyone, bacon cobs are served, get your glass of Bucks Fizz". Kev was scuttling about with his camera, "I need a picture of you motley crew for posterity". He took half dozen pictures and then the bus driver was honking his horn for them all to get on the bus. This was going to be a nervous moment for John. He wasn't sure what kind of reaction he would get with Sandra sitting next to him.

They all got on the bus settling into their respective seats. Pant's on Your Head Bob had commandeered the back seat so he could tell his jokes, much to Cheryl's annoyance.

Carol Lestar was the first to comment. "We should all be safe today, we have two coppers on the bus to contend with". Steve was next. "Nice to see a pretty one though" this was Steve's way of supporting John. I'll agree with that Steve lad" said Jack Etchings, which cost him a clip round the ear from Shelley. John decided to speak. "Any tips Kev?" "I have two nailed on winners" said Kev. "Tell us then". Kev said "Growler in the 2.55pm and Miss Prickly Dickly in the 4.10pm". Everyone fell about laughing. John turned to Sandra and said "I fancy Miss Prickly Dickly" She smiled and said "Then you need to earn the right Mr Gammon" and she turned her head with a little smile on her face and looked out of the window towards the beautiful countryside.

Bob had started his jokes. "Have you heard this one? "A man walks into a bar with a giraffe. He orders a pint for him and a double brandy for the giraffe. He stands on a stool and gives the brandy to the giraffe who downs it in one"" Steve heckles him "Come on Bob spit it out" "It's nearly over Steve. "The giraffe promptly falls over, taking up the bar area, the guy finishes his pint and starts to leave. The landlord seeing this runs from behind the bar, with his red dickie bow, just a quick reference there Kev" "Bloody hell Bob hurry up, we're nearly there" said Shelly. "Be patient Shelley" and he carried on "The landlord says you can't leave that lying there! The man says, it isn't a lion it's a giraffe".

Sandra was the only one who laughed, everyone else just groaned.

They arrived at the course, it was packed, everyone in their race day outfits. "Have you picked any horses yet John?" "Not yet Sandra, let's get a race card and go into the champagne bar, Kev said he has reserved a table for us all". Sure enough Kev had done them proud they not only had a table, but they also had their own personal waitress and a young man to take their bets if they wanted to stay inside. John studied for a while then decided on Coconut is Lucky. "That will still be running at 5.00pm mate" said Steve. "Ok smart arse what are you going for? said John. "The Coal Face it's 3/1. The one you picked is 33/1 you muppet" "Well we will see at the end of the day" said John. Most of the table went for Steve's horse. Sandra went with John, ten pounds to win. "At least do it each way John" "No Steve, you don't fancy a horse to come second!".

They all got over the first fence ok, then at the second, three fell which left five still in the race at the third from home two more fell. Leaving Moonstruck three furlongs in front of The Coal Face and Coconut is Lucky looking beat into third place. "Told you to do it each way, it should finish John and you would have got a fifth of 33/1!!" As they came to the last, Moonstruck hit the jump badly and almost unseated it's jockey. The whole table was up and shouting on The Coal Face when Coconut is Lucky came steaming through to beat it by a short neck.

"You jammy git Gammon, how do you do it?" "Pure skill, Steve pure skill" replied John. Sandra threw her arms round John and whispered "I think you have just earned the right" They got back £660.00 plus their stake. John asked "What did you have Kev?", who was looking quite forlorn. "I had Majestic King" said Kev "Didn't that fell early on?" "Alright bloody Templegate, plenty more races to come" said Kev.

In the next two races John and Sandra won nothing. Next up was the race for Kev's first tip, Growler. Everyone put a tenner on it at 8/1, which would mean a potential win of £880, plus the stake money back, if it came in. "The pressure is on now Kev" "No pressure Jack, I have been watching this horse all season" "I like a confident man Kev" "Don't get fruity with my husband Steven", and Doreen laughed.

The race started and finished with Growler leading the whole way to win. Kev beamed as he took the plaudits of everyone with Bob singing "He's a Jolly Good Fellow". In the next two races nobody on the table had a horse finish. Now it was time for Kev's next tip. Steve said they should all put £30.00 in each after having that good win. "It's a good price 4/1, joint favourite with Mixing My Toasties". They all agreed and Kev said that out of the two tips, this one was a cert, his tipster had told him.

The race started with Miss Prickly Dicky near the back of the field, Mixing My Toasties was lying third. The final two furlongs came and Miss Prickly Dicky was fifth, Mixing My Toasties third, with Eagle

High two lengths in front. They were all safely over the last for the long run in. These three were neck and neck, the whole table were shouting and cheering Shelly knocked her Proseco all over Carol Lestar, both ladies too drunk to care. At the line Eagle High just stole it from Kev's tip. "Never mind mate, it had a good run" Kev was gutted. Doreen knew the look. "How much did you put on?" asked Doreen "I had £200 on the nose Doreen" "Well that serves you right!".

The rest of the day passed by and nobody else won anything more. Back on the bus they were all giving John and Sandra some friendly stick. "You'll be able to buy Saron an engagement ring, now John" Bob blurted from the back seat. "He'll need a fuller wallet for Saron, she comes from good stock, fake diamonds will be no good for her John" Steve shouted. "Behave you lot".

Sandra was rubbing the inside of John's thigh, very discreetly.

They arrived at the Headless Women. "This looks quaint Kev" "It is Carol. It's so called, because legend had it, that the landlord in 1756 got so fed up with his wife's nagging, he cut her head off". They all left the bus Carol tripped over, but blamed it on the fact that she wasn't used to stiletto heels, as she got back up somewhat bedraggled.

The Headless Women was in a small village called Ibley. It only had a few farmhouses and a pub. The pub had survived because of it's good food reputation and the tourist trade. Many of whom came to see where Queen Victoria had stayed for just one night in 1889. Her carriage had been subjected to a storm, she had been staying at Chatsworth House and was on her way back to London, when an almighty storm erupted. Her equerries felt it best to rest for the night to let the storm die down. Queen

Victoria was to sleep in one of the guest bedrooms, but before she retired for the night she apparently played the piano for the locals. So the piano remains in the same place as it had then and nobody has ever been allowed to play it since. The tourists come in the droves and take pictures of their friends, families etc. sat at it, hopelessly reliving the tale.

"Ok, listen, everybody the drinks are on me after my win in the first race. Get what you want" said John. They all had a couple more beers. The meal was a fixed menu of Prawn cocktail followed by Fish and Chips and Black Forest Gateaux. "You have done this as a wind up Kev, haven't you?" "To be honest Jack, yes I have, they do lovely food though, but when the owner asked me what we wanted to eat. I said a fixed menu, then I remembered the Beefeater Steak Houses in the 70's and everybody used them and this was what everyone used to have. I thought it would be a laugh" "Oh you are funny Kev", Shelley shouted. Three hours passed and it was time to get back to the Spinning Jenny. Everyone on the bus was singing. Doreen had decided that everyone had to sing a song. First up was Kev, with his rendition of My Way. Then Steve got up and sang The Gambler by Kenny Rodgers. John did Bananarama number with Sandra. Shelley, Doreen and Cheryl did It's in His Kiss by Cher. Bob and Jack got the biggest laugh with their rendition of Don't Go Breaking My Heart, the Elton John and Kiki Dee Classic.

They arrived back at the Spinning Jenny having dropped Bob and Cheryl off and then Jack and Shelley off on the way. Shelley was holding Cheryl up. Cheryl kept on saying "Where was cutie pie?". Bob was keeping well back with Jack.

"Nightcap John?" "Why not mate, we've had a great day" "Brandy's all round please

Doreen" "Don't think Carol needs anymore, she's asleep by the fire. She can sleep in one of the guest rooms tonight".

Steve stood talking to John. "Bloody hell mate, she 'aint half keen on you" "We are just work colleagues Steve" said John "Bollocks John, I know you remember? How are you getting back? Let's have a taxi back to our place you'll have an excuse ready for Saron then. Jo will put you in separate rooms, but the place is so big, once we say goodnight we will be at the other end of the house, so you are sorted" "You're a top man" said John. Steve called for a taxi and within ten minutes it was outside. "Come on let's drink up. Thanks for a great day Doreen, Kev" said Steve. "You're all very welcome thanks for coming guys".

Outside Steve said to John, "Do you and Sandra want to come back to ours for a night cap? You could stay over, we've plenty of room John" John asked "What do you think Sandra?" "Wwell that would be nice Steve, Jo, thank you".

Once back at Steve and Jo's house, they all had another couple of whiskies. Eventually Jo showed Sandra to her room and John to his. "We are in the North Wing, so if you need anything, just go down stairs and help yourselves. Good night Sandra" "Goodnight Jo, thanks" said Sandra. Jo turned to John and said, "Come on John, I will show you to your room". John turned and winked at Sandra and then followed Jo down the corridor. "Thanks Jo" "No problem John, sleep well, goodnight".

John waited ten minutes and then sneaked down the corridor to Sandra's room. He knocked softly on the door. Sandra answered it in a fluffy white bath robe. John's eye's almost popped out of his head. He leaned forward and they kissed for what seemed like forever. Sandra fell back onto the big mattress of the four poster bed. She was teasing John and he was teasing her. Eventually they made love. It wasn't like last time. The passion felt very different, like there was more meaning. It was no longer just lust. After they had finished, she lay in his arms stroking his chest and twirling the hair's on his chest with her fingers. Softly Sandra said, "John that was so beautiful, I could cry" "Don't do that" said John "It will ruin a special day" "This room is so beautiful.The wallpaper, the four poster bed, the oak panelling, everything, they have done an amazing job on this house" "Yeah they have Sandra" said John.

"Why do you still want to do this John?" "I can't explain", he said "I feel like a kid in a sweet shop, but I am frightened of making that commitment". "John you know Saron, Joni, Jeannette and Sheba they all fancy you and I am no different". John thought for a minute, thinking she missed Angelina out, but said "Oh I don't know about that"

"Yes you do John, because you play us all" "If you didn't want to be here Sandra, you wouldn't. You have walked away before" "Only because I want to keep some dignity at least John, there has to come a time when you want somebody special in your life that you can't carry on like this" "I know Sandra, trust me I know". Not another word was spoken.

The early morning daylight was shining brightly through a crack in the curtains when there was a knock on the door. "Shit, quick Sandra answer" said John. "Hello" she said. "Oh Hi Sandra, Jo sent me up to tell you breakfast is ready" "Oh ok thank you

Steve" "John must have gone for a run or something he isn't in his room" Steve couldn't help but let out a little snigger. John wanted to say something but he thought Sandra might object so he stayed silent. "Don't know Steve, I will be down in a minute" said Sandra "Ok" said Steve and left.

"John you are going to have to make out that you have been for a run" said Sandra quickly. "Don't worry, Steve won't say anything". "Well you go down first and then I will come down five minutes later" said Sandra.

John arrived just as Jo had put his breakfast out. "Steve said you've been for a run John?". Steve nearly choked on his sausage. "You ok sweetheart" asked Jo. "Yeah fine Jo, a bit of sausage went down the wrong hole". Sandra joined them, "Be careful with that sausage Sandra, they can be dangerous" said Steve and he winked at John.

They all sat around the table enjoying each other's company and chatting about the previous day. Steve offered, "I'll take you back to the Spinning Jenny for your car John, is that ok?". John and Sandra got their stuff together and Steve drove them back for John's car. "I tell you what Sandra, John will make somebody a good husband one day. You could hardly tell he had slept in his bed last night". Sandra just smiled. Steve dropped them off and Sandra pecked him on the cheek, thanked him for his hospitality and she walked over to John's car. John shook Steve's hand. "Thanks mate I owe you one" "No problem mate just make sure Sandra avoids choking on sausage like I nearly did". John whispered in Steve's ear "I'll get you back Offside" and they both laughed.

John started his car up and drove Sandra home. "Do you think Steve knew we slept together?" she asked. John put his innocent face on and said "No, it's just how Steve is, he is full of innuendo towards me" I'm not surprised, you do leave yourself open for it Mr Gammon". She kissed John and said, "thank you for a lovely day and an even more lovely night John". John kissed her and she got out of the car and waved him off.

The big test was yet to come. What was he going to tell Saron?. He arrived at Hittington Post Office Cottage just has Saron and Angelina were putting the last of the boxes into her car.

"Well, well, well, if it isn't the dirty stop out. I was worried about you, so I phoned Jo and Steve. She said you stopped at theirs last night" "I'd a lot to drink and then they said did I want a night cap and before you know it, it's 2.00am in the morning, so I wouldn't have been able to get a taxi back anyway" "I'm only joking John, so you had a good time then?". Angelina was looking at him she knew there was more to it than Saron thought. Luckily Jo hadn't mentioned Sandra so it looked like he was in the clear.

"How's the move going?", he asked. "It's the last of the boxes John, can't wait for Monday to come. We are really looking forward to getting our teeth into it" "I think you will both be very successful. The punters will come for miles to see not one, but two pretty girls behind the bar" "You old smoothie Gammon" said Saron and laughed.

"What are you doing about a chef?" "Well we are ripping the kitchen out and modernising it, so initially it will be just sandwiches and pork pies on the bar. Oh forgot to say, we are doing a little leaving party for Denis and Clara on Monday, so will you tell Carl and all those at the station that drink there please" "Yeah no problem. Are you sleeping at the cottage tonight?" "Yeah I will come back John, but it will be later on. They have been so good with us" said Saron. "Who's moving Denis and Clara out?" "Bob and Cheryl, and Jack and Shelley" "So where are they going to?" "They bought a little cottage about fifteen years ago in Pritwich. They had a lot done to it last year in anticipation of retiring".

"Listen John, we best get going. I will see you tonight". John pecked Saron on the cheek and as he did he caught the eye of Angelina, she gave him a cheeky grin.

John headed inside the cottage. It was a beautiful morning, so he decided to go for a good walk. John set off from Hittington and walked down the side of the duck pond and then climbed steadily for about fifteen minutes until he was on Hittington Moor. The view was tremendous. The sky was light blue with cotton wool ball clouds. The wild flowers were out and bobbing their heads in the fields as he made his way towards Lingnor, a small village with three pubs, a decent fish and chip shop and a couple of art galleries that pandered to the needs of the walking fraternity.

John walked along the cobbled streets of this quaint little village, just as he passed the fish and chip shop and before climbing again toward Cowdale, he heard a shout.

"Mr Gammon how are you?". John turned around to see Sheba hanging over the wall. "Hello Sheba, how are you?" "Yes, good thanks just lambing at the moment. In fact you can give me a hand if you don't mind. This one is struggling a bit think. She has got three inside her".

John jumped over the wall and held the ewe whilst Sheba got to work sorting her out. In no time at all the first two lambs were out and they appeared healthy enough but the third one didn't look so good. Sheba gave the ewe the third lamb, but it didn't want to know. She wrapped it up and said she had to get it back to the sheds to sort it out.

"What will happen now Sheba if the mother has rejected it?" "I will skin one of the lambs that died earlier off another ewe and as she only had one, I will wrap this one in the dead lamb's skin and in general the ewe will then become it's surrogate mother" "Wow, I never realised that Sheba. Look I will let you get on" "Thanks for the help John".

John nearly forgot "Oh, meant to say, the girls are having a retirement party for Denis and Clara at the Tow'd Man on Monday night" "Oh great, probably see you there then John". Sheba set off up the field. She wore a checked cloth cap, shirt, waistcoat, trousers and Hunter Wellies looking every inch the shepherdess. John smiled to himself. How contented she seemed to be and how lovely that must feel in your job.

John carried on with his walk, eventually arriving in Cowdale. It was almost lunchtime but he decided to carry on walking toward Monkdale to have his dinner in The Sloppy Quiche Café. John got there at 1.20pm.

"Afternoon Karen" he said "Afternoon stranger, how are you?" "Good thanks, how are you and Jimmy?" "Rushed off our feet, but we shouldn't complain. Is it just a drink or are you having some food John?" "Think I will have a dinner Karen" said John. "Ok sit down and I will bring you a menu over. What do you want to drink?" "Just a nice black coffee, no sugar, please Karen". Karen obliged and brought back a menu. "We also have a few specials on, John. We have Wiggly Diggly stew with Stilton dumplings and that comes with mash potatoes, green beans and carrots. We also have Lasagne Jimmy, which is homemade Lasagne with a

Monkdale salad or we have Karen's Sloppy Quiche a choice of broccoli and cheese or cheese, onion and toasted walnuts. I'll give you a minute John whilst I serve these walkers" "Thanks Karen it all sounds great". Finally John decided on the roast beef dinner with horseradish mash, roast potatoes and a medley of Monkdale vegetables.

The food arrived and Karen was laughing. "What's so funny Jigley?" asked John. "Jimmy put you extra on, he said it would help with the walking". The plate was overflowing and the medley of vegetables consisted of broccoli, carrot, green beans, red cabbage and sprouts, enough to feed John for a week. John was a big eater he cleared the plate in no time. The café had almost cleared, so Jimmy came out of the kitchen and sat with John.

"How are you mate?" asked Jimmy. "Not bad Jimmy thanks" replied John, "are you keeping busy?" "It's been crazy John, from the first day we opened up and with the theme nights that Karen thought up, we are fully booked every time" "Good to hear Jimmy, you two deserve the success". Karen arrived with a dessert. "Here you are John, on the house. You can't leave without trying Jimmy's new dessert" "Blimey Karen, I can hardly walk now, what is it?" "Jimmy calls it a Cowdale Swingle, don't ask me why", she said, "don't think you know yourself, do you Jimmy?" Ha laughed, "It was just a name that came into my head" "Go on then what is it?" asked John. "Its basically egg custard on a digestive biscuit base, covered in dark chocolate which covers the whole dessert, then on top of that is a pineapple ring and that is encased in dark chocolate, sprinkled with coconut and a scoop of Dilley Dale Crunch Ice Cream on the side". John took a mouthful. "Blimey Jimmy, I think that's the nicest thing I have ever tasted" "Don't say that John" said Karen, "we won't get his head through the kitchen door". Jimmy just laughed. John stood up, "Right I'd better pay you and start on my travels again. The food was great thank, you both very much" "No problem John, see you soon".

John set off through Monkdale. The pathway was adorned with so many beautiful colours on each side, it resembled the colours in a Monet painting. John had done a further two miles and was back up on high ground heading back towards Hittington Dale when his phone rang.

"Mr John Gammon" said the voice, "Yes, who is this?", asked John. "This is Sergeant Flood from Sheffield Police Sir" "How can I help you?" "Well Sir, a lady reported that she hadn't seen her neighbour all day yesterday, nor today. So as a courtesy call, we popped round to the address and I am afraid we found the gentleman living there, dead in bed. The only number contained in his phone was yours Mr Gammon. The lady said you were the gentleman's nephew" "Yes that's correct Sergeant" said John "I'm afraid I'm out walking at the moment, but I should be back at my cottage in about two hours. I'll drive straight up there" "Mr Gammon, Sir, there isn't anything you can do here, other than start making some arrangements for his funeral. Your Uncle did leave a letter, which said it was to be opened only by John Gammon upon his death. I am assuming all his affairs will be noted in this letter".

"Look Sergeant if you could take the letter to the station I will come over and collect it" said John. "Ok Sir, I will possibly be off duty by then, but I will leave it with the desk sergeant. If you could bring some identity with you please Sir" "Not a problem Sergeant, I understand".

John wasn't sure how he was feeling as he walked the six miles back to the Old Post Office cottage. He felt numb. It was his biological dad who had just died, but he didn't really know him at all. Phil had been his dad and that was the thought that kept coming back inside his head.

He phoned Saron. She didn't answer, but called back a few minutes later. "Hi John, sorry I missed your call. What have you been up today?". John, for some unexplained reason, just blurted out his news. "Uncle Graham is dead" "Oh John, I am so sorry. What happened?" John explained to Saron about the neighbour and that he was going to drive up to Sheffield to pick up this letter. "Give me a call on your way back, we should be done here and I will meet you" said Saron. "Ok" and John cut off the call.

It was 6.00pm when John arrived at Tinsley Road Police Station Sheffield. "Good evening Sergeant. I have come to collect a letter from my recently deceased Uncle. Your Sergeant Flood left it for me" said

John. "Just a minute Sir, what's your name please?" "John Gammon" "Just give me a minute Mr Gammon". The Desk Sergeant came back with a large brown envelope. "Have you got some identification Sir?" John took out his warrant card. The desk Sergeant looked at it. "I do apologise Sir, you are a legend in the Peak District, my wife is from Bixton, so I have been following your career. I am very sorry for your loss" "Thanks Sergeant". John took the envelope, left the star struck Sergeant and headed back to the car. Once he was back in the car he opened the envelope and read the contents.

"Dear John

You will never know the pain I have felt. From when you were a little boy growing up knowing I could never be the real father in your life. I won't go into the remorse I felt toward my brother Philip, this isn't the time to say these things, but just know I was a good man.

The bungalow I live in now, I only rent but I do have other properties. My whole estate has been left for you to do as you wish with. Living over here, your Mum and Dad never really knew how successful I had been and I never liked to brag, hence the little bungalow I live in now.

I am quite sure with the things I have left you. If you so wished, you would not have to work again, but knowing you have my genes you will need to be the best at what you do and retirement was never for me.

I feel blessed that you eventually heard the truth and that you were man enough to accept the word from your lovely mum and you didn't judge her, it is a rare quality you have son.

I know you found it hard with me and I understood that, but seeing you and knowing you knew, gave me comfort these last few months. I have battled this illness for some time and I know now that time is no longer something I have".

John at this point had to stop while he cleared a tear from his eye and gathered his thoughts.

"I guess when the man in the big chair say's he is taking you, it doesn't matter how much money you throw at specialists etc., he will take you if he wants you. John, if you don't mind, I want to be buried at Cowdale Church, next to my Grandad Harold Gammon. I looked up to him so much whilst growing up. He taught me the principles of business and life's rules of which he had many, let me tell you.

I wish two have hymns at the service. "Abide With Me" and "All things Bright and Beautiful".

John knew that these were his Mum's favourite hymns and he wondered if that was why Uncle Graham chosen them.

"When I leave the church I would like them to play "Don't Cry Daddy" by Elvis Presley. I wish to have my wake at the Spinning Jenny and the bar is to be a free one, please John.

Well Son, and I make no excuses now for calling you son, live your life to the full and enjoy every moment. The best preparation for tomorrow, is doing your best today. Love the meek, take care of the poor, share your wealth, invest your time for the good but always love what God has given you.

Goodbye Son, I will be watching over you".

John put the letter down and was unable to control his emotions. These were the words of a good man that made a mistake all those years ago and never really managed to forgive himself. John composed himself and rung Saron. "Are you ok John?" "Yes, I'm fine, where shall we meet?" "Let's meet up at the Spinning Jenny" "Ok I will be about fifty minutes" said John and with that he left.

John made good time and was at the Spinning Jenny spot on time. "Hey lad, I'm so sorry for your loss, your Uncle Graham was a lovely man there were no airs and graces with Graham he treated everyone as his equal" "Thanks Kev" said John "Must have been a bit of a shock?" said Kev. "Yes it was, I thought it would be at least a few weeks more, Kev to be honest". Doreen heard John telling Kev and she came over and gave John a big hug. "Uncle Graham wants his wake to be held here, if you can do that?" said John "Don't care what's happening John, if that's what he wanted I will make sure it he gets his wish, just let me know when" "I will". Saron had got John a double brandy, she seemed to know him better than he knew himself.

"Come on let's sit down" she said to John. John went through what had happened and then produced the letter. Saron started reading it, but cried all the way through. "John he really loved you. The poor man must have been in such anguish for so many years" "I know and there's me thinking selfishly about myself" John replied. "Don't beat yourself up, you had to have time to get used to it and you didn't have the time as it worked out. Look I'm just nipping to the toilet, my make-up is running".

Whilst Saron had gone to the ladies, Kev came over with another double brandy for John. "Are you alright lad?" "Kev can I tell you something?". Kev spoke quickly, "Before you do John, I need to tell you something. I was out on a night out with your dad many years ago, you were probably only about eleven then. We were in a bar in Ackbourne and a guy who used to live round here, Sam Hufton, I think was his name. Well he started giving your dad some grief about what a looker your mum was. Then he said "did you and your youth share her because you looked like Graham", your dad wasn't a violent man, but he got up and knocked this guy all around the pub. I had to pull him off him or he would have killed him. I managed to get him away and into the Land Rover and we drove back halfway to Hittington. He broke down and told me just what you are about to tell me. To be honest, I wasn't surprised because you were the spitting imagine of Graham, John". "So you knew?" John said "Did anyone else know?" "No John, and I never told anybody. Me and Phil never spoke about that night ever again. John they were both nice lads. Sometimes in life things happen which you don't have control of, but remember they both loved you lad" "Thanks

Kev for those words and for being a good friend to me" "Come on then John, let's have a drink, Graham would not want us all being miserable".

John shouted up "Drinks all round from my uncle Graham". A voice came from the small room at the side. "Top Man Mr Gammon, mines a double vodka and diet coke" "Hello Carol, I wondered when you would appear" "Love you too lover boy" and she laughed.

It was almost closing time and Saron said she would drive back to the cottage. John was pretty much out of it, so she took him to bed and covered up him and she slept in the spare room.

The following morning John said his head felt like the road works on the M25. "Serves you right" smiled Saron. "Thanks for the sympathy vote, Saron" "Only joking with you, come on get ready and I will take you for your car".

John's head was banging as he drove to Bixton Police Station. "Morning Sergeant Yap" "Good Morning Sir" "What sort of weekend have we had in the wonderful world of Bixton Police Station?" asked John. "Nothing much to report Sir, a few fights in the town Saturday night, but nothing major" "Ok thanks Sergeant".

Gammon climbed the stairs to his office and was met by Milton. "Good morning Sir" "Yes good morning Carl, would you get everyone together please, for a briefing, in the incident room, in fifteen minutes?" "No problem Sir" said Milton as he left to get everyone assembled.

"Ok, good morning everyone. Trust you have all had a good weekend and are ready to press ahead and find this bloody serial killer. Any movement anybody?" "I have been trying to figure out why he or she takes the left ear of their victims and leaves this stick man drawing" stated Inspector Smarty. "And what's your conclusion Inspector Smarty?" asked John. Smarty put his thoughts forward, "Well the ear thing was a punishment for poaching and stealing in the 16th and 17th centuries. The stick man I am struggling with, does anyone have any ideas on that? And why does he leave a drawing at the scene of the crime and another one at a church? It doesn't make sense Sir".

"What does make sense with these weirdo's Inspector? Right what have we got? Victim one Maria Dooley, Scooper what have you found out about Maria?" Scooper answered, "Background checks have come up with no criminal records. Her bank and building society accounts show no unusual activity. She appears to have been in the wrong place, at the wrong time Sir" "What about all these boyfriends?" "Danny Stevo seems to be the boyfriend everyone associates her with, except that is, Mr and Mrs Dooley, who say they have met her boyfriend, Rupert Bare. Mr Bare is well known to us all. A spoilt rich kid who seems to enjoy causing trouble but can't defend himself when it kicks off" "So this guy has got a temper then?" "Yes Sir" "Ok, let's keep a close eye on him. What about Mr Stevo?" said John. "He seems to be well liked, he wasn't aware Maria was seeing anyone else, just seems to be a nice guy Sir, now we also have the added complication of Mr Bilkin, the guy who works in the gardens at Chatsworth. From what we can see, he is just a fantasist Sir, no real harm in him. His work colleague on other hand, is a different kettle of fish. Lacey has previous for beating up his ex-wife and her boyfriend some five years back. He was also cautioned about a fracas with a woman in December last year, at Wonka's nightclub in Bixton, but all charges were dropped by the lady in question, one Diane Astley".

"Have you spoken with Miss Astley yet?" asked John. "No Sir" "Right, well let's make that a priority. The guy that found the body, Mr Wang, what's the tie up between him and the second victim Poppy Chi?" "She was his niece Sir?" "What have we got on Mr

Wang anything?" "Nothing Sir, squeaky clean" "Right, I want Inspector Lee and Smarty to re-interview Lacey and put some pressure on him. Sergeant Milton bring Rupert Bare back in and let's see if he winds up easily?".

"Ok, let's move onto Poppy Chi. What have we got Scooper?" "Well" said Scooper, "it appears that Poppy fell into bad company at University, her friend Rosie Wilson said that she had met Billy Holland, and from that day she was besotted with him and that he had got her into drugs. We have interviewed Holland. He is certainly playing on the wrong side of the law. He lives in a big house, but has no obvious forms of income" "Right, get his bank details and go through them in some detail" Joh continued "Chan Chi we haven't located as yet. His drinking den is The Queens on Buckle Street, Derby, Sergeant Wisey, I want you hanging round there until you see Chi. Do not attempt to communicate with him just radio in and I will send a team of officers to bring him in for questioning. I believe this man to be very dangerous, so I repeat, do not try and apprehend. What else do we know about Poppy? Her father was a high ranking diplomat. She was adopted by Mr and Mrs Chi because her real mother was their cleaner in China and she couldn't afford to bring her up. She appears to have had a good relationship with her adopted parents. Mr Chi gave her £10,000 because she said she wanted to go travelling to New Zealand but she apparently spent that money on heroin. Billy Holland denies any involvement with Poppie's addiction. I don't believe him so I want this bastard nailing on something, do you get my drift?". The room all nodded in agreement. Finally John said, "Ok everyone, thanks for your time, we'll reconvene tomorrow at 11.00am".

Gammon left the incident room and was met by Sergeant Yap. "Sir, I've just taken a call from a Mr Denis Clark, over at Cowdale Church, another body has been found" "Shit! That's all I need" said John "Ok, Milton and Scooper come with me".

Gammon, Scooper and Milton arrived at Cowdale Church. Denis Clark met them. Clark was a diminutive man with round John Lennon type glasses and was balding, but had a small pony tail. He looked and dressed like an aging academic. He went to shake Gammon's hand, but Gammon noticed blood on Clark's cuffs and thumb. "Just a minute Mr Clark, is that the victim's blood" Clarke replied, "Probably, she was still alive when I found her, so I tried to help her, but the paramedic said she had died. Then your forensic team arrived and put this tent up".

Something wasn't sitting comfortably with Gammon. "Just wait there Mr Clark" he ordered. Gammon walked over to the forensic team. He put his head inside the tent. He could see a woman lay on the ground covered in blood, her left ear was missing and she had been very badly beaten. Her face was swollen, she was almost unrecognisable.

"Any idea who she is?" asked John. "Not yet Chief Inspector". Gammon walked back to Clark. "I think it would be best if we spoke down at the station Mr Clark" "You will have to wait a minute while I lock the church up" "Are you the church warden Mr Clark?" "No Sir, I am the lead campanologist. I was checking the bells and the rota for a wedding on Saturday. I think the young lady I found is the bride to be. I am ringing the bells for the wedding on Saturday. Her name is Alice Beadman, she is marrying David Lansky. They live together in Cowdale, which I always thought was wrong". Again Gammon could feel the hairs on the back of his neck go up, there was something odd about this guy. "Ok Mr Clark. Lock the church up and we can get down to Bixton and take a statement".

They arrived back at Bixton and Clark was put in interview room one.

"Sergeant Milton, I want some discreet enquires made on our Mr Clark. Who are his friends? Where does he drink? What are his habits etc. Spend some time in the pub. That usually gets some results on these things" "Ok Sir, sounds ideal to me" "Only ideal if you get me some results Milton". Milton left with his instructions.

"Sandra, get one of the other officers to get some background checks done on Mr Clark, then come into the interview room". Gammon ordered a coffee for him, Scooper and Mr Clark.

Scooper joined Gammon. "Ok Mr Clark, if you could run through exactly how you found the body" "I was on my way to check the church bells and as I entered the church yard........" "What time was that Denis? I am ok to call you Denis?" asked the Inspector. "Yes Sir, that's ok. When I got near to the old yew tree, I could hear moaning and that's when I found Alice Beadman, she was still alive. I have done first aid training, so I tried to help her. I then called the ambulance service" "And what time would you say that was Mr Clark?" "I would say, about 10.00am" "So they arrived at what time?" "It was 10.28am" "How can you be so precise?" "I looked at my watch Sir, because I like to watch a TV program in the week and it's on at 11.00am and I didn't want to miss it".

This all seemed a bit strange to John. How could a guy who found this poor girl be worrying about a TV program? "So you tried to help, prior to the ambulance arriving?" "Yes" "Could she speak?" "Yes, she did say something. She mumbled Chinaman" "Chinaman Mr Clark, are you sure?" "It sounded like that to me". There was no emotion in Clarks voice, he was very matter of fact the whole of the time they were taking his statement.

John continued, "So, you said you were going to the Church to check the bells for Alice's wedding next Saturday, correct?" "Yes, everything should be in good order, it's a big day" "So did you leave Alice at all after you had found her?" "No, Sir, I stayed with her until the ambulance arrived" "After the ambulance arrived, then what happened?" "I called your lot because as I said, I watch a TV program in the week and I wanted to know if I could go now that the ambulance was there".

"So you never actually left the scene?" "No" "After we spoke at the church, you said before you could come to the station you had to lock the church up Denis?". Clark went quiet for a minute, then he changed his story. "Oh I remember now. I went in the Church to wash my hands they were covered in blood. Oh also forgot, I found this on her body".

Clark produced a drawing of a stick man. Gammon felt cold knowing this was another murder by the killer. The piece of paper was heavily stained in blood. "Just excuse us a minute Denis, would you like another coffee?" "No, I will be fine thank you". Gammon went outside with Scooper. "Get this down to forensics, I don't think it will be any good to us, but he got it out of his pocket and it may have fibres on it or something that we can tie to the other notes found on Maria and Poppy" "Do you think he is our killer John?" "I don't know Sandra, he certainly is a bit weird though. I also want his background check doing immediately, let's see if Denis Clark as a record Sandra?" "Ok Sir".

Gammon went back in to the interview room. Clark was sat whistling "the wedding march".

"Are you ok Denis?" "Yes, I'm fine, can I go now?" "Ok Denis, but we may need to speak with you again during the course of our investigations". Clark left the station still whistling. Gammon shook his head. "Another nutter Sir?" asked Sergeant Yap. "We appear to have a town full of them Sergeant Yap". Gammon proceeded to his office and waited for confirmation of the death of Alice Beadman so that he could inform the family.

The results soon came through. Dental records showed it was Alice Beadman of Three Chimney Pots Cottage, Cowdale. The report also said she had been sexually violated, very badly beaten and her left ear had been removed from her body. Gammon called down to Sergeant Yap. "Sergeant get Milton out the front with a car will you? I have the sorry task of informing her family of Alice's demise" "Ok Sir, right away".

Gammon put on his coat. This was one part of the job he hated, but always insisted on doing it himself. His thoughts were, if he hated it so much, then there was a big chance other officers did too and he never expected anybody to do something he wasn't prepared to do himself.

Milton and Gammon arrived in the picturesque village of Cowdale, with its little village pond and the beautiful church that sat slightly on a mound. It was believed to have been built by the Saxon's with a spire added during the Norman reign of Britain. This was not going to be easy job, the poor guy they were going to see was to be married to the girl of his dreams on Saturday and now some sad bastard had taken those hopes and dreams away from him.

They walked up the cobbled path to the front door of the cottage. You could tell they were a young couple. The designer curtains draped lovingly in the window recess. The lawn was immaculately cut with beautiful flowers of every colour adorning the borders. Gammon knocked on the door. After a few seconds the door opened and a man opened the door. "Mr Lansky?" "Yes". Gammon and Milton showed their warrant cards. "Can we come in?" "Eh? Yes, I guess so, if this is about the row the other night, it just got out of hand" said Lansky. "What row was that then Mr Lansky?" "Alice had been out on her hen night and was pretty drunk when she came in about 2.00am. I had waited up. She told me she had seen Rupert, her ex-boyfriend. I was pretty annoyed. I have told him before to leave us alone, but he's a prick. Sorry for that".

"Mr Lansky, you need to sit down, we have some bad news for you. I am afraid Alice

Beadman was found murdered in Cowdale Churchyard last night". Lansky started shaking "I didn't hit her very hard, she just kept going on and on about her ex" "So you hit Alice?" "Yes twice, the first time I just used the back of my hand, but she came back at me with the poker. I was just defending myself. After the second blow she stormed out and said that the wedding was off. I sat down and just drank myself to sleep".

"Let me get this straight, you didn't follow her then?" "No Sir, I was too upset" "You will need to come to the station for us to take a statement Mr Lansky. Could you tell me where Alice Beadsman's parents live?" said John. "They did live here, but they were killed in motorbike accident in France three years ago. Micky Beadman was mad on bikes and they used to tour everywhere on their holidays" "How long were you two together?" "About two and a half year's altogether. I met Alice through her dad because I'm into bikes too, so after he died we kept in touch and slowly we got together" said Lansky. John continued, "That accent's not from round here, where are you from?" "I'm originally from St Austell, in Cornwall, I moved up here" "Ok. Well we will take you back to Bixton and Sergeant Milton will take a statement. Get your coat Mr Lansky".

It was 4.30pm once Lansky's statement was completed, so Gammon gave him a lift back and then went back to the cottage to get changed for Denis and Clara's leaving party at the Tow'd Man. On entering the cottage there was post on the mat, two letter's for Saron and one for him.

John made himself a coffee then sat down to read his post. The letter was from the solicitors Gillespie and Souther of London Road, Derby.

"Dear Mr Gammon,

I am writing to confirm that you are the sole beneficiary of the will of the late Graham John Gammon".

John didn't know his Uncle Graham had a middle name and certainly didn't know it was John. He felt the weirdest sensation come over him his Mum and Dad had called him after his biological father. Phil could not have known at this point. The letter carried on.

"You may or may not know but Mr Gammon was a very wealthy gentleman, and because of that his affairs, whilst in order, will need attention before I can meet with you and meter out Mr Gammon's instructions. I expect this to take me quite a few days and then I will contact you to come to my office for the formal will reading. If you have any questions or concerns, please do not hesitate to contact me or my PA Mary Logan at this address.

Yours sincerely

Tam Gillespie LLB TEP"

John was quite staggered by the letter it appears that Uncle Graham was truly a wealthy man, but why did he feel the need to hide it.

John finished his coffee and went to change for the party at the Tow'd Man. He was just about to leave the cottage when his phone rang.

"Chief Constable William Cruickshank Lincolnshire Police here" said the voice on the phone. "How can I help you Sir?" said John, "Just a head's up Chief Inspector, I have been instructed to release my Head of Forensics to come to Bixton to head up your Forensic Team" "Oh right" said John "do we have a name Sir?" "Yes he is the top man in his field, his name is Michael John Walvin, we know him as John. You will find he is very thorough Chief Inspector, not a lot gets by John. He will start at Bixton in one week's time and I am sure you and your officers will give him your full support" "Not a problem Sir, thanks for the heads up". With that the phone line went dead. Gammon didn't have chance to say that he thought he knew John Walvin. John had spent about three months at Lincolnshire Police Headquarters on a murder case, some ten years back and he was sure it would be the same man. He too was one of the forces rising stars.

John dressed and headed for the Tow'd Man he could see from the car park the pub was full. "Evening John, how are you?" "Can't complain Bob" "Here let me get you one. What do you fancy?" "What you drinking Bob?" "I'm on "Man in Trouble" from the local brewery" John laughed, "Go on then mate, I'll try one of those please".

John nodded across to Saron and Angelina, they were both mega busy. Bob returned with John's beer and was quick with the quip, "It's not taken you long Mr Gammon". John gave him a puzzled look. "Nice to see you too Bob" "Always nice to see you Sheba, you know that". This cost Bob a dig in the ribs from Cheryl.

John was stood with his back to the room, when he felt a light tap on his shoulder.

"Annie, how lovely to see you" he smiled. "Can I have a quick word John?" "Of course" and John ushered Annie to one side. "What's the matter Annie?" "I have something to tell you John. Remember when your life was saved John?" "I do, how will I ever repay you Annie?" the old lady replied, "It's not me you have to repay John. Just remember my words to you. Live a good life, help others and have no evil in you" "Well that's what I try to do Annie?" "You see John, I know that you went to the safe house in Chesterfield where Brian Lund was staying". John looked at her, "Annie how do you know that?" Annie whispered to him "I have been able to see things since I was a child John".

John felt like a naughty school kid and then Annie dropped a bombshell. "John I will be leaving tonight" "But I thought you were staying with Saron's mother now?" he replied. "I don't mean that John. I am leaving this world" she said. John was aghast, "What?" "My work here is done John and I know it will be tonight".

John was lost for words. He knew if Annie said this, there was every likelihood that it would happen.

"Come on misery guts, come and have a dance" and Sheba tugged on John's sleeve.

Annie looked at John, "Go John, and remember what I have told you" and she kissed John on the cheek.

The night was a massive success for Saron and Angelina. Denis stood up with Clara and thanked everyone for their custom over the years and announced they had purchased a bungalow in Pritwich for their retirement, so they would be staying local.

Saron caught up with John and asked him if he was staying. John declined. He was still deeply concerned with what Annie had said earlier. He wandered over to Annie, she looked fine, but still John felt anxious.

John looked at his watch it was almost midnight, as he turned around, there was a loud scream from Saron's mother. Annie had got up to put her coat on and had fallen to the floor. John tried to administer the kiss of life but it was no good she had gone. This amazing lady who had saved his life had now predicted her own demise, but not before warning John about his future. How did she know all this? Saron held her mother, they were both heartbroken, luckily most of the crowd had gone, there was only Shelley and Jack, Saron, Angelina and Saron's mum. John called for an ambulance and explained what had happened.

By the time Annie's body had been seen by a doctor and she pronounced dead at the scene. Her body had been taken away and it was now almost 2.15am. Jack and Shelley had gone home, so it just left Angelina, Saron and her mum with John.

Angelina made them all a brandy coffee and they sat chatting. Saron's mother said "Annie had asked if you would be here tonight John?" "Why?" asked Saron. "She just said 'I need to speak to him'" said Saron's Mother. "Did she?" "Yes, she did actually and she told me she would be leaving this life tonight". Saron let out a cry of despair. "Don't worry Saron, she was quite happy. She told me her life's work was done here".

John decided to stay the night after all, especially with it now being so late. Saron bottled up behind the bar and then went upstairs to John, who was now fast asleep.

It was 8.00am and John woke up with a start. "Are you ok John?" asked Saron. "I think so, I've had a really bad dream. I dreamt Annie was dead" "Saron spoke softly, "It wasn't a dream John" "Wow, she was an incredible lady Saron" "You know she thought a lot of you John" "I wonder, why me?" "She told my mother that you were a good man, who sometimes loses his way" "I guess we all do that, hey?" "I guess so John, but she did think you were special" "Look Saron, I'd best get off to work. Did I tell you that your replacement is a chap called, Michael John Walvin?" Saron was awestruck, "Wow he is absolutely the best in the country on Forensics. Anybody working in our industry tries to emulate him, John he is the best in the business".

ANNIE TANNEY

Gammon set off for Bixton, mindful of what had happened. He now had two more funerals to attend, Uncle Graham's and Annie's and he was still no further forward in the serial killer case.

"Morning Sir" "Morning Sergeant Yap, any problems from last night?" "Nothing at all Sir, Monday nights are always quiet in Bixton and surrounding areas".

Inspector Smarty appeared. "Morning Sir, can I have a word?" "Of course Inspector Smarty".

Gammon pulled away from the front desk. "I had a conversation last night with an informant and apparently Denis Clark, the bell ringer guy, has been inside. My information spent time in the nick with him, he said he really is a nasty piece of work and he only knew he was living here because my informant's wife does the flowers at the church. He went to pick her up and Clark was there. His wife told him, he called himself Denis Clark and that he rang the bells at church. My informant said he didn't let Clark see him and he doesn't want Clark to know who he is, as he has built a new life here and his wife didn't know about his past. Sir, Clark who found one of the victims, had been away for aggravated assault on a prostitute twelve year ago".

John was surprised, "Why do we have no record of this?" "because his name, back then, was Wally Bickman. He changed it to Denis Clark when he came to live here" "Has he any other convictions as Wally Bickman?" asked John, Inspector Smarty replied "Oh yes, he was done for living of immoral earnings. He was arrested, but not charged, for passing counterfeit money. He apparently beat a next door neighbour so badly and was arrested for grievous bodily harm. However, the neighbour withdrew his statement saying he had been mistaken. He is a bad egg Sir" "Right, let's get Mr Clark back in here Smarty. Good work" and Smarty left.

"Milton, dig deeper for some more intel on this piece of crap. Also, Milton, would you ask if forensics have stated what time Alice Beadman died?" "They have Sir, they said somewhere between 9.30am and 11.30am".

"Ok Milton, radio through to Smarty and tell him to ensure that Clark has his solicitor with him when he brings him in" "Ok Sir".

Gammon proceeded to his office. Was Clark the killer? He had found the victim, he had Alice's blood on him. He'd changed his name and had previous form.

It was 11.30am when Yap informed Gammon that Denis Clark and his solicitor Michael Prati had arrived and were in interview room one. "Ok Sergeant, get Sergeant Wisey in there. I will be down in a minute".

Gammon made his way to the interview room. Wisey had the interview tape set up and ready to run. Gammon began the interview. "I am Chief Inspector John Gammon and this is my colleague, Sergeant Wisey. Today's interview with Mr Denis Clark and his solicitor Mr Michael Prati is with regard to the on-going investigations into the murders of Maria Dooley, Poppy Chi and Alice Beadman, of which Mr Clark found the third victim. Alice Beadman was still alive when he found her, but he stated that he tried to keep her alive but was unsuccessful".

"Mr Clark, or can I call you Denis?" "You can call me Denis" "Ok Denis, would you run through events that led up to you finding Miss Beadman?". "I had walked to Cowdale Church to check that everything was ok for the wedding of Miss Beadman. I was in the church from 8.30am" John interrupted, "Can I stop you there Denis. Is this a normal procedure that you would do before any wedding?" "Yes" was the reply. "Explain to me why please?" "Well Inspector, I like to ensure that the practise we put in, is served well on the day" "That doesn't really answer my question Denis, does it?" "Look, I just make sure everything is in place for my team of bell ringers" "Ok Denis, so just a few more questions. How long have you lived round here?" "I moved to Cowdale a good few years ago Mr Gammon". John replied "I can tell by your accent you must have come down from Scotland, correct?" "No, my family moved from Scotland when I was five. My father followed the steel work to Corby in Northamptonshire" "You haven't lost your accent Denis?". "There are more Scottish people in Corby than English people, so I guess that's why" "So have you ever been in trouble with the police before?".

Clark squirmed in his seat on hearing the question. Clark turned and spoke to Michael Prati, turned back and replied "No comment". John pressed on with the questioning, "Is that 'no comment' because you have then Denis? Or should I call you Wally?". Clark again looked embarrassed. "Your family name is Bickman, isn't it Denis? You were christened Walter Bickman weren't you?". Again, Clarke conferred with Prati. Prati then spoke. "My client has the right to change his name by deed poll, this is not an offence" "You are correct Mr Prati, but it is an offence to pervert the course of justice and your client never mentioned his previous convictions, and because of his name change he was dodged under our radar".

Mr Prati answered. "My client would like it put on record that he served his sentences for his misdemeanours and only changed his name because of police harassment. To the point that, he also moved out of the area, to live here in the Peak District". "Mr Prati, I cannot comment on why Mr Clarke chose to move areas and change his name. I can only comment at my uneasiness at his deceit" "Mr Gammon", said Clark "I have put that life behind me. I go to church, I ring the bells at Cowdale and I hold down a permanent job. Because I went to try and help this poor girl I am now being vilified by you and I don't think this is fair".

"What isn't fair Denis, is that I have three girls that were mutilated, sexually assaulted and then murdered, and I have grieving families and friends to whom I cannot give closure to. Do not talk to me about what's fair!! Where do you work Denis?" "I work in the food packing department at Pippa's Frozen Foods in Lingcliffe" "How long have you worked there?" "Eleven years, Sir" "I am again, going to name the three girls that are involved in this investigation, and I want you to tell me if you know any of them. Maria Dooley, Poppy Chi and Alice Beadman, who you found at Cowdale Church. Did you know Maria?" "Yes, but only because she worked for a short time at Pippa's Frozen Foods where I work" "Did you ever engage in conversation with Maria or socialise with her?", asked John. "I may have said hello to her in passing, but I never socialised with her" "Did you know Poppy Chi?" "Yes, but only because she used to work in the Chinese in Ackbourne. I think her uncle owned it" "So you had met Poppy then?" "As I said Sir, only if I went for a Chinese meal. She worked on the till but I haven't seen her for a long time" "How often did you use the Chinese Denis?" "Twice, sometimes three times a week" "Finally, Alice Beadman, the lady you found and whose blood you had on your clothes?" "Miss Beadman arranged with the vicar to have the bells rung at her wedding, so yes, I met with her on a couple of occasions".

"From where I'm sat Denis you must be concerned, you knew all three victims. You were actually placed at the scene of Alice Beadman's demise. You worked with Maria Dooley and you had contact with Poppy Chi. Have you got an alibi for any of the nights that these girls were murdered?". Clark replied "I was at Bubley Church, near

Ackbourne, until 10.00pm and I know that looks bad because that was where Maria was found, but honestly Mr Gammon. I am not a killer. I know I have been bad in the past, but I am a changed man, that is why I came to live here in the Peak District, to start a new life"

"I will decide that Denis. Where were you on the night of Poppy Chi's murder?" "I can't remember Mr Gammon. Were you anywhere near Rowksley Woods?" "No, I don't think so" said Clark. "How can you be sure? You just said you didn't know where you were!! I need more than that Denis". "Ok, I will tell you. I'm seeing a lady, she works with me at Pippa's Frozen Food" "What's her name?" "She's married Mr Gammon" "I don't give a rolling doughnut, Denis I want her name" "It's Mrs Deborah Newton" sighed Clark, "she works in the HR Department" "Does she know about your past Denis?" "No, of course not! I am trying to rebuild my life Mr Gammon".

John straightened up his posture, "Denis Clark, I am holding you for forty eight hours while we check out some of your statement". With that Gammon left Sergeant Wisey to take Clark down into the holding cell. Gammon called Inspector Scooper. "Sandra you are coming with me to Pippa's Frozen Foods in Lingcliffe".

Gammon and Scooper set off, it was almost 2.30pm when they pulled into a visitor parking space at Pippa's Frozen Foods. They showed their warrant cards at reception and said they wanted to speak with Mrs Newton in private. The receptionist showed them to a meeting room down the corridor from reception. The room was adorned with awards the factory had won on their supply of products to Marks and Spencer's, Waitrose and even Harrods's in London. The owner Pippa Nedsram had built the business from scratch, after leaving university with a Business degree. The business was a big employer in the area. Gammon and Scooper sat down. The receptionist brought them a coffee each. Deborah Newton arrived. She was in her mid-forties with shoulder length, brown hair and she wore a smart business suit. Mrs Newton put out her hand, "How can I help you?".

John Began, "You are Mrs Deborah Newton from the HR Department here at Pippa's Frozen Foods is that correct?" "Yes, I am head of HR. Could you tell me what this is about please?" "I will cut to the chase Mrs Newton. We have Denis Clark in custody at Bixton Police Station". Gammon was watching for a reaction and was concerned when she didn't show any. "What has that got to do with me?" She asked. John replied, "Mr Clark has said he was with you on the night of Poppy Chi's murder" "Why would he be with me?" she said. Again she showed no feelings. Gammon thought she was either a very good actress, or she genuinely didn't have anything to do with Clark. "Just to put the record straight, Denis Clark has made a statement saying that basically you and he are having an affair". Yet again Mrs Newton wasn't fazed, although she did show some degree of annoyance. "Are you saying you are not in a relationship with Denis Clark?" "Most definitely not" she snapped, "I hardly know the man" "So you cannot vouch for him being with you on the night of Poppy Chi's murder?" "I was at home that night, it was my little girl's birthday party, so I was hardly going to be with Mr Clark, was I?" "Can anybody substantiate your alibi Mrs Newton?" "Yes, two or three of the girls from my department and Morag from reception, whom you have just met", she said. John turned to Scooper. "Inspector Scooper, would you just go and verify with

Morag that what Mrs Newton has told us is correct, please?". Scooper did as instructed.

John turned his attention back to Mrs Newton. "Mrs Newton, why do you think Denis Clark would lie?" "He is a fantasist Mr Gammon. I have had one occasion where I had to speak to him because he had harassed Maria Dooley. She worked here. We should have sacked him, but Maria asked if we would just give him a warning. I hear Maria was murdered, she was a lovely girl Mr Gammon". Scooper came back said that Mrs Newton's story had checked out. "I'm sorry to have troubled you Mrs Newton. Thank you for the coffee", and they left.

"Do you think Clark is our man Sir?" asked Scooper. "I'm not sure Sandra, it all seems a bit too easy for my liking" "What are you going to do with him Sir?" "Let him stew for a couple of days I think".

Gammon took the scenic route back to the station, it would soon be summer in the Peaks and the countryside looked amazing. Beautiful, lush green grass, dotted with wild orchids, adorning the fields. As they approached the station, Gammon's Uncle Graham's solicitor called.

"Mr Gammon, I will be ready to read the will next Tuesday at 2.00pm if that's ok?" "Yes that will be fine. You mentioned you were sorting the funeral Mr Gillespie" "I was just about to say, the funeral will be two days after the reading of the will. Your Uncle Graham asked to be buried at Rowksley Church, but I will discuss this further with you on Tuesday". "Ok Mr Gillespie, I will see you Tuesday".

Scooper spoke, "Sorry to hear about your Uncle, John" "Thank you, I knew he had only a limited time left Sandra, but he went quicker than expected" "Are you renting Saron's place now John?" "Yes until my place down at my Mum's farm is done" "I suppose Saron is busy with the pub and all that now, but if you ever want some company, give me a call" and she smiled that seductive smile before getting out of the car at the station.

John was thinking to himself that Saron taking the pub might not be a bad thing after all. He had his freedom again. Just then the phone rang it was Saron. "John, Mum is sorting Annie's funeral out, are you going to do a reading?" "I think I should Saron, seeing that she saved my life" "I thought you might want to John" "Just while you are on Saron, Uncle Graham's funeral is next Thursday" "Oh John, I am so sorry, I won't be able to be with you. We have Peak District Tourism people coming to discuss our grading for the pub" said Saron sadly. "Don't worry" replied John, "I understand" "Are you coming up tonight?" "I'll see what time I get done" "Ok, hopefully see you later" "Yeah, bye" and John hung up.

Gammon arrived at the station and headed towards his office. He met Sergeant Milton on the stairs. "Afternoon Sir" "Afternoon Carl, how is Mr Clark?" "As far as I am aware, he has been a model detainee Sir. Are we charging him tomorrow?" "I don't think I have enough and it all seems too easy to be honest Carl" "What do you mean Sir?" "Well he has previous, he found a victim, he worked with another of the victims and he bought Chinese food where the other victim used to work" "It looks like he is being set up Sir" "Well either that or he is very careless. I don't want to charge him only to find out later it wasn't him and these are all coincidences Carl" "Yes, I agree Sir, we can't have another Alison case on our hands" "Can you imagine the press Carl, if we get this one wrong?" "Right Sir, just finishing. I'm taking Joni to see Grease at Bixton Opera House tonight" "Have a nice evening Carl" said John. "Thanks Sir".

Gammon had just got to his office door, when Inspector Scooper collared him. "What are we doing about Denis Clark Sir?" she asked. "Leave him sweating for tonight and release him tomorrow, but inform him he can't travel anywhere as he is still part of the ongoing investigations" replied John. "I thought we had him bang to rights Sir" "Something's not quite right here Sandra. I can't afford to charge him unless we are one hundred percent sure" "Well on another point Sir, do you fancy a meal tonight? The Sloppy Quiche is doing a Greek night and I thought you might be at a loose end with Saron working" and she smiled at him. "Why not, I'll pick you up at 8.00pm" "Ok I'll book for 8.30pm then".

What could possibly be wrong with an innocent meal with a pretty girl?, he thought. After checking his email, Gammon left for home. Choosing to take the scenic route the countryside looked amazing. As Gammon drove down the valley, he remembered the little house that sat just above Hittington Dale. As a child his brother John and their friends used to pretend that the little house was occupied by German soldiers and they were the British that had to regain the house. They had spent many happy hours playing war games at the house and the surrounding fields. It wasn't until many years later that the house had been bought by the National Trust, as it was believed to be one of the places where Anthony Babington and his associates plotted to kill Queen Elizabeth, in order to restore a Catholic Queen onto the throne of England in 1586. The small house now stood majestically on a hill looking down at the traffic and tourism as if to say "Well look at me, didn't I do well?".

John arrived back at the Post Office Cottage, showered, changed and then left to pick up Sandra from Pritwich. Sandra met him at the gate. As usual she looked a million dollars, she was certainly a stunning girl and he knew he was wrong take her out, especially with him still being in a relationship with Saron, although he now felt the pub was taking up all Saron's time. Maybe it was time to end their relationship and let her concentrate on her business. Sandra climbed in the Jaguar. She was dressed in a tight fitting blue dress that was just above her knees. Emblazoned on the dress, was a peacock, her shoes matched the dress and she had a small leather black coat on, which complemented her look.

"Very nice Miss Scooper" said John approvingly. "Why thank you John" she said smiling. "Are we ok for 8.30pm then Sandra?" "Yes Karen said 8.30pm was fine". They arrived shortly after at the Sloppy

Quiche, just after parking at Up The Steps Maggie's and walking down Monkdale. Karen Jigley met them. "Good evening you two. I've sat you by the window if that's ok? Can I take your coats?"

Karen showed them to the table. "What would you like to drink?" "Do you fancy an Ouzo Sandra?" "Yes, why not John, last time I had one of those was in Crete with some friends a lot of years ago" "Ok. Two Ouzo's with lemonade please Karen". "Jimmy hasn't done a special board tonight everything we have is on the menu". John and Sandra perused the menu and when Karen returned with the drinks they ordered. "What would you like Sandra?" "Can I have the Dolmades, followed by Lamb Kleftiko, please Karen. John?" "I'll have the Green Pea Fava, followed by the Chicken Gyros" "Both good choices it'll be with you soon" and Karen left with the orders.

"John, I know you don't want to talk about work when we are out, but this Denis Clark character, are you sure we should let him go tomorrow?" "I know what you are saying Sandra, but it's a decision I can't be wrong on again. The Alison case very nearly ruined my career and unless I have something really concrete I can't chance it" "But what if he is our man and goes on to kill another girl?" "That's a chance I have to take Sandra. We have checked his house out and found nothing. Forensics didn't find any fibres from his coat, on the other two victims and we have no DNA connecting him, other than on the victim he found".

Just then Karen arrived with the starters, "More drinks you two?" "Yeah, make them doubles this time please Karen". As she left Sandra turned to John. "If I didn't know better Chief Inspector, I would say you were trying to get me drunk, so you could have your wicked way" and she glanced that seductive smile at John. "As if" John replied.

With the starter polished off and the main course almost a distant memory, Sandra decided to try her luck. "Are you still seeing as much of Saron John?" "No, not really, she is pretty much totally focused on the pub these days. Why do you ask?" "Isn't that obvious John?". Karen saved John's blushes as she arrived to take the dessert order. "Would you like coffees or a sweet?" "Yes please and let's have two Brandy floaters please Karen" "John can we share a Tiramisu?" "Fine by me" answered John. "Another good choice" said Karen "Jimmy's Tiramisu is quite big and to die for".

The dessert arrived and Karen wasn't wrong, the Tiramisu could have fed four people never mind two. "That was absolutely fabulous Karen" said John and paid the bill. "Have a safe journey you two" she said. "Thanks Karen and thank Jimmy, the food was excellent" "The Jigley's aim to please John" said Karen, as John and Sandra left.

As they wandered back along Monkdale, Sandra cuddled into John "This is so nice John". John was thinking the same and how it all felt so natural. "I guess we had best have a drink at Up The Steps Maggie's seeing as we have been parked in their car park all night" said John. "Any excuse Mr Gammon" and Sandra laughed.

The pub was quite busy but not with many faces that John knew. "There you go then, good health" "What is it John?" "A Port and Brandy" he replied. "Now I know you want your wicked way, am I staying tonight John?" "If you want too Sandra" "Do you want me too?" "Of course I do".

Copious amounts of Port and Brandy later, the pub was empty except for John and Sandra. "I think we'd best get a taxi back don't you?" John asked up to the bar "Excuse me, could you order me a taxi please?". A lone voice came from the snug, it was Jack Etchings. "I'll take you home lad, just let me finish this pint" "Thanks Jack, didn't know you were in". "I've been playing dominoes for the Spinning Jenny" "Where's Shelley? It's not like you two not to be out together?" "She's babysitting for the eldest lad", replied Jack, "Come on let's get you home". Jack dropped them in the square at Hittington. "See you later, Thanks Jack" said John. "Do you think he will tell Saron?" asked Sandra. "No. Jack doesn't do gossip, he won't even mention he has seen me to his Shelley. He's a good guy, Jack never get's involved with other people's business" "How lucky is that then?" and Sandra laughed.

As they wander over to the cottage, Sandra linked John's arm. "How weird is this, me staying at Saron's place?" "Never thought of it like that Sandra" said John. They entered the kitchen, "Would you like a drink or a coffee" "Have you got any Brandy John?" "Only the best, Remy Martin" and he laughed. "Bring it up, while I freshen up John".

John had all on not showing his pleasure at the thought of a night with Sandra. He poured two Brandies and gingerly walked up the little staircase to the bedroom. Sandra wasn't in there, so John put the glasses on the bedside table, turned both bedside lights on and turned off the main bedroom light. John waited a good five minutes before getting out of the bed and headed for the bathroom. The bathroom door was open, but there was no sign of Sandra, so he called out. "Sandra, Sandra" "In here John", the voice was coming from the single bedroom.

John opened the door and Sandra was sat up in bed reading one of Saron's Marie

Claire magazines she had left. "What are you doing?" asked John. "Well, I was going to have my glass of Brandy and then go to sleep why?" "Oh" said John, picking his words carefully, he said "I thought you might want to sleep with me?" "No John, I don't think that would be right John. You share your bed with Saron".

John was now totally confused, but he knew deep down Sandra was right. He gave Sandra the Brandy, pecked her on the cheek and left for his own bedroom. Sandra smiled to herself, she knew John was quite infatuated with her and she also knew this move would keep him keen. Sandra drank her brandy and snuggled under the covers feeling quite pleased with herself.

Sandra was up early, showered and had made some toast while John was showering. John felt a little bit uneasy when he came down. "Look Sandra, sorry for presuming last night" "Forget it John, only rights right in my book, but thank you for a lovely evening".

Sandra knew she had John wanting more and possibly for the first time she felt some control over the situation. "Are you going to run me to Pritwich to pick up my car?" "Yes no problem" "Ok well lets have breakfast and get going then". As they left the cottage a bright red tractor came through the village and pipped. "Oh shit, that was Sheba Filey, John, isn't she big mates with Saron?" "Yes she is, I guess I will have some explaining to do".

John dropped Sandra off in Pritwich and headed back to Bixton Station. "Sergeant Yap, can you call Denis Clark's solicitor and ask him to attend at 10.00am this morning please?" "Ok Sir. Oh, by the way, there is a Mr Michael John Walvin in the conference room waiting to see you".

John headed for the conference room. John Walvin stood up to shake John's hand. He was about six feet tall with a good head of hair and would be in his late fifties. "Well if it isn't John Gammon, not sure if you remember me John" "I certainly do" said John "how are you keeping?" "Yeah pretty good thanks. When they asked me to transfer here as Head of Forensics, I wasn't sure. Then they said I would be working with Chief Inspector Gammon, the penny dropped, so I jumped at the chance" "Well Wally that was very nice of you" "You were always a man to remember things John, you even remembered my nickname of Wally".

"Great to have you on board mate, I will arrange a meeting in the incident room with the rest of the team, so I can bring you up to speed" "Sergeant Yap, would you get John a coffee and then tell the team I want an update at 11.00am in the incident room" "Will do Sir. Denis Clark's solicitor is here"

"Ok, put him in interview room one with Clark and Milton, then take John down to Forensics and introduce him to his team please Sergeant Yap. I'll speak with you in a bit Wally" said John. "Ok John thanks" said Walvin.

Gammon climbed the stairs to his office. He wanted to have a quick check on his emails and post, while they were sorting out Denis Clark and his solicitor. One of Gammon's emails was a bit concerning, it was from a Sergeant Glamp of Dewsbury West Yorkshire Police.

"Chief Inspector Gammon,

I am emailing you with a concern I have whilst I was working the streets of Dewsbury last night and I thought I should let you know. I arrested a drunken man at 1.44am this morning. He was being unusually violent and just being a general nuisance around some of the young girls when they were spilling out of the clubs.

The gentleman in question was a Mr Rupert Bare, he apparently was on a stag night and had lost his party, so carried on drinking alone and eventually he had had too much and became obnoxious with the revellers. It wasn't just that, it was more of what he was saying that concerned me. He was telling anyone that would listen, that he was the serial killer in the Peak District and to watch out because he collected ears. People thought he was just drunk, but I am formerly from Micklock so I tend to follow your cases. Knowing some background on your current case, I thought I'd best let you know. Mr Bare was released this morning with a caution with regard to his future behaviour".

Best regards

Liam Glamp.

Sergeant Dewsbury Police.

Gammon fired back a quick reply thanking Sergeant Glamp for his information. A couple of things bothered Gammon. Why would anyone go out bragging that they had murdered these girls and mutilated them? He thought it was time he got Mr Bare back in. Gammon left the office to go to the incident room and informed Sergeant Yap to send Inspector Lee to pick up Mr Bare.

Milton started the tape. "Chief Inspector Gammon has now entered the room". John began the interview. "Mr Clarke, after due consideration with regards to your interview yesterday, I have decided to release you. It is on the strict understanding that you are not to leave Derbyshire without first getting prior permission from Bixton Constabulary. You will surrender your passport and should you break this regulation, you will be automatically arrested. Do I make myself clear Mr Clark?" "Yes, but I haven't done anything" "If that is the case, the fullness of time will confirm that, but until then you are still a suspect in a triple murder case. Good day Mr Clark" and Gammon left the room. He wasn't sure if he had done the right thing but previous mistakes were dictating to him this time.

As Gammon left the interview room Inspector Lee was taking Rupert Bare into interview room two. Gammon followed him in. "Do you want a solicitor to be present Mr Bare?" "No, why do I need one?" John continued, "We need you to help us with our ongoing inquiries into the murder and mutilation of three young women" Bare replied, "I've told you everything I know" "Last night I believe you were on a stag night in Dewsbury Mr Bare, is that correct?" "Yes, it was Lucas Radbourne's stag night we shared a flat together when I was at University. What has this got to do with the nutter that is killing these women?" "I believe you were arrested last night for being drunk and disorderly and from what I am told you are lucky not to have been charged with sexual harassment" "What?!, I was just having a bit if fun with a gang of girls" said Bare. "Does your fun run to telling a certain few of the girls that you would cut their ears off and that you were the killer of the murdered girls?" "Ok, look I was drunk. I'm sorry". John leant forward, "Can you tell me where you were on the nights of these girl's murders?". Bare shifted in his seat, "I want my solicitor, you are trying to implicate me in these murders and I am not having it" "Ok Mr Bare, call your solicitor and when he arrives we will reconvene" John turned to Milton, "Milton escort Mr Bare to a phone, allow him to call his solicitor and then put him in a holding cell. We have a meeting in the incident room in ten minutes so get a move on".

Gammon made his way down to the incident room to prepare for the meeting. Slowly the room began to fill up and Milton arrived, just a few minutes late. "Ok everyone, I have called this meeting today to introduce our new Head of Forensics, Mr Michael John Walvin MRCP. I knew John, as he likes to be called, many years ago when we were both starting out on our career paths. You will find John to be very thorough and meticulous in his work, so let's welcome John to the team". Everyone clapped and John smiled, although feeling a little embarrassed by all the attention.

"Ok, let's get down to some facts. Murder victim one, Maria Dooley. Found at Bubley near Ackbourne by a Mr Wang, who is the Uncle of the second victim Poppy Chi. Maria's left ear had been cut from her body, I am guessing as some kind of macabre trophy, she had been sexually assaulted and a picture of the stick man was close by and a further picture of a stick man was found at Monkdale Church. What do we know Inspector Lee?". Lee took up the conversation, "Maria was a normal working girl from a good family. Maria appears to have had quite a few male friends with two in particular. Danny Stevo, Danny is believed to be her long term boyfriend, although it seems she had been seeing a Mr Rupert Bare from Cowdale Hall at the same time. The Bare family are well connected within the local area. Rupert it appears, after having spoken to several local people, is perceived as a bit of a spoilt brat. Not particularly well liked and a bit of a pest around women. I believe DCI Gammon is currently interviewing this man for the second time" "Thank you Inspector Lee".

John continued, "I have Rupert Bare in a holding cell, waiting on his solicitor. He had been on a stag night, last night, in Dewsbury of all places and was bragging to anyone that would listen, that he was our killer. My feeling is that he isn't, but I need some conformation of his whereabouts on the nights of the three murders".

"Ok Inspector Scooper. Second Victim Poppy Chi" said John. Scooper continued, "We have still not been able to apprehend her step brother. Her step brother is Chen, we have through investigations, found he runs the streets of Ackbourne and Bixton, but he keeps a very low profile. Poppy was from a place called Ibley, which is close to Monkdale, she was found in the woods at Rowksley by the game-keeper. She had the same injuries and circumstances as our first victim Maria Dooley. There's quite a lot going on here. We have spoken with her best friend, from her University days, and she gave us the name of a man who she believed Poppy had started seeing, Billy Holland. Her friend believed he was a really bad influence and that he has got her into the drugs scene. Billy Holland was interviewed, but released. We are currently looking into his finances and he seems to have a lavish lifestyle, but no perceived income. The third thing here is, Mr Wang, who found the first victim Maria Dooley, is also Poppy's Uncle".

"Ok" said John, "let's look at our third victim, Alice Beadman. She was due to be married to a David Lansky, they were already living together in a small cottage in Cowdale. Lansky admitted that on the night of her murder, they had had an argument and that Alice had stormed off saying the wedding was over. He said, he didn't follow her and that night she became victim number three. Alice was found by Denis Clark, who I have interviewed at length. Clark appears to be a fantasist with previous convictions. On the face of it all your instincts would put Clark in the frame but somehow I have a feeling that it's all too easy and our killer wants us to think this way. Right lets go through what we have".

"Mr Wang, owner of a Chinese restaurant in Ackbourne, knew Maria Dooley through going into his shop. Wang is Uncle to Poppy Chi. Albert Lockwood found Poppy Chi, although I think we can count him out after interviewing him. Denis Clark found Alice Beadman, but I think we should leave our thoughts open on Mr Clark".

"Our other suspects are, Rupert Bare. Local toff implicated in the murder of Maria Dooley and was actually bragging on a night out in Dewsbury that he is the serial killer. Personally I think he is just a prat, but keep him on the board. Danny Stevo. Believed to be the long term boyfriend, I think we can count him out also. Andrew Bilkin. Not a full shilling, this one believed he was Maria's boyfriend, again keep him on the board but not high on my suspects list. On the other hand, we have Mr Tony Lacey, could well be that there is something not quite right about this guy".

"Chen Chi, step brother to Poppy, and not a nice character, I want this man bringing in for some serious questioning. Billy Holland, whilst I am pretty sure he makes his money dealing, I don't think he is our serial killer".

"David Lansky, boyfriend of Alice Beadman. Again he sits low on my suspects list. Denis Clark, however, ticks all the boxes but it just seems to be too easy, leave him on the board".

"Have we anymore thoughts on why the killer is so brutal and why he takes the victims left ear every time? Can anybody shed any light on the drawings and why is there one at the murder scene and one at a church?" concluded John.

"Sir, I have been doing a bit of digging". John made light of the situation, "I hope we get some good vegetables this year then

Sergeant Milton!!" A ripple of laughter went around the room. "Not that digging Sir. I have been looking at old rituals of mutilation and I came across one in Scotland. A James Gavin of Douglas, Lanarkshire had his ears cut off for refusing to renounce his religious faith. I have looked into this and found Maria Dooley was a Catholic and Alice Beadman was also a Catholic, but her boyfriend told me they didn't tell the vicar or they would not have been allowed to marry at Cowdale Church" "Good work Milton. What about Poppy Chi? surely she wasn't a Catholic?" Milton replied "Her parents said she wasn't brought up with religion, but speaking with her friend Rosie, she told me that Poppy had been to Catholic Church with her many times".

John was impressed, "Brilliant Sergeant Milton, now we appear to have a connection. Any thoughts on the stick man drawings anyone?" "I found out that stick men drawings go way back in time and have been used in China for hundreds of years for linguistic symbols" advised Inspector Smarty. "This is getting very interesting, well done Smarty. So we might deduce that we have either somebody who dislikes religion, and in particular, Catholic's, and we now know the stick figure were used in China. Look, I think we all have enough to go on for now. Sergeant Wisey, you and Inspector Lee get out amongst the bad lads and get Chan Chi brought in for questioning. Scooper, let's do some more digging on Tony Lacey. Milton let's do some thorough back ground checks on Mr Wang and Poppy's parents. Please try to be discreet. Ok. we will give it a week then reconvene. Good luck everyone".

John left the room and walked back to his office and his mobile rang. "Mr Gammon?" "Yes how can I help you?" "It's Tam Gillespie's PA here, he wondered if you could call this afternoon for the reading of your late Uncles will" "Yes what time?" asked John "Would today at 3.30pm be ok?"

John grabbed a coffee and then headed to the solicitors. Gillespie's PA showed him into the oak panelled office. On the wall was a painting of a gentleman with bushy sideburns looking very inch a Victorian Gentleman of some repute. "Please, sit down Mr Gammon. Would you like a coffee?" "Yes please" replied John, as he sat in front of the huge desk. The PA scurried off. Gillespie had half round glasses perched precariously on the end of his rather large bulbous nose.

The solicitor opened a cream coloured scroll and began to read the document out loud.

"This is the last will and testament of Graham John Gammon and therefore supersedes all others.

"I Graham John Gammon, on this date of July 4th 1978, as witnessed by Emily Victoria Gammon, being of sound mind and body do bequeath my whole estate to my only son, John Gammon.

My three houses, Number one 'Travail Manor' in Barnsley, with two hundred and twenty acres, mostly laid to pasture. Number two my house 'De Darley Manor', Dilley Dale, Derbyshire, a six bed-roomed detached home with four acres. Number three my house, 'Cotton Manor House' in Hittington Dale, a twelve bed roomed Elizabethan Manor House set in twelve acres.

My personal belongings which are stored at Ringway Secure lock ups in Barnsley, and my personal monitory wealth with updated amounts to the sum of three and a half million pounds.

ANNIE TANNEY

I would ask that my son, John Gammon, looks after Ceefor my cat until she dies. I wish that the persons presently living in my properties not be asked to leave until their deaths and at that point they may be sold and any monies raised then be given to my son, John Gammon.

I wish two have hymns 'Abide With Me' and 'All Things Bright and Beautiful', played at my funeral".

John knew that was his Mum's favourite hymn and he wondered if that was why Uncle Graham had chosen it.

"When I leave the church, I would like to have played 'Don't Cry Daddy' by Elvis Presley. I wish to have my wake at the Spinning Jenny and the bar is to be free please John.

All there is left to say is "Remember John, you can't fall if you don't climb and there is no fun stopping on the ground". Take care, my son, I am so very proud of you"

Mr Gillespie looked up from the scroll, "That concludes the reading of the will. I will forward all the documentation for the houses to you. I will need your bank account details to forward your Uncle's money. The funeral has all been arranged with the service to take place at Rowksley Church at 10.00am this Thursday. The burial will be next to Graham Gammons, granddad in the churchyard at Rowksley. The wake is organised to follow at the Spinning Jenny in Swinster". At that Mr Gillespie stood up and shook John's hand. "You are a very wealthy man Mr Gammon". John was still shocked at what he had just heard and he left the office in a daze.

John needed to talk to somebody, but he wasn't sure who. He opted for Sandra, so he rang her. "Hey are you free tonight?" "Well I could be, what's the matter John?".

Gammon explained what had happened at the will reading. "Look, I'll meet you at Up The Steps Maggie in about twenty minutes John" "Ok Sandra, thanks, I will head there now".

John arrived at the pub, ordered a Port and Brandy for Sandra, and a pint of Glowing Times for himself. John sat in the corner near the fire and waited for Sandra. Sandra arrived, "Sorry about the state of me, I have come straight from work. Thanks for the drink John, but why haven't you spoke with Saron about this? Not that I mind, but I am curious?" "She's too busy with the pub Sandra".

Sandra was intrigued. "Ok, so the solicitor told you, that you have all these massive properties, his personal belongings in a lock up and three and a half million in money. What are you going to do, John, retire?" "I've been thinking while I was waiting for you and the words Annie Tanney said to me before she died keep ringing in my ears" "What did she say John?" "She told me to 'Live a good life, help others and have no evil in me'" "Pretty profound words John", said Sandra. "I know you are going to think I'm crazy but I think she knew about the will and I think she was telling me to give it away and help others". Sandra's jaw dropped, she couldn't believe what she was hearing. "Listen John, you've had a massive shock. Take some time to think this through. At least wait until after you have buried your Uncle" "Yes ok, you are right Sandra, I just feel like Annie is with me telling me what to do" "Well I'm telling you I need another drink!" and she flashed hre mischievous smile.

"Sorry Sandra, do you want anything to eat?" "Are you eating?" she asked. "Might as well" "Can I have the bacon and brie baguette please?" John ordered adding steak sandwich for himself. It was getting up for 10.30pm by the time they had finished. They had laughed the whole night, Sandra was just the tonic John needed. "Are you staying tonight Sandra?" "I don't want to stay at yours, John, it doesn't seem right. Mum has got Rosie, so you can stay at mine if you want?" "Ok", said John, "shall we get a taxi and you can drop me off in the morning for my car?" "Anything for you, Mr Gammon" said Sandra.

They arrived at Sandra's cottage. It was pleasantly decorated with a modern kitchen, a dining room, a nice size living room with a multi-fuel stove and a stunning old stone fire-place. Upstairs there were two bedrooms and a large bathroom.

"You pour us a red wine and bring it up" said Sandra. "I think I have done that one before, which room will you be in?" "With you of course" and she smiled at John. Sandra made her way upstairs while John sorted the wine.

John took the wine up to the bedroom. Sandra was already in bed. She took the glass of wine from him, sipped it and placed the glass on the bed side table. John removed the cover and passionately kissed Sandra. Sandra was receptive and they were soon in a passionate embrace. They were locked in a full embrace and time just ebbed away, their feelings were so intense. Eventually they lay in each other's arms exhausted.

"John that wasn't just lust was it?" said stated. "I don't know, Sandra you seem to play with my head, it's like you enjoy dangling me" "That's a bit rich coming from you John!" "Look I didn't mean anything wrong, I really enjoy your company and of course the love making" he explained. "So why are we playing silly games?" "It's the commitment thing, I just can't do it Sandra". They lay, entwined in each other's arms and fell asleep.

"John, breakfast" shouted Sandra. John thought he was dreaming. Sandra called up again, "Come on sleepy head, your coffee and toast are going cold" "Coming" he replied. John put on his trousers and shirt and made his way downstairs. Sandra wearing a baggy red tee shirt. John kissed her and tried to take it further. Sandra was quick to stop him. "No chance Gammon, I need my breakfast and I have to take you for your car, so behave" "Ok Miss Frosty Knickers" he teased her "Give over Gammon".

Breakfast finished, they both showered and Sandra took John for his car. "I will be late in today, John, I have to take Rosie to the dentist" "Didn't take you long to use the boss then?" he replied "Behave Gammon go and get in your car". John kissed Sandra long and hard then walked to his car smiling to himself as he watched Sandra pull away.

John decided there and then he had to come clean with Saron, although he knew it wouldn't go down well, he couldn't carry on like this but thought it best to wait until after Annie Tanney's burial.

John drove home, changed his clothes and headed for work. There were major road-works on the way into Bixton, which he'd forgotten about, So instead of taking the half hour detour, he was now sat in the traffic waiting patiently. He switched on the radio and tuned into Radio 2. Dolly Parton and Kenny Rodgers were singing Islands In the Stream, it was a tune that brought back all sorts of memories.

Suddenly the peace and quire was disturbed, there was the car behind honking his horn, John had drifted off to sleep and the cars in front had set off leaving John just sat there. "I must be contented" he thought to himself.

As he neared Bixton station his mind wandered to what he should do about the money and the property his Uncle Graham had left him.

John finally landed at the station. "Good Morning Sir" "Hello Di, nice to see you, are you on days today?" "Yes Sir, Sergeant Yap is on holiday so I am doing the next two days and Sergeant Wisey is doing the next two nights" replied Di. "Ok, how is everything?" asked John. "Quiet Sir, but it's the Cheese Rolling tournament at Hittington Wakes on Saturday and they also have that Toe wrestling match too. It will be mayhem, you know how these young farm lads get with a smell of the barmaids apron" "It kicked off last year didn't it?" remarked John. "Yes it was the tug of war competition that caused that, Pritwich beat Hittington Dale in the final, and they are great rivals so it all kicked off. Fifteen arrests that night" answered Di. "Blimey, remind me to go away from Hittington on Saturday night Di" and Gammon chuckled as he climbed the stairs to his office.

Gammon spent the first two hours going through his emails and then his post. He had about twelve letters left to look at, when he came across a card. Gammon opened the card. It had letters cut out of a newspaper stuck inside and it simply said "Gammon why don't you go back to London? We don't want you here. You will never catch me, you Plod, I have three ears in my collection. When will you realise you are no match for me. I might be tempted to stop killing if you leave and go back to London. So you see, you have all the next victims' destinies in your hands. You choose. You only have until Saturday and to prove that I am not playing, I will send you a present Gammon". The card finished with a picture of a stick man.

Gammon immediately rang down to Forensics. "Wally, can you get up to my office. I have something to show you?" "On my way John" replied Walvin. John Walvin appeared at the office door a few minutes later. "Come in John, take a look at this and then see if you can get any DNA from it please" said John. "It looks like you have upset somebody here John" "It's the usual thing with these nutters Wally". "What are you going to do?" asked Walvin and John replied, "I'll tell you what I am not going to do, and that's go back to London, well not until I have nailed this bastard" "Right let me go and see what I can do for you John". Wally left the office and Gammon finished off his mail. Nothing more of any interest came from the rest of his mail. It was now 2.20pm, Gammon decided to finish early. He wanted to speak to Doreen to ensure the solicitor had catered for enough food for his Uncle Graham's funeral.

Gammon drove away from Bixton Police station with his thoughts on the funeral. Did he write down some things to say at the funeral? Or should he just get up and speak from the heart? He chose the latter, because that's what Uncle Graham would have done.

"Afternoon Doreen" John greeted her. "What are you doing at the pub at this time of day young Mr Gammon?" "Well actually I have come to see you about Uncle Graham's funeral. I wanted to make sure the solicitor has catered for enough people" Doreen replied, "Well he told me to cater for eighty people, but your Uncle Graham was well liked round here, so I am doing it for one hundred and twenty" John thought out loud, "I'm guessing that there may be a lot of people from Sheffield attending, you know, business folk. Doreen, did you know about how wealthy Uncle Graham was, and about his properties and businesses?" "Yes John, but I think he only ever told me and Kev. He stayed at the pub once, I think it was when Kev bid on Cotton House at Hittington Dale. Graham never wanted anybody to know what he owned, he was a humble man John" "I know" said John. Doreen continued, "I have said this before, but sometimes when I see you, I always say to Kev 'bloody hell John Gammon you are so like Graham' it's unbelievable, even how you walk. Your Uncle Graham could have had any woman he wanted round here, but I never knew of anybody that he went out with. He would come down years back for the Wakes and the odd New Year's Eve and the local girls were like bee's round a honey pot. So you see it's in the Gammon genes, hey young John?" and she laughed. Little did she know he thought to himself. "Listen John, don't worry, it's all sorted, just sorry you have yet another family member to bury".

"Well on that note Doreen, I'll try a pint of Pedigree". Kevin, appeared from out of the cellar. "Kev, come and pour your mate a pint of Pedigree, I've got food to sort"

"You're early John, having a bad day?" asked Kev. "Nah, just checking on the funeral arrangements" John sighed. Kev looked concerned, "Are you alright lad?" "I'm ok thanks Kev, just not sure what to say at the funeral. Should I say that Graham was my dad" "Look lad, there's nowt to gain by doing that, nobody need ever know. Graham lived with the guilt and torment for all those years thinking Phil never knew. You have to remember as well, Graham never got over your Mum, and it must have hurt seeing her so happy with your Dad" "Suppose you are right Kev" "Listen lad, let's a have a brandy a piece to celebrate his life, my treat" "Never turn down a Brandy Kev".

"How are Saron and Angelina doing at the Tow'd Man?" "I'm not sure Kev, they have a lot on, so have I, so Saron and I haven't seen each other for a bit". Kevin turned to John, "I know you lad, you are trying to call it a day aren't you?". John sighed again "To be honest Kev, I can't see it working now she has the responsibility of the pub" "It's a big commitment John, it's a 24/7 life I'm afraid".

Kev changed the subject, "How's work going? a nasty business, these murders, John?" "Yes, we have a few likely suspects" replied John. "I won't ask John" "I couldn't tell you Kev, even if I wanted to" "I know that lad". John sat quietly for a moment and said, "Listen mate, I'm going to nip up and see Saron. I need to know when Annie Tanney's funeral is". Kev nodded his approval, "Ok lad, we'll see you at the wake if not before" "Ok mate thanks for the brandy" "Anytime take care lad". John drove to the Tow'd Man, the scenery was spectacularly beautiful. Lush green fields filled with small wild flowers adorned the views like a huge patchwork quilt of colours.

John arrived at the Tow'd Man. Angelina was busy putting hanging baskets up. They had purchased new picnic tables, which had all been painted in a lovely, Farrow and Ball blue.

"Hey John, how are you?" said Angelina. "I'm good thanks, is Saron in?" "Yes, she's down the cellar, giving it a lick of paint. Have you come to help" Angelina asked with a smirk. "Ha, ha funny lady" replied John. "I think so Mr Gammon" said Angelina.

Saron heard John's voice and came up from the cellar. John raised an eyebrow, "Nice attire Saron". Saron had on bright blue bib and brace overalls, turned up to just below her knees, with a pale blue shirt which was now splattered in cream emulsion. John smiled to himself, there was only Saron that could make painting overalls look so sexy. "Never mind taking the mickey Gammon, have you come to help? I was beginning to think you had done a runner, it's that long since I have seen you".

"I would love to help you Saron, but I am sure I have my sock draw to tidy out" and John laughed. "Very funny PC Plod, come on, I will make you a coffee" and she turned to walk away. Angelina carried on with her jobs outside while Saron and John headed into the kitchen.

"Wow what a difference a couple of weeks can make. Nice kitchen Saron" said John "Angelina sorted it John, she will be doing the cooking so it was only fair she had things how she wanted" "Have you been busy?" "Last night was probably the first quiet night since we took over. I guess all the locals have been and had a look. We are hoping once Jayne Thornley-Coil has got the letting rooms done, then the walkers will take up any slack times during the winter season".

"Anyway, enough of me, how are you John?" "Thought I'd best check when Annie's funeral is?" the mention of Annie's funeral made Saron feel guilty. "John, I am so sorry about not being able to make your Uncle Grahams funeral" "Don't worry Saron, it's not a big problem" "Well Annie's funeral is on Monday next week, will you be coming?" said Saron. "Of course, I owe Annie so much Saron". "John, would you like to leave from the hall with me and Mum?" "No thanks Saron, I'll meet you at the church. What time is the service?" "It's 3.00pm at Pritwich Church and then afterwards at the Sycamore in Pritwich. I'm sorry I haven't seen you, the pub is taking up all my time. We haven't really sorted any staff yet, that may have to wait until everything is finished. You could come up here though John, if you are having a drink I will be behind the bar anyway". John didn't rise to the comment, seeing Saron again had sent his feelings all over the place. She was such a nice person and she had done so much for him, and yet he'd slept with Sandra only last night. What kind of person was he?

John said to Saron, "We had Uncle Grahams will read the other day" "Well I hope he left you something" said Saron. John was quick to reply, "Saron he left me everything" "I thought he rented his bungalow?" she said "It turns out he was mega wealthy. He owned three country houses, he had antiques that are in a lock up and he left me something like three and half million pounds". Saron's jaw dropped. "My God! that is some will. I didn't realise he was that wealthy. Why did he live in rented accommodation though?" "He never wanted anyone round here to think he was flash, so he simply hid his fortune from everyone" said John. "So what are you going to do with it all John?" "You are going to think I am crazy Saron, but I think I am going to give the houses to the people that live in them. The money I am going to give to Dilley Dale Hospital. The hospital has always been under threat from closure and it is only a cottage hospital".

"Look John, it's nothing to do with me what you do with your inheritance, but have you thought this through?" said Saron. "On the night that Annie died, when she told me she was dying, I felt she was trying to tell me something", said John. "Why what did she say?" "She said 'live a good life, help others and have no evil in you'" "Well that doesn't mean she wanted you to give your inheritance away John" said Saron and John replied, "It's hard to explain Saron, I felt her presence when the will was be read, I could feel her by my side. It is like fate, she saved my life Saron, I have to do some good in my life" "Well you know best John" said Saron sounding slightly miffed. "Look Saron, I am hardly short of money, I have the holiday cottages at the farm, I earn a good wage, so what do I need a fortune for?" "If it makes you feel better John, it's your money".

"Look John, I have loads to do, why don't you nip home, get changed and come back up for when we open at six?" "I'll see what I feel like. I have to speak at Uncle Graham's funeral and also Annie's, so I better get working on what I have to say" "Ok, well If I see you, I see you". John kissed Saron and she went back to the painting in the cellar.

Angelina was just coming down the steps from hanging up the baskets. "Are you ok John?" "Yes thanks Angelina, are you?" "Yes. Look we haven't spoken since you know what, and I just want to say, I don't regret what happened but if it's affected our friendship then I do regret it" "Look, let's just forget it ever happened, it's too complicated Angelina" "Fine by me John" Angelina replied.

John left Angelina and got back in his car he planned to nip back home, shower and then go out. He had almost got home when his phone rang. "Sir Di Trimble here, I have a woman wanting to speak with you" "What about Sergeant?" "She won't say" said Trimble. "Well can't one of the other Inspectors talk with her?" asked John, annoyed. "I've tried that, she is insistent that she will only speak with you" "Ok Di, I'll spin round and I'll be about twenty minutes. Get her some coffee and I will be as quick as I can" "Ok Sir".

Gammon was cursing his luck, but was also intrigued. He arrived at Bixton station and headed straight to the desk Sergeant.

"Ok Di where is this mystery lady?" "She's in interview room one". John headed to the room. When he opened the door he was met with a timid lady with short blonde hair, reasonably dressed. She looked like she could have been quite a good looking girl at some time, but she appeared dragged down by time in her appearance now.

"Chief Inspector John Gammon and you are?" said Gammon. "Rachel Lacey" replied the woman. "How can I help you?" "If I were to tell you something, would my husband get to know Mr Gammon?" "I can't guarantee that Rachel, but what I can guarantee is, if you withhold evidence which may lead to the arrest of any individuals involved in a crime, then you too would also be charged. Shall we start again?".

"It's my husband Mr Gammon" "What about your husband?" "His name is Tony Lacey, he works in the greenhouses at Chatsworth" she said. "Yes, I know Mr Lacey" said John. "The other night, when that young girl was murdered at Cowdale, he came home at 2.30 in the morning. I got up and went downstairs. He'd stripped off his clothes and he was putting them in the washing machine" "Well I agree it's an odd time, but it's hardly a crime" "Mr Gammon his shirt was covered in blood. When I asked what he was doing, he hit me and told me to go back to bed. The next day I took his washing out of the machine while he was having his breakfast. The blood stains were still there but he snatched the clothes from me and went outside. We have a dustbin that we burn leaves in, he put his clothes in there and burnt them".

"Did he give you a reason?" asked John. "I didn't dare ask Mr Gammon. He is a violent man and even worse when he has been drinking. He quite often comes home in the early hours of the morning and tries to molest me and if I resist he calls me names and hits me. I have to give in because I don't want my daughter to hear him" she confessed. "So, just to re-cap, Mrs Lacey, you think your husband may have been involved in Alice Beadman's murder?" "I don't know Sir, but I know he has had many affairs whilst we have been married" "Is he a local man?" Mrs Lacey replied "He was born in Liverpool, but he came to live down here with his Grandma and Granddad when he was twelve. I met him on a horticultural course, we started dating then I fell pregnant with my daughter Molly. My dad was quite strict, so we had to get married and I knew from the start it was a massive mistake, but I had nowhere to go". "Look Mrs Lacey, it will be difficult for us to trace anything with regard to your husband but I will assign an officer to watch his movements. This will be the best chance, because if he is our killer, he will kill again. Thank you for coming forward, I realise the risk you are taking and I will keep you out of this until we have something positive. If you remember anything, or you have anymore information, please contact me. Here is my card, any time day or night" "Thank you Mr Gammon, I had to tell you, it's been playing on my mind" "Take care Mrs Lacey, I will be in touch" and Gammon showed her out.

"Is in Inspector Smarty in his office?" "Yes he is Sir" "Ok thank you". Gammon made his way to Dave Smarty's office, shutting the door behind him after he went in. "Blimey am I in trouble Sir?" "No quite the opposite" and Gammon set about telling Smarty what he had just heard from Rachel Lacey. "I want you to put this guy under surveillance at night, have all the overtime you want Dave, and only report back to me on this. "Ok Sir, I will start tonight" said Smarty. John turned to Di, "Get his address Sergeant Trimble, it's on file as we have already interviewed this guy. Dave, be very careful" warned John. "I will, no problem Sir".

"Right Di, I am off" said John finally. "I'm sorry about that Sir, but she was insistent she spoke with you only" "No problem, what time are you on until?" "10.00pm Sir, Sergeant Yap is at the Derby versus QPR game". "How is he doing Di?" "He's a nice guy, we help each other out with the shifts. Mind you I did think Sergeant Hanney was a nice guy, don't think I will make detective Sir" said Di. "He fooled all of us Di goodnight" "Goodnight Sir".

Gammon set off back to Hittington, he had a text on his phone from Sandra, it just said "thanks for a nice night, shame I haven't got a babysitter tonight" John could feel the old guard go up. What was the matter with him? As soon as anyone started getting close to him, he shut them out.

"I need a drink" he thought, so he headed for the Spinning Jenny. The car park was quite full, he wandered down the small steps and into the bar area. Joni was behind the bar. "Hey John how are you?" "Good thanks Joni, what about you?" "Yeah ok, have you heard me and Carl have decided to split?" "No" said John, "he never said, but to be honest we are so busy at work we don't get much time to speak. Sorry to hear about that" "To be honest John, he isn't over his last relationship, so it's best we move on" "I was in the Wobbly man the other week and Rick was saying how he missed you not working with him and how he could not get good enough staff since you left" Joni smiled, "I heard he isn't selling now John. Right what would you like?". "Can I have a pint of Dilley Dale Dark. What percentage is it?" he asked. "Blimey John, it's 8.3%" "Don't worry, I'll just have one, now you have started to pour it. You're busy tonight" "It's Hittington Dale Ladies Bake Off Quiz night. They have one twice a year and the proceeds go towards a bus trip to the NEC to The Good Food Show". Joni went off to serve two couples at the far end of the bar, so John sat alone at the bar. He felt a nip to his bum and turned round.

"Sheba was that you?" he asked. "Who could resist the John Gammon bum?" she laughed, her white teeth lighting up her face. "Whoops only just seen who is on the bar, don't want to upset Joni" "Why would she be upset Sheba?" "Are you blind Gammon? She is besotted with you. Us mere mortals don't stand a chance". Joni came over and served Sheba although she was courteous she wasn't friendly. Sheba picked the drinks up, but as she left the bar she turned to John and said, in a voice just loud enough for Joni to hear, "If you get too many you are welcome to stay at mine, I looked after you the last time" Joni let Sheba go and then came over to quiz John. "Another conquest John?" she asked. "No nothing like that, I slept on Sheba's sofa a bit back nothing else" "Wish I could believe that. Where is the lovely Saron tonight? Thought you'd be propping the bar up at the Tow'd Man these days".

"We aren't living together anymore Joni. She has the pub and I have her old cottage until the farm cottages are complete" "Oh, so you are not with her then?" "You know me Joni, I'm not committed to anyone" said John. "Oh I know you John, trust me" and she went off to serve some other customers.

John looked round to see Shelley Etchings with Sheba making their way to the bar.

"Would you like drink ladies?" "Never turn down a drink from a handsome copper John" "Thought not Shelley, where's Jack tonight?" "Watching football John, it's a girl's night out tonight". Sheba jumped in quick, "Hang on Shelley we don't mind speaking with handsome looking men though" "Grab your coat Gammon, you've pulled" and Shelley laughed.

"Come on ladies, what are you having?" "I'll have a brandy and port please John" said Shelley, "Sheba?" "What do you recommend handsome?" she said. Joni stood waiting to get the drinks, annoyance all over her face. "I know, I will have a glass of Proseco, please John" "Ok, a Brandy and port, and a Proseco please Joni". The girls got their drinks and as Sheba was leaving she whispered in John's ear "The offer is still open". Sheba smiled, flicked her long black hair and followed Shelley in to the other bar. John decided to call it a night with the funeral being tomorrow. "Good night Joni" he said. "You're going are you?" "Yes Joni, big day tomorrow" "Good luck John, keep your chin up" and she smiled.

John arrived back at the cottage, on entering the kitchen he found a brown jiffy bag with his name on it. He opened it inside there was a letter rolled up with two elastic bands round it. John carefully slid the elastic bands off the rolled up paper and to his horror a human ear fell on the kitchen table. The paper had letter's cut out of newspapers stuck to it. It just said, "I warned you Gammon, don't tempt me ha, ha".

Gammon immediately called Sergeant Milton. "Sergeant, would you call at my place? I need you to collect something and take it into work for me" "On my way Sir". Carl Milton arrived shortly after and Gammon showed him the ear and the letter. "I need John Walvin to look at this first thing tomorrow. I'm not in work as I have my Uncle's funeral but call me about 3.00pm. We should be at the Spinning Jenny by then" "I guess we are looking for another body now Sir" said Milton. "I think you assume correctly Carl" said John. Milton left the cottage with his grisly package. John decided to crack open the Jameson's Whisky, it always helped him to think. Had they interviewed the killer? In some respects the killer had dropped his guard by hand delivering the Jiffy bag to John's house. Surely this meant he was local.

After a couple of glasses of whisky he made his way to bed. He had just fallen asleep when his mobile started vibrating. Saron was calling. Half asleep John answered, "Hello" "John I'm a bit concerned. This guy keeps coming in the pub and he is really weird. He doesn't appear to know anyone, so I don't think he is local, but he keeps trying to chat me up and tonight he kept saying what lovely ears I had". "Saron, don't think I am not interested but it's Uncle Graham's funeral tomorrow and I am shattered. He will just be some weirdo from a neighbouring village. If you are that concerned, call Denis tomorrow and see if he knows who he is "John, I don't know what I have done to you, but you seem so disinterested in me. I'll let you get some sleep" and she ended the call. John lay back. "Bloody women, I will never understand them" he muttered. John woke at 8.15am, made his breakfast, ironed his clothes and showered.

He left the cottage and drove down to Rowksley. He couldn't believe how many funerals he had attended in the short time he had been back in the Peak District and he wasn't sure how he felt about burying his genetic father.

John was shown to the front of the church, which was already quite full. Rowksley was a beautiful old church, it's stained glass windows behind the alter, shone coloured lights onto the coffin like a kaleidoscope. On the left side of the church, all the pews were full. The side John was sat at was now almost full too. To John's surprise, Sandra Scooper arrived, dressed head to toe in black and she wore a small hat with a black net veil. Sandra sat down next to John and in a quiet voice asked John if he was ok. John nodded and Sandra reached across and squeezed his hand affectionately, a gesture to say, 'I am here for you'.

The vicar climbed into the pulpit, he spoke clearly. "Graham's only surviving nephew, John, would like to thank you all for coming here today to celebrate the life of his Uncle Graham. I will read a short passage from the bible. This from 14:1:6

Do not let your hearts be troubled.
Trust in God and trust in me.

In my Father's house there are many rooms, if it were not so, I would have told you.

I am going there to prepare a place for you.
I will come back to take you, to be with me, that you may also be where I am.

You know the way to the place where I am going.

Thomas said to him "Lord we don't know where you are going, so how can we know the way?"

Jesus answered "I am the way and the truth and the life. No one comes to the Father except through me"

Reverend Lindy then said, "Please stand for our first hymn 'Abide With Me'". The congregation stood up and as is normal at funerals only a few sang, most people mouthed the words, but made no sound. The vicar then asked everyone to be seated while John gave his reading.

"First of all, thank you all very much for coming today. I know some of you have had very long journey's. Uncle Graham was my dad's brother. It was only after I lost my Mum, I got to really know Uncle Graham. Dad, as you know, was the farmer and Uncle Graham the business man. He had been very successful as I'm sure some of the people here today can vouch for that. The thing that stood out about Uncle

Graham was that money was not his driving force. He didn't like people to know he had wealth as most of you know".

"I remember me and my brother Adam going fishing with Uncle Graham. We spent the whole day on Micklock Lake and never caught a fish, but he told us that we had. When I questioned him and said if we had, where were they? He said that they had been on the hook, but had wriggled away at the last minute, but any fish that did that, were re-caught by the bailiff and taken to Rowksley fish and chip shop for the people that caught them to eat for their supper. Well as little boys this seemed magical and we duly headed for Rowksley Fish and Chip Shop for a sit down supper. He had already spoken to the owner, so when we arrived the waitress came to the table and asked me and Adam if we wanted our catches done in breadcrumbs or batter. After a few minutes the owner and the waitress came out with our Fish and Chips and the owner asked everyone for a round of applause for our local fishermen. Everyone clapped and we felt very special. Uncle Graham had this knack of making people feel special".

"I decide to just read from the heart today with no notes, but I did research a poem that sums Uncle Graham up".

Footprints in the Sand.

One night I dreamed I was walking
Along the beach with the Lord
Many scenes from my life flashed across the sky
In each scene I noticed footprints
Sometimes there were two sets of footprints
Other times there was only one
This bothered me because I noticed
During the low periods of my life when
I was suffering from anguish, sorrow or defeat
I could see only one set of footprints
So I said to the Lord, You promised me,
Lord that if I followed you

You would walk with me always.
But I noticed during the most trying periods
Of my life, there has only been one set of prints in the sand
Why when I needed you most
Have you not been there for me?
The Lord replied
The times when you have seen one set of footprints
It was then that I carried you.

"Uncle Graham was always there for anyone in need and I guess he carried many people in his life, but whatever he did it was never for gain".

John could see Doreen wiping a tear from her cheek.

John finished his reading and the vicar returned to the pulpit. If you would like to stand for our final hymn 'All Things Bright and Beautiful'. John could picture his Mum stood at the farmhouse kitchen sink singing this hymn, while he and Adam played farms on the kitchen table. He knew Uncle Graham would have known this was her favourite and this was possibly his final compliment to a woman he never stopped loving, but who he knew he could never be with.

The hymn finished and the vicar announced that there would be a buffet at the Spinning Jenny and all were invited. The coffin was then lifted and carried out. As it left the church, the song "Don't Cry Daddy" by Elvis Presley was playing. Sandra asked John if he wanted her to go with him to the grave side. John nodded. At the grave-side there was only Sandra, John, Kev and Doreen. The vicar said a small prayer and they lowered the coffin into the ground. Each person threw a small amount of soil on to the coffin and then they left the grave-side.

ANNIE TANNEY

The Spinning Jenny was packed. John spent a lot of time thanking everyone for coming to the funeral. He had a curious moment. A lady he had noticed, who would have been in her late sixties and who clearly had been a pretty lady, waited until John was on his own and she came over and introduced herself.

"My name is Maggie Else, I knew Graham very well" she said. "Pleased to meet you, Is it Mrs Else?" "Please call me Maggie" "Ok, Maggie it is, so how did you know Uncle Graham?" asked John. "I met Graham in 1963, I was twenty years old, you've probably worked out I am seventy three John". Surprised John said, "You know my name Maggie?" "I know a lot more than you think. I wanted to be a model and your Uncle Graham got me sorted. I then got a break in films and eventually became a Bond Girl" "Really? how interesting" said John, "So where do you live Maggie?" "I live in Hittington Dale at Cotton Manor House". John quickly realised that this was one of Uncle Grahams houses he had been left.

Maggie went on "I fell on hard times, but your Uncle Graham was always there for me, I live in his house rent free. He was such lovely man, John". John still didn't say anything about owning Maggie's house. "He never told me he was poorly, I saw him about three months ago and he seemed in good spirits. He was such a good looking man all the girls wanted to be with him, me included. I'm going to shock you now, but I once asked him if he was gay, because I could not understand why he never took up any of the offers he received. Over a bottle of Red wine he told me his secret, but he swore me to secrecy". Intrigued john asked Maggie, "What was his secret?" Maggie then said, "He told me about your Mum and you. He never got over the guilt. Your Mum was a lovely lady and beautiful as well. Graham knew what they had done was wrong and he fought with his feelings until the day he died. For that reason he was never interested in anyone else and threw himself into his business. John would you like to come for afternoon tea next Sunday? I have so much to tell you" "Yes, that would be lovely, Maggie". Maggie leaned forward kissed John on the cheek before leaving.

Sandra came over, "Are you ok? Who was that?" "It's a long story, but I have a feeling I have more surprises round the corner. Come on let's have a drink" said John. Sandra looked at him confused. John hadn't noticed Joni was working, until he got to the bar. "Oh hi Joni" "What can I get you John?" "I'll have a double brandy please". Joni scowled at Sandra, "What would you like?" "I'll have a large red wine please". Joni went off to get the drinks. "What's her problem? Let me guess another one in love with Mr Gammon" and she laughed.

Joni placed the drinks on the bar and went off to serve somebody at the far side of the bar. John and Sandra moved away. "Nice piece you did for Graham just then John" "Thanks Kev" said John. "I think you summed him up well" said Doreen, "That was a lovely reading John, your family would have been proud of you" "John are you ok?" "Fine thanks Shelley, it's very good of you and Jack to come today". Shelly said, "Graham was a kind, generous man. We both had the utmost respect for him. God took one of the good guys today John". John said "Well let's all have a drink and celebrate his life. That is what he wanted. Same again please Joni".

The bar slowly emptied, most of the people that had travelled had left, it virtually came down to the usual crew. Steve and Jo, Cheryl and Bob, Jack and Shelley, Kev and Doreen, John and Sandra and Carol Lestar.

John ordered another round just has his phone rang. "Excuse me" he said. It was John Walvin, "Hi John, hope you are ok, but you said to call you if I found anything. Not good news John" "Why" "Well the DNA from the ear matches Sergeant Wisey". John was stunned, "What?? Are you sure?" "One hundred percent, John" said Walvin. "I thought Wisey was at work?" "Apparently Dave Smarty said he had asked for two days off but never gave a reason" replied Walvin. John fired away, "Has anybody been round to his flat? He rents one on Buckle Street in Bixton. Get Sergeant Milton to go round to his flat and tell him to call me please Wally" "Ok John, sorry about the bad news it must be a hard enough day as it is today" "No problem Wally, it comes with territory as you know. I'm more concerned about young Wisey to be honest" said Gammon. "Well it doesn't sound good to be honest, John" "Ok, well thanks Wally,

I'll wait for Sergeant Milton to call me". John went back to join his friends.

"John would you find it disrespectful to your Uncle Graham if we had a game of Jack's" "Not at all, in fact I bet he would think it was a great idea. Not sure you lot will at the end though" laughed John.

They started off the game, John dealt the cards. Scooper got to name the first drink. "Gin, please Joni". Jack got the next drink, "Put a Port in it Joni" "Bloody hell Jack, Gin and Port what you trying to do? Bloody kill us?" "It'll put hairs on your chest Carol" said Jack. "I think she's already got them, haven't you Carol?" "Piss off Lineman" said Carol. "Stop trying to annoy people Steve" "Only my bit of fun" said Steve. Jo scowled at him, which meant he'd to cut it out. The third Jack out of the pack landed at Bob. "I always end up out of pocket at this flippin' game, I do". "Stop whinging and pay up" said Cheryl. "You're as bad you never bring your purse out" "Women's prerogative Bob" said Shelley. "It's certainly Cheryl's, Shelley". Bob paid his due and then the fourth Jack came out. Again it landed on Sandra Scooper. "Oh no, look what you have done to me Jack". Jack laughed "Come on lass, down in one or you have to buy a round". Sandra drank it quickly. "That was awful". Of course everyone who hadn't had to drink it laughed.

The game carried on, with poor Cheryl getting three drinking Jack's, one after the other. Brandy and Pernod, followed by Vodka and Tia Maria and then Whisky with a Cherry Brandy. That almost finished poor Cheryl. Off she went distinctly sickly in colour. The other poor infortunate Jack drinker was Scooper, although she had gaps in between but she had won five times, so sensible conversation wasn't forth coming with these two. Everyone else had won one or two. It was now almost midnight and taxis' were called for everyone. Steve sidled up to John, "Are you two an item now then" "Behave Offside" said John. "I'll take that as a 'Yes' then" said Steve smugly.

John and Sandra's taxi finally arrived, Sandra fell asleep leaning on John, on the way to his house in Hittington. John got Sandra out of the car and inside. He managed to get her upstairs and lay her on the bed. Sandra was mumbling about how she loved John and that he would be better with her than Saron.

The following morning John had heard Sandra moving about upstairs and popped some bread in the toaster. Sandra came down stairs. "Morning Sandra" said John. "What the hell happened John? I feel like I have been hit by a train and my head feels like I have got Cozy Powell and his drum kit in there. Have you got any Asprin?" John smiled at her, "I've just put the box next to your coffee" "John I really don't think I can make work today, I feel so ill. I just want to go back to bed". "Before you do that, have a couple of slices of toast if you are taking tablets".

Sandra took one look at the toast and ran to the downstairs toilet. John grinned, "I'll take that as a 'no' then with regard to the toast. Listen Sandra I'm off to work. I will phone you at lunchtime". All he could hear was Sandra retching. John grabbed his keys and set off for work.

As soon as he got to work, he called Sergeant Milton to his office. "What happened to the phone call Carl?" snapped Gammon. "I did phone you Sir "Let me check". Gammon felt in his pocket for his phone. "Shit! I must have left it at the pub. Sorry about that Carl, what did you find out? Where is Wisey?" Milton answered,

"His flat was immaculate Sir. The landlord let me in, he said he hadn't seen him for two days. He seemed like a curtain twitcher, so he would have known". "Right, this is getting serious. Call all the hospitals in a thirty mile radius and see if anybody has been admitted, who fits his description and with these injuries" "Yes Sir" said Milton and left.

"Sir have you got a minute?" "What's the problem Sergeant Yap?" asked John. "It's Sergeant Wisey Sir, you do know he is gay?" "Well I kind of guessed, but why would that be a problem Yap?". "Oh no problem Sir, but I know he used to hang out, on his nights off, at the Pink Lady Bar and Grill in Bixton. It's got a bit of a reputation with the young lads. They go out on stag parties and then when they've had a belly full of beer in the pubs, they try and get into the Pink Lady, so most Saturday nights it all kicks off".

Inspector Smarty was just walking past the office. "Smarty get down to the Pink Lady, see if anybody know where Wisey might be?" "Sir, that's a……." "Before you say anymore Smarty, we know it's a gay bar. Take Inspector Lee with you if it bothers you that much" said John. Smarty and Lee set off for The Pink Lady. "Thanks for that Sergeant we will make a detective of you yet".

Gammon climbed the stairs, grabbed a coffee and headed for his office. The amount of post on his desk never ceased to amaze Gammon, he would no sooner clear his desk one day, then the following day it was overflowing again. Gammon waded through a third of the pile when a call came through from Smarty.

"Sir we have just spoken to somebody that call's himself Simon Twinky. He works behind the bar and does a bit of a stage show" "Too much information Smarty, just the facts please" said John grinning to himself. "Don't think it's his real name Sir, but he said the people that use the bar on a regular basis don't use their real names. He said that Wisey was known has Prince Charming, he said he was a regular two nights ago and that he left the bar with a stranger. Twinky said he thought he could have been of Chinese origin, but he didn't get a good look at him". "Is there any CCTV footage Smarty?". "They have cameras but they don't record, he said if they did, nobody would come in" "Ok you two come back to the station" "Ok Sir".

Gammon phoned Sandra. "How are you?" he asked, "John I feel so ill. I can't remember anything about yesterday. Did I show myself up? I feel so bad it was a funeral after all" "Don't be silly, Uncle Graham would have loved that we celebrated his life that way. Are you up yet?" "No just phoned Mum, she is sorting Rosie out. Sorry, I am going to have to go and be sick again" and the phone went dead.

As soon as Smarty and Lee got back Gammon called a meeting in the incident room. "As you are now all aware I have received a left ear in the post. Forensics have checked it out and I am sorry to say the match is that of Sergeant Wisey". There were still one or two of the team who weren't aware of the incident and a gasp rang round the room. "I would not normally disclose a person's private life, but Sergeant Wisey was a gay man". Again surprise was evident in the room. "Whilst there is nothing wrong with Sergeant Wisey's preferences, my concern is for his safety. He will have lost a lot of blood but there are no reported cases anywhere in a thirty mile radius of

Bixton. It is early days yet, but I am not getting a good feeling about this".

"Yes, Inspector Smarty?" "Sir, the person who was seen leaving the Pink Lady with Sergeant Wisey was possibly of Chinese origin. Does the CCTV show that?" "No Sergeant Milton, they don't switch it on for obvious reasons. He was seen leaving by a Simon Twinky, the bar person and sometime entertainer" said John.

"The Chinese guy we are looking, Chan Chi, could it have been him?" asked John "Twinky said he didn't get a good enough look. Look if we can find Chan and surely all our resources must have a clue as to where he is, then we could always do a line up. Chan seems to have disappeared off the radar. Milton after this meeting, me and you are going to hunt down Chan". "Ok Sir". "Right everyone I want Wisey finding and time is important here, he maybe being held

hostage for some reason, he may have inadvertently dropped on our killer. Whichever way, he is a colleague and we need to find him. That's all thank you. Come on Milton let's get off to Derby".
"Where do we start Sir?" "The Queens Arms on Buckle Street, that's where he run's his operations from" said Gammon.

Gammon and Milton arrived at The Queens. It was a typical town pub, quite an old exterior in a rough end of the city. It was the sort of place, even if you were desperate for a drink, you may want to avoid. Milton pushed open the twin doors. The brass door handles were so dirty they barely resembled brass. There were two steps down into quite a large area. The pub was quite busy for the time of day. There were two pool tables, both had lads playing them, your usual scroats, arrogant, mouthing and off dressed in jeans and hoodies. The whole place smacked of dodgy dealing.

Gammon ordered two drinks from the young girl behind the bar, who was covered head to toe in tattoos. Crazy for such a young girl. She was the type that never looks at you. There were a few older guys studying the racing papers at the far end of the bar. Most of the tables were taken up, two of the tables had girls on them clearly dressed for their occupation of walking the streets. "You never know Carl we might drop lucky let's sit and watch" instructed Gammon.

They had been sat at the bar for almost two hours, when a big guy walked in. He was quite badly knocked about and had a limp. He ordered a drink and went and sat down. John ordered two more drinks and bought the girl behind the bar a drink.

"Who's that? He looks like he's been in the wars" asked Gammon. The young girl replied, "It's Billy Steele". Gammon knew the name and had seen him maybe once or twice because he worked for Lund. But his face was so badly swollen and was all lacerated, he didn't recognise him. "Right Carl, you stay there, I am going to have a word with Mr Steele" and John went over to where Steele was sat. "Well if it's not Billy Steele, mind if I sit down?" "What do you want Gammon?" "I didn't recognise you Billy, been in a fight have we?" "Piss off Gammon, I'm doing nothing wrong, I just came in for a quiet pint" snarled Steele. "Working for a new boss are we, now that Lund has got what he deserved?" "I don't work for anyone. I'm on disability pension since my accident" replied Steele. "Would that be the accident in the Drovers Arms, where Chan smashed a glass in your face, then kicked you half to death and left you in a wheelie bin Billy?" "No comment Mr

Gammon". "Are you really that thick? Don't you want your revenge on Chan?". Gammon could see by Billy's persona that he was getting to him.

"Look Gammon what do you want?" asked Steele, "I want to know where Chan Chi is?" "Look I can't talk here, people are watching, this is his turf. Meet me at the Café in the Park in Micklock. I won't be staying long, but I will fill you in" "Thanks Billy, I will be there at 3.00pm tomorrow" concluded Gammon.

Gammon went back to Carl. "You look pleased with yourself Sir" said Milton. "Come on Carl, I'll tell you all on the way back". As they got up to leave, one of the pond life, a man in his early thirties with a scar across his eye and his left cheek, bumped into Carl. "Steady!!" said Milton. "Thought I could smell something" and he got up close to Carl, "I know what it is now,

Pig Shit". The man then glared at Carl and walked away. Luckily Billy Steele had left, so he hadn't seen the confrontation and the fact that the pub knew they were police. Billy would possibly have not turned up the next day, if the pub locals knew who he had been talking too.

"Come on Carl, I think our cover is blown, lets head back to Bixton". On the way back Gammon told Carl about the meeting he was going to have with Billy Steele at the Café in The Park in Micklock. "Bit of an odd place for him to want to meet Sir?" "Think he's working on the assumption that not many of Chan's men would be in the park" said Gammon.

It was almost 5.00pm when they arrived back at Bixton Police Station. Gammon headed straight for the desk Sergeant. "Any news on Wisey yet, Sergeant Yap?" "Nothing Sir, all the lads have been out looking for him but no joy" "I was just hoping Sergeant" said Gammon. "We all are Sir" replied Yap. "Right, well if we have no other problems, I will see you tomorrow" and Gammon left the Station. When he got in the car he called Sandra. "How are you?" he asked, "Still not good John, I'm at home. Look I am really sorry about this, what did you say to them at work?" "Just said you phoned with a migraine" "Thanks John, sorry to put you in a position like this, I'm never drinking again". John laughed, "You'll be fine by morning" "Ok, see you then" said Sandra.

As he ended the call with Sandra, he got another call from Jayne Thornley-Coil. "John, just to let you know, all three cottages are now complete. They have been fully decorated and if you find anything you are not happy with please call me and I will get it sorted. I have inspected them personally and they are of the highest quality" "Thank you Jayne. Listen, I'm going to the Spinning Jenny now, if you want to bring your invoice, I'll pay you tonight" he offered. "There's no need for that John, I know you are good for it" "Jayne, I prefer to pay when I job is done, I have my cheque book in the car" "Ok I will see you in half an hour" she said. "Great" he replied.

John arrived at the Spinning Jenny and ordered a pint of Pedigree. The bar was empty with only Kevin working. "How are you John" he asked. "Good mate. It's bit quiet tonight" said John. "Tow'd Man have got a grand opening party on, I thought you would have been there John" "Not heard anything mate" "Oh, have you and Saron called it a day?" enquired Kev. Just then John's mobile rang.

"John? Why are you ignoring me? I have rung several times, it's our opening night tonight and I wanted you to come" "Sorry

Saron, I don't have any missed calls" "Whatever John. You know where I am if you want to come" and she ended the call. Kev raised an eyebrow, "Looks like you have upset somebody John" "Apparently so, Saron has been trying to get hold of me about tonight". Just then Jayne Thornley-Coil arrived. Kev looked at John. "Bloody hell John, you lead a dangerous life both professionally and privately" he said quietly. "Hi Jayne what would you like?" asked John. "Just a soda and lime please John. Shall we sit over there in the corner?" "Ok, I'll bring the drinks over". Jayne Thornley-Coil had on a brown pin stripe business suit, with a cream blouse and brown shoes.

John sat down. "Sorry about the attire John, I came straight from the office" "You look very smart" remarked John. "I usually like to wear jeans and leather jackets. My brother say's I am a rock chick" and she laughed "What music do you like John?" "I like Motown and Northern Soul, not that I can dance or anything, I just like the music. What about you?" "Bon Jovi, Alice Cooper, I do like a bit of Motown to dance to if I'm at a party" she said. "Are you married Jayne?" "Not anymore. I tried it and I didn't like it. I have been too busy building my business up. Saron sent me an email saying they were having the grand opening of the pub tonight, so I suppose you are going up there too?" John replied. "I'm unsure yet, it's quite busy at work and I'm waiting on some developments, so it might be an early night for me".

"Right let me show you some pictures of the holiday cottages before you pay me" said Jayne. The three holiday cottages looked immaculate. Beautiful gardens at the rear with patios, there were small dry stone walls dividing each cottage and parking areas for two vehicles at each property. "When will you rent them out John?" "I'm not sure yet, but I am thinking of having one for myself" "A word of advice John, don't. You'll be at the mercy of the holiday makers twenty four hours a day. I would put them with a holiday letting company. They do everything for you so you have no hassle, just a nice fat cheque each month" "That sounds like a good idea, do you know anyone?" asked John, "Well actually, one of my companies does this, Thornley-Coil Dream Cottages" "I see, nice sales pitch there Jayne!" "No I didn't mean anything" "Only joking Jayne, it's a great idea".

"Right first of all, what do I owe you for the renovations?" asked John, cheque book at the ready. "Are you holding your breath?" asked Jayne "it's £114,000.00 in total". "Well that came in under budget Jayne. I think you quoted £118,485.00 originally" said John. "There were some savings on the fixtures and fittings John" "I'm well pleased with that Jayne, are you sure?" "Absolutely

John, just pass my good name on" "Oh I will, I promise" and John wrote a cheque out for £115,000.00 and handed it to Jayne. "You've overpaid me John" "That's a thank you Jayne, from me" "Well look John, I'm going home to get changed. If you would like me to quote for managing the holiday cottages, just let me know" "Yes, I definitely think it's a good idea" replied John. "Ok, I will let you have something through by Wednesday next week. With Easter not too far away, you'll need to get them advertised" Jayne recommended. "Right, I might see you later. I'm going to the Tow'd Man for the party" "Ok Jayne, I'll see how things work out" and Jayne left.

John's phone began buzzing, it was a text from Saron, the message read:- "I was going to tell you tonight, but I might as well get it over with now. I tried to call you numerous times today and I was a bit worried when you didn't answer. I drove down to see if you were at home, just as Sandra Scooper was leaving the cottage. I know I shouldn't have entered your home without your permission, but I just needed to know if I was being mucked about. I went in the house and drying on the side, were two cups, two plates and two glasses, so I went upstairs and sure enough there was my proof. A note from Sandra saying she was sorry for getting so drunk but she loved the time spent with you. Now call me naïve John, even you might have been able to wriggle out of all that, but the black knickers on the bedpost sealed it for me. So don't come up here tonight, I am too angry. I still think you should be at Annie's funeral on Monday, but go straight to the church. Me and you are over".

'Well I guess that's me told' he thought.

"Are you having a drink John?" the familiar voice of Carol Lestar carried through to where he was sat. "Go on then Carol, I'll have a brandy, please" "Double?" "Go on then" and John wandered over to the bar.

"What time are you going to the Tow'd Man John? Shall we share a taxi?" "I'm not going Carol, got a lot on at work" said John. "Are you two not an item anymore then?" asked Carol "Don't think so" he replied. "Well I did wonder with you being with Sandra at the funeral" "I'm not with anyone now Carol". Carol smiled, "You've always got me, lover boy" and she planted a big kiss on his cheek. This made Kev chuckle causing his red dickie bow to bounce up and down.

Steve and Jo came in asking the same questions. They all had a few more drinks and then left in a taxi for the Tow'd Man, leaving just Kev and John again. "Kev do you know a lady called Maggie Else?" "Yes why John?" "Well Uncle Graham left me her house as part of his will, but the will states that I cannot sell it until Maggie vacates. Anyway she came over and introduced herself to me at the funeral and I am going for tea on Sunday".

"Maggie is a lovely lady, did you not recognise her? Maybe it was before your time. She had been in the movies. She starred with all the big stars from the sixties. She was in 'Cradle to Grave' which was a horror movie. She was the lead part in 'Mr Bumble', that was about her love for a schoolteacher. It was quite controversial at the time. Her most famous film were the ones made into a Trilogy, they were 'Windswept Daffodils'. It was about a small girl growing up in Oldham and a day trip to the open fields of the Peak District. 'Those Satanic Mills' which was the same girl's life growing up from sixteen to twenty seven. The final one was 'Dreams Really Do Come

True'. This was about how, by luck, she escaped the drudgery of her former years. After those she appeared on TV in programs like 'Blankety Blank' and 'Celebrity Squares', then she just disappeared of our screens. She is very rarely seen now John" said Kev. "What was her association with Uncle Graham?" asked John. "I don't know the full story, its best if she tells you. You should be very honoured if you have been invited for afternoon tea John"

"Can't wait Kev. Listen mate I'm going to have an early night" replied John. "I think I'll lock up early. Doreen has gone up to the party with the girls from here, so I'll get locked up and get some sleep before she get's back, full of alcohol and wanting to tell me she loves me" laughed Kev. "You should be so lucky Kev" and John laughed. "Away with you buggerlugs".

John drove back and in no time it was the following morning. With the arrangements in place to see Jimmy Steele at the Café in the Park in Micklock in the afternoon, John decided to drive down to the holiday cottages to have a look. Then he was going to see the solicitor to discuss what he wanted to do with his inheritance.

John approached the farm and noticed straight away that the holiday cottages looked stunning. Each with it's own copper nameplate. Cottage one, was called 'Squirrel Nut Cottage'. Cottage two, was called 'Adams Retreat, named so after his brother. Cottage three was called "Phil and Emily's Homestead".

"Morning John" "Good morning Roger, how are you?" "Pretty good mate thanks. They have made a lovely job of the cottages are you moving into one?" said Roger cheerily. "No, I've decided to rent all three out for holiday lets Roger. How are you doing with the farm?" "Not bad John. I have to say though, if I didn't own it, I couldn't make a living from it. Milk prices are that low, it's ridiculous. Me and my lad are going on a farmers protest march in June" "Don't blame you mate" said John.

John had a look around the kitchens. They were of a very high spec. Each cottage had two large bedrooms and both had en-suite facilities. John felt quite proud of what Jayne had achieved. He had decided not to work on his Mum's house and side barn just yet. It was the memory of his parents that was still too painful for him to begin any work. He spent a couple of hours looking round. Shouted his goodbyes to Roger and left for the solicitors.

ANNIE TANNEY

Tam Gillespie's PA informed him that John had arrived. "Come in John take a seat" he offered a chair. The office always seemed so professional, with it's oak panelling and leather chairs. Gillespie opened the conversation. "Everything is now settled John and transferred into your name. The people residing in your properties will all receive letters outlining your Uncle Grahams wishes, which will be sent out today. The money has been put into your bank account and the keys for the lock up are here for you. I have instructed the lock up company that you will be in touch, here is a full inventory of what should be there".

Gillespie handed John an A4 brown envelope. "You are a very lucky man John. Will you be finishing work?" John replied "I want to give everything away". Tam Gillespie almost choked on his Earl Grey tea. "Are you serious, John?" "Yes Mr Gillespie. Some time ago I was at death's door and was saved by a very special lady. I know why I was saved, I believe it was to do some good with my inheritance" "John, you are probably in shock, take some time before you make any rash decisions please. Let's meet up in two months time, when things have settled down" "I won't change my mind" said John. Gillespie responded, "As your solicitor, I would feel more comfortable if you took my advice". "Ok, I'll take the time, but trust me I won't change my mind" "Just think about it and I will see you in a couple of months when you have had consider your options. In between times, sit down and write some instructions, as to what you would like me to do John".

John shook Gillespie's hand and left to meet Billy Steele.

Micklock Park was in a beautiful setting, with plenty of activities for people to enjoy. John walked down the path to the café. People were playing tennis and children were splashing in the little pool. Their parents looking on, wishing they dare get in with them, it being so warm a day. The little steam train was full to capacity as it made it's way in a circular route round the park.

The café was quite busy, but John found a table near a window so he could see Billy Steele approach. He ordered a cup of coffee and a piece of carrot cake while he waited. John had been sat for almost two hours with no sign of Billy. He decided that Billy had bottled it and wasn't going to turn up, so John left. He called into the station. There still no news on Wisey or anything else. He felt a little deflated, he was hoping for some news of Wisey.

John decided to go home and write an aphorism for Annie, he wanted it to be good, he owed the lady so much but he hardly knew her. As John approached the cottage Scooper called him. "Hi John, are you ok?" "Yes fine Sandra you?" "Well I'm not sure. I've just received a text from Saron and she's going on about us" "What did she say" asked John. "She said she was disappointed in me, but always knew I would get my claws into you. She then said she wished me luck because you would hurt me the same way that you have hurt her and Joni" relayed Sandra. John told her "She saw you leave the cottage and went in. She still has a key and she found your note and a pair of your undies on the bed post" "Oh John I am so sorry" "Don't worry, it would have come out at some point. We were drifting apart since she took the pub anyway Sandra. What you doing tonight?" "Rosie is in a school play and then Mum wants to go out for dinner" said Sandra. "Ok, well I will see you tomorrow" replied John. "Ok and again, sorry about the note and the underwear" "No problem Sandra, have a nice night".

John got back home, poured himself a Jameson's Irish Whisky and started to write for the funeral. What do you say about a woman that did so much for other people in her life? John was still at it, three quarters of a bottle of whisky later. He decided what he hadn't written by now, must mean the rest had to come from the heart, so he climbed the stairs to bed.

John woke to the sound of the birds singing, he could hear the little lambs bleating for their mothers. He showered and went downstairs, made a coffee, put his laptop in its case and opened the kitchen door to set off for work. To his horror there were two men tied to the oak tree in the garden. Both were covered in blood and had been severely beaten. John ran over to them. The first person he could recognise was Billy Steele, minus his left ear. He looked even worse than he did when John last saw him. John felt for a pulse there was nothing. He then went to look at the next guy. He also had been severely beaten and to his horror he realised it was Sergeant Wisey. He felt for a pulse and could just feel one, albeit very faint.

John quickly called for the Emergency Services. Wisey was unconscious but still had a faint pulse. John released the ropes that were holding the two men to the tree. He held Wisey, praying that the ambulance would be quick. It took only ten minutes for them to arrive. The paramedics came and took over. They radioed ahead to the hospital and took Wisey off in the ambulance.

Smarty, Scooper and Milton arrived with Forensics. John Walvin cleared the crime scene. "How was Wisey Sir" "Not good Smarty, he had a pulse although very weak" "The poor man, it must have been our killer". John replied "I'm not so sure of that Sandra, I don't know who my money is on for these two. Billy Steele didn't show yesterday at Micklock. I think one of those scumbags in the Queens have contacted Chan to tell them Billy was talking to us". "But what about Wisey?" asked Carl. "Not sure on that, unless Chan swings the other way and Wisey had sussed out who he was, perhaps? Right let's get back to the station and let the Forensic lads see what they can find for us" ordered Gammon.

As Gammon entered the station he was met with a sober looking Sergeant Yap. "Bad news, I'm afraid Sir. Sergeant Wisey was pronounced dead on arrival, at Bixton hospital" "Right Ian, call the station together, we'll meet in the incident room please" "Yes, will do Sir".

The room was full. "Well team, it with a very heavy heart, that I can tell to you that Sergeant Wisey was pronounced dead on arrival at Bixton hospital. Which means we not only have a serial killer to find and bring to justice, we also a cop killer. Both the men found this morning had been tied to a tree at my cottage in Hartington. They had been beaten to a pulp and both had the trademark left ear cut off".

Gammon continued, "Billy Steele had been a henchman of Brian Lund's, before Lund himself was killed. Apparently Chan Chi, who ran the other half of Derby, had seized his chance to announce his take over in the pub, Billy got up to leave and he was beaten up by Chan. A couple of days ago I spoke with Billy Steele, not my favourite person, but I wanted to know the whereabouts of Chan. Billy agreed to meet with me at the Café in the Park in Micklock to give me information. I am pretty sure that Chan was informed about me speaking with Steele and I assume he either had him killed, or did the deed himself. With regard to Sergeant Wisey, I am also surmising that Chan maybe gay and had picked up Sergeant Wisey. I am also guessing that Chan found out that Wisey was a copper and that maybe Chan had bragged about things to him unknowingly, so he had to shut him up. The cutting off of the ears I think is just supposed to put us of the scent, we have not had any stick men drawings that we know of for these two victims".

"I want the Queens Arms raiding and anything we can bust the place on I want.

Drugs, using the place to run prostitutes, whatever we can find to shut it down and flush out Chan. Take rapid response on this, I want Inspectors Smarty and Lee to head this, along with Milton. Scooper you are coming with me, get your coat" "Looks like you have pulled Sandra" said Lee. Gammon shot Inspector Lee a scowl and they all scurried out of the room.

Scooper and Gammon headed for the car. "Where are we going Sir?" "I want to see Billy Holland and see if I can lean on him for Chan's whereabouts. If anyone knows where he is it will be Billy". They arrived at Holland's house. "Wow Sir, how can he afford this?" asked Sandra. "I'm not really bothered at the moment Sandra. We have bigger fish to fry". Sandra thought John seemed tetchy, so didn't pursue her thoughts.

After knocking on the door for what seemed like forever, Billy Holland appeared he clearly was under the influence of something, drugs or alcohol. "Mr Holland, nice to see you are fully compos mentis, I would like a word" and Gammon barged his way into the hall way. "Hey, you can't come in here without a warrant". Billy stood in a pair of track suit bottoms with an off-white tee shirt with a picture of Billy Idol emblazoned across the front and a pair of leather sandals. The house smelt sweet, a sure sign that marijuana was being used. On the hall table was a line of coke. "What's this Billy, your talcum powder?" asked John.

Just then a young girl, possibly eighteen years of age, came from the front room. She wore a black tee-shirt with Bon Jovi on it and very little else on. She shouted to Billy "Anymore Charlie, Billy?". Billy yelled back at her, "Shut up you stupid cow". Gammon ignored him, "Arrest her Scooper, call for the drugs lads from Derby to come and go through this place". Billy started protesting "Mr Gammon, can't we work something out hey? The drugs are only recreational" "Like they were for Poppy Chi eh? You low life scum bag. What have you got, that would possibly stop me, arresting you and your girlfriend for possession of Class A drugs? I'm sure when the boys look round here they will find a few more secrets. You have cocked up this time Billy boy haven't you?"

"Mr Gammon. I'll tell you where Chan is" offered Billy. "What and that's it?" said Gammon. "What else do you want?" whined Billy. "Last night a police officer and former henchman of Brian Lund's, was murdered. Their left ears cut off and they were tied to a tree outside my house. So, I want the name of the person or person's that have done this, your choice, Billy boy". "Look, give me a few days to locate Chan and to dig around. I will call you, but you can't implicate me in any of this or I am a dead man walking" Gammon considered the offer, "Ok Billy you have until Wednesday next week or you will be going down for a stretch. Release the young lady Inspector". Gammon walked over to her. "What's your name?" The girl looked away. "You tell me right now or I *will* arrest you" "Kylie" she replied. "Kylie what? Minogue?" Gammon snapped. "No Kylie Dooley Sir". "Miss Dooley, are you related to Maria and Lexi Dooley?" "They are my sisters". Gammon frowned, "Just a minute, when I spoke with your parents after the death of your sister, they never mentioned they had another daughter" "We don't get on. I left home when I was fifteen. They don't know where I am, so please don't tell them" begged Kylie. "Why did you run away from home Kylie?" "They were always on my case. Our Maria could do no wrong and Lexi was the quiet one, but I guess I am the black sheep" "You're certainly that, how old are you?" "Twenty three" she replied. Gammon was quite shocked at that, he would have said she was no more than eighteen.

"How do you know Mr Holland?" Gammon asked. Kylie hesitated. "Come on, how do you know Mr Holland?" he asked again. "I met him in a late night kebab shop" "Have you been on the game?" "Are you going to arrest me?" she asked. "That depends, Kylie". "Yes" she said, "and I still am. I work for Chan Chi".

"Scooper, make us all a drink. I want to know about this" said John. Gammon took Kylie into the living room. At this point she got upset. "He will kill me Mr Gammon, if he knows I have spoken with you" Gammon tried to calm her down, "Nobody is going to kill anybody, just calm down. Tell me about Billy?" "Like I said, I met Billy at the Kebab shop on Dung Lane in Derby. I had a goodnight with the punters so Mr Chan gave me an extra fiver back. I was hungry so I went for a kebab and a coffee. Billy came in and bought then for me". "Did he get you onto drugs?". Just then Billy came in with Sandra and the coffees. "Come on Mr Gammon this isn't fair" said Holland. "Let me tell you something Billy. You have no income from working, so I already believe you deal or how can you sustain this lifestyle? Let me tell you something else, I think the deal here is that you supply Chan's girl's with drugs, which keeps them on the streets for Chan, and I am guessing he takes a cut as well from you Kylie?" Holland looked away. She nodded. "Now that's confirmed, we are now making some progress" said Gammon. Kylie sniffled, "Billy, I'm sorry. Holland just looked at Kylie. John saw the exchange of looks and said, "You touch Kylie, Billy and all bets are off. Do I make myself clear" "I'm not a violent man Mr Gammon" "You may not be, but I am!!".

"Kylie, I need information on Chan. How many girls does he run?" Kylie looked at Billy. "Just bloody tell him, it's too late now you silly cow" spat Holland. Kylie said "I think he has about twenty five girls in the South of Derby, but don't know how many more since he has took the North side. I have never worked up there Mr Gammon". Gammon spoke "Right Billy and you Kylie, everything said today has been in confidence, but trust me if you don't deliver Chan to me, I will arrest you Kyle and I will let it be known that you have been informing the police Billy about Chan. With that I will let you get back to your party. You have until Wednesday".

Gammon and Scooper left. "That was some result Sir" "Yes quite pleased about that Sandra. I will drop you back at the station for your car. Can you get your Mum to look after Rosie on Saturday? I fancy a walk and a few beers" "I should think so, I will call you and let you know tonight". Gammon dropped Sandra off at the station and decided to call at Up The Steps Maggie's for a drink. The car park was quite full and he thought about going somewhere else but he spotted Jayne Thornley-Coil's red cabriolet BMW in the car park. He wandered into the bar area and sure enough Jayne was sat with Pete Barrington. Pete nodded and Jayne said "Are you sitting with us John?" "I'm only having a quick drink Jayne but thanks" "Oh come and sit down, we are having a right laugh" she said "Ok" replied John.

John turned and ordered a pint of Lead Miner, "Would you two like another drink?" "I'll have the same as you John thanks" said Pete. "Jayne, what about you?", asked John. "Can I have a Proseco with Chambord please?" "Yes no problem". John brought the drinks and sat down. "So what are you two celebrating?" enquired John. "Well we have finished your job" said Pete. "And let me say how pleased I am with them Pete, great job" "No problem John". "We have finished the Tow'd Man project and Jayne just told me we have won a massive job at Micklock Moor the Old Alison House". Impressed John asked, "Really has it sold?" "Yes they are turning it into a five star hotel" "Well done you two". Jayne replied, "Me and Pete generally have a good drink when a project is finished and passed off, but we have been that busy we are celebrating two jobs being passed off and a new big project ahead, so all is rosy in the garden as they say". "That's great Jayne" .

Four drinks later and both Jayne and Pete were getting very merry. In the back room there was a retirement party going on and the DJ put on Smokey Robinson 'Behind a

Painted Smile'. Jayne grabbed Pete and they went off for a dance. It was almost half an hour before they came back.

Joni came in with Danni Beau. Danni apparently worked with the guy who was retiring. "Hey John, what are you doing sat here on your own?" asked Joni. "I just called for a quick drink and met Jayne Thornley-Coil and Pete Barrington, so sat having a beer with them". Pete saw Joni and threw his arms round her. "How are you my dear? It's been so long". "You old Smoothy" she said and Pete chuckled. Pete made some introductions, "This Jayne Thornley-Coil a good friend and work colleague, this is a dear friend Joni and this is the famous Danni Beau, Jayne". "Pleased to meet you both, the music in there is brill" said Jayne. Danni offered "Why don't we all go in there, he is a friend of mine, he won't mind?" John stood to leave, "I think I will get off" "Oh no you don't Gammon", said Jayne.

Joni shot John a look. "No I really must go" said John. Jayne dragged him protesting to the dance floor and made him dance to 'Poison' by Alice Cooper. She looked the part with her rock chick clothes on. Faded jeans, ripped at the knee, black boots that her jeans were tucked into, a Johnny Rotten tee shirt and a large silver cross round her neck.

When the record was finished Danni found them a table. Joni saw her chance, as the next record came on. "You like this one, if I remember John?". 'The Night" by Frankie Vali was John's favourite, so he danced. Joni asked him about Saron. John said they had split, that the pub was taking all her time up, so there was no point. "So what about you and Carl?" he asked, "No, it's over John, I think we were basically still grieving and we both happened to be at a low point in our lives. We are still friends and always will be that won't change. So what now for you, how do you know Jayne?" "She's the Architect and Project Manager on the holiday cottages at the farm. They have made a fantastic job. I will show you when you have some free time if you want". "Yeah that would be nice, send me a text or call me John" said Joni.

They left the dance floor and John made his excuses and left. On his way home he called Sandra to see if she was still on for the walk. "Hi John, yeah Mum's having Rosie, do I need walking boots? Where are we going?" "I am taking you on Kindle Scout, so you will need some good boots" he said. "That's ok, I have some, it's just been a long time since I wore them John. What time shall I be ready for?" "I'll pick you up at 7.30am so be ready. It will take half an hour to get to the set off point. I thought we could walk for a few hours then stop for a breakfast". "Sounds great John, I'll see you in the morning".

John arrived back at the cottage where John Walvin and his assistant were working under the bright arc lights erected in his garden for the job in hand. "Nearly done

John" said Walvin "Have you found much Wally?" asked John in reply. "Unsure at the moment, we'll know more when we get it analysed. John you always were impatient" "Sorry mate you know what it's like" answered Gammon.

John just entered the house when Saron rang. "Listen John, I am sorry for my recent attitude towards you, I am a bit stressed at the pub and that creepy guy keeps coming in. He is weird John, he really is, but that's no excuse for my behaviour, after I found that stuff at the cottage. It just annoyed me so much. I have calmed down now, so I thought it best to apologise to you. I would still like to be friends John" said Saron. John was unsure what to say. "I understand" replied John, "and of course we will still be mates". John could hear Saron getting upset, so he cut short the call.

John poured himself a Jameson's and set off for bed. It was soon 6.30am John showered, made a coffee and got himself ready to pick Sandra up. The journey from Hittington to Pritwich was stunning the winding roads were littered with small hedgerows either side which meant you could see for miles across the lush green fields. Just before the turning for Pritwich, Lord Cote-Heath had a herd of Llamas in one of his fields, which whilst unusual, blended in well with the countryside.

John turned for Pritwich. On the first corner in the village there was a small sweetshop that John could remember using as a kid, when he and Steve Lineman would go on a cycling adventure. They'd call at the little shop for a bottle of Panda and a Sherbet Dib-Dab, a paper tube full of fizzy sherbet with a liquorice stick in it. 'Happy days' he thought. He was surprised to see the shop was still open. Mrs Chateau, as the locals called her, had been on holiday to France with her husband Ernie in 1967 and that was the only time that she had ever had a holiday or left the village. Anybody that came into the shop, especially if they were holidaymakers, were subject to at least ten minutes of Mrs Chateau's holiday memories from France. As John drove past the shop, he could see her putting out the carrots on a stand, covered with fake grass. She waved to John, although she hadn't seen him for probably thirty years, so he wasn't sure if she remembered him or was just waving because that's what she did. John waved back and carried on past the duck pond and the Sycamore pub, which was now run by Rita and Tony Sherriff. John thought he should make the effort and call and see them soon. John pulled up at the beautiful ornate gates of Pritwich Hall, where Sandra was waiting for him.

"Morning Sandra" said John, "Morning Mr Gammon" she replied. "I like your bobble hat" Sandra laughed, "Mum knitted it, so she insisted I wear it, she thinks I will get cold!!" Sandra's bobble hat was red and pink with a massive yellow bobble on the top. "Well it's good to see you have decent walking clothes on". She had a Rab quilted coat, black leggings and boots. "I thought you might pitch up in four inch heels to wind me up Sandra" "Nah, I am saving them for later" and she laughed.

They arrived at the bottom of Kinder Scout. Sandra looked up at the skyline. "Wow John, that looks awesome" "Wait until we get on the top, you can literally see for miles Sandra". It took almost an hour to arrive at the vantage point. John pointed out Swinster and Micklock. "Look you can actually seeing Bixton from here" said John enthusiastically. "Don't think I'll bother

John, I see enough of that place during the week" and she laughed.

They walked for another hour through brambles and moorland. Then John took a cut down, half way down the valley. John showed Sandra 'Crinkly Ladder'. A natural waterfall, that over time, had carved a crinkly pathway down through the valley. "Not far now, Sandra. We can stop and have some breakfast". John helped Sandra across another stile, they walked down the field, arriving at the Wriggly Tin Café, so called because of its tin metal roof. "How quaint, John" remarked Sandra. Once inside they ordered two mugs of tea and two farmers' breakfasts.
John confided in Sandra, "I'm going to see a lady that lives in one of the houses Uncle Graham left me" "What's her name John?" "It's Maggie Else" said John. "Really?, I remember mum and dad talking about her years ago, she was a famous actress. What

was her stage name?" she asked John. "I don't know Sandra. She introduced herself to me at the funeral and she asked me to go for afternoon tea. I think she's a bit of a recluse these days, but I am sure from what I hear, she was a big movie star". "The reason I remember her, was Mum and Dad were going to a New Year's Eve party at the Cote-Heath's and dad was teasing mum saying he hoped Maggie would be there as she had a figure like Marilyn Monroe". "Should be an interesting afternoon" said John.

The breakfasts arrived and the waitress placed them on the table in front of them. "Oh my God, John, I will never eat all this" exclaimed Sandra. "Give it a go" laughed John, "you'll be fine". "Just look at it! Three sausages, four pieces of bacon, two pieces of black pudding, hash browns, mushrooms, grilled tomatoes, beans and two fried eggs!!". Sandra had no sooner finished listing all that was on her plate when the waitress came back with two slices of buttered toast each and two rounds of buttered bread each. Sandra's face was a picture. "What you laughing at Gammon?" "You forgot to mention the fried bread your eggs are sitting on", and he laughed. It took almost half an hour for John to demolish his breakfast and Sandra a further fifteen minutes to even get close to finishing hers. "Right shall we set off back for the car?" asked John. "How far is it John? I can hardly walk after that breakfast, I'm that stuffed" said Sandra patting her belly. "It's only three fields away" he replied. "Thank goodness for that, I'm not sure I could walk much further". John paid the bill and they set off across the fields for the car.

"What time have you got to be back for Rosie, Sandra?" "Mum is having her overnight" "Oh great" said John. "Why?" asked Sandra. "I want to show something

else while we are up this way" "Don't you get saucy Gammon" "No, I'm not soft girl, nothing like that, but I have to show you this".
John headed for a small hamlet called Stinton-in-the-Peak. About fourteen years ago, they found what they believed, is the only surviving Coronation Crown of Edward the Confessor. They entered the little Hamlet of Stinton and John pulled into the car park of the village pub. Aptly named the 'Flying Alders', an unbeaten race horse owned by the Duke of Devonshire, who, reportedly turned down the chance to sell the horse for it's weight in gold. "Ok Gammon, I am guessing you are taking me to the pub?" "Too right I am, this where the Crown is kept in a glass case above the bar" said John, proud of his local history knowledge.

The Flying Alders was a quaint village pub, set out how they used to be with a best end, that was surprisingly large, and a small snug. John took Sandra in the snug. "John this is lovely" she said. "I haven't been for years Sandra, but if it's the same landlord and landlady they are really nice people". "What can I get you?" said the chap behind the bar, "Bloody hell, it's John Gammon how are you?" "I didn't think you would remember me?" said John. "Once met, never forgotten, anyway you are always in the news around here lad. What brings you up here?". "We've been walking and I wanted to show Sandra the Crown" said John. "Well I will tell you what, seeing that it's you John, I will take it out of the glass case for you. We've had people coming for miles to see it, we have even had Prince Charles in here once. You two are probably only the second people to touch it since Charles did when he visited in 2003" said the landlord proudly.

The Crown was made of gold with fancy spiked pieces all round it, just like those you see on cast-iron railings, but these were made of gold. All round the perimeter were precious jewels. Terry told Sandra the story. Edward reigned from 1042 to 1066 and was considered to be the last Anglo Saxon King by many. Sandra touched the crown, then being a police officer she could not help herself and asked the question. "Isn't it dangerous for it to be on show like this?" "Every night it is taken by a guard to a safe place and returned the following day, every day" Terry advised her. "Who pays for that?" "Her Majesty the Queen of England" said Terry. "Why would you do that?" asked Sandra. "It is said that Edward gave the Crown to the village of Stinton before his death. He had visited Derbyshire three weeks before he died and had stayed at this very pub. When he left, the landlord of the day, found the Crown under the bed with a note from Edward asking him to keep it as he had a premonition that England would fall to William the Conqueror and that he would never get his Crown back. They would never think it would be left in the village of Stinton. Sadly he died before the battle of 1066, but the legend says that if the Crown is removed from Stinton, the monarchy will fall".

"Wow that is really interesting Terry, thank you" said Sandra. Terry put the crown back in its glass case and pulled John a pint of Confessor ale. "What about you my dear?", Sandra asked, "Can I have a gin and tonic please" "You certainly can. Well, I still can't believe John Gammon is in my pub. Do you remember when we played for Brickwell in the Hope Valley Football League? He was even bloody good at football!!" "Why does that not surprise me Terry" said Sandra.

They sat down and chatted away, enjoying each other's company. "Another drink you two?" asked Terry. "No you're ok Terry thanks, we're having a bit of a ride round" "Well don't wait so long to come and see us you two". "Thank you Terry, for showing me and letting me touch the Crown" "Anything for a pretty girl, hey John?" John laughed, "Come on Sandra, let's leave the old silver tongue. Cheers Terry we'll see you soon".

"Now what John?" asked Sandra, "Shall we call at the Spinning Jenny?" asked John. "Why not" she replied, "Off we go James, and don't spare the horses" and Sandra gave out a loud laugh.

They reached the Spinning Jenny and walked down the steps into the bar. "Good evening landlord" said John. "Hello John, Sandra how are you both? Looks like you have been for a stroll" "Some stroll Kev, he has had me walking up hill and down dale. We ended up in Stinton-in-the-Peak at The Flying Alders" "Has Terry still got it John?"

"Yes still there Kev" replied John. "He has had that place as long as me and Doreen have had the Spinning Jenny. Nice lad Terry. Right what can I do you for" and he chuckled. "Pint of Pedigree for me Kev, Sandra?" "Brandy and Port please Kev" she said. "What about me gorgeous copper?" came a voice from nowhere. "Hello Carol" said John. "Hello my little favourite" replied Carol and as was her way, she planted a kiss on his cheek.

"Have you heard about the trouble up at the Tow'd Man?" asked Carol. "No, what?" asked John. "Some weirdo has been going in and had been very suggestive to Saron and Angelina and last night it all kicked off. Apparently Angelina was arrested, she hit the guy so hard he ended up in hospital. The locals said they had never seen anything like it, it was like watching Bruce Lee when it all happened" "Oh blimey, I suppose I will find out more about it on my return to work on Monday" said John.

John, Sandra and Carol sat with Bob and Cheryl it was a pleasant evening and they left just around midnight. Sandra was a little tipsy. By the time they got back to the cottage, she fell asleep in minutes, so John went in the spare room. The following morning Sandra was up bright and early, she showered and was about to leave a note when John came downstairs. "I'd best shoot off John, I don't want to put on mum too much" she said. "I understand" replied John, "I have got afternoon tea with Maggie Else this afternoon, so I will give you a call later". Sandra leaned forward and gave John a peck on the cheek her mum was waiting for her in the car by the cottage gate.

John showered, grabbed a coffee and thought he'd best nip into work to find out what had happened with Angelina. On arrival at Bixton Di Trimble was on the desk. "Morning Sir, what are you doing here on a Sunday?" "I have come to see Angelina" "She's in cell three Sir" said Di. "Give me the keys Di" and Gammon walked down the corridor to cell three. Angelina looked surprised to see him. "John what are you doing here?" "What the hell happened last night? The guy is in a bad way Angelina" said John.

"This guy was being very suggestive to Saron and touched her a couple of times inappropriately. She had told me, but with me being in the kitchen most of the time I haven't seen any of it. Last night we shut the kitchen early, as it had been dead, so I went in the bar and we were taking turns serving. When Saron sat at the bar on her own, this guy starts saying things to her, I clocked it and told him to keep his thoughts to himself or he could leave. He then went in to an abusive rant calling us disgusting names. He then lunged forward at Saron and grabbed her around the chest, I shot round the bar and he threw a punch at me. As you know I am trained, so I chopped him in the throat and he dropped like a sack of potatoes. Apparently he was a bad asthmatic so then he struggled to breath. We called an ambulance and then Sergeant Milton arrested me. Really could do without this John" "Ok let me see what I can dig up on this guy" said John. "Thanks I owe you one" and she smiled.

John went to his office and called the hospital. He explained who he was and asked if they had any records on the guy. The name came back as Glen Tully, so Gammon entered his name into the Police computer. 'Bingo' he thought when the information came up on the screen. Glen Tully was serving three life sentences for rape and murder. The judge at his trial recommended that he never saw the light of day again and that he was a menace to society. The next bit of bad news was that he had escaped from Leicester prison six months previously and had appeared to just disappear.

Gammon now had a plan he went back down to speak with Angelina and he told her the news. "Right Angelina, this is what we'll do. You say you recognised the guy from a tattoo of a maiden on his right hand and that you were making a citizen's arrest. He became violent and you feared for yours and Saron's lives, so your training took him out. It will never get as far as the courts. I'm going to get on with my work and we will release you shortly, with no charge". "John, thank you so much. If you ever get fed up of playing the field, put me on your list" her eyes sparkled and John smiled.
Gammon held a meeting with Milton and Angelina, he also informed Leicester Police

where Tully was and what had happened, so it was a win, win situation for everyone except Tully. Milton did question why Angelina hadn't mentioned this when he arrested her. Gammon smiled and just said "You've alot to learn young Carl".

It was getting up for 2.00pm, so John set off for Maggie Else's. John arrived at Cotton Manor House in Hittington Dale and he began to feel a little nervous. He wasn't sure what Maggie was going to reveal about Uncle Graham.

He parked his car in front of the house, there was big statue of a mermaid with water coming out of her mouth. There were three rounded, stone steps that led to the big double oak doors. John pulled the lever next to the door which played a peel of bells. A young lady dressed in black, with a white cap, the kind of attire that you would see in Victorian style coffee shops in Harrogate and places, answered the doors. John informed her, "John Gammon, to see Miss Else" "Come in Mr Gammon" she said. The entrance hall had a huge round oak table taking centre spot, with a fantastic colourful flower arrangement in the middle of it. "If you would like to come through to the drawing room Mr Gammon" the young lady said. This felt weird to John. Here he was in a house he owned, which was unbelievably grand, yet this was the first time he had seen it.

Maggie Else greeted John. In the drawing room there were pictures of Maggie with Frank Sinatra, Richard Nixon all the famous people of the time. "John how lovely to see you, please take a seat, would you like a sherry?" "Yes please Maggie. I must say what a beautiful house you have" "I like to think so, although it isn't mine. I will show you round after we have had afternoon tea. So you are Graham's nephew? You are so like him". John thought it best to be honest with Maggie she clearly wasn't a gossip and hardly went out. "Actually Maggie, Graham was my father" "I'm not surprised, when I met you at his funeral it was like meeting him when we were both younger. I suppose you are intrigued why I asked you over John". "Well I a bit, if I am honest" replied John.

"Let me take you back to when I met Graham Gammon for the first time". Maggie daintily sipped her sherry and began her story. "It was March 29th 1963 when I met Graham. I was twenty years old. Graham had started making his way in the world and I had done a bit of modelling and wanted desperately to get into films, I guess just like all the young girls in the day. People always commented that they thought I looked like Jean Shrimpton. Graham was big friend of Ian Larkin, the photographer for Vanity Fair and Harpers magazines. I lived in a little village called Merryfield, in West Yorkshire. and I met Graham at a club in Sheffield called Scamps. All the girls were round him, he looked like a cross between George Best and Sean Connery. Graham asked me to dance and we struck up a friendship. I told him of my aspirations, so that Sunday he picked me up in his Jaguar and took me to London to meet Ian Larkin. You should have seen the curtains twitching on our street when he pulled up in this shiny Jag. I felt like a million dollars. Ian took some tasteful pictures and within six months I was in all the top magazines".

Maggie leaned forward and showed John some pictures of her in an old Vogue magazine. He thought she was stunning.

"Did you and Uncle Graham get close?" "Patience John, I will tell you more in a bit. I was modelling for about six months when I got my first screen test for the film. 'The Desperate Days of Ivy March', I played Ivy's sister Lauren. The film won an Oscar, I was nominated but didn't win that year. I did four more films and won an Oscar for the film 'Desperate Measures' about a working class girl in the sixties. I knew when I first saw the script this could be big for me. I didn't need to research the part I had lived the life prior to breaking into the film industry".

"The award was presented by Lauren Bacall, your Uncle Graham was in the audience that night and at the party afterwards. I always remember Cubby Broccoli asking Graham if he had thought of getting into films with his looks". John just smiled, like he always did, he knew it would not have been for his Uncle. Maggie continued "After the party that night, he stayed at my house. I so wanted to have a relationship with Graham, but he wouldn't for some reason, that is not until later in this story".

The afternoon tea arrived, all nicely presented on a three tier silver server, small cakes on the bottom tier, then smoked salmon sandwiches cut into triangles, with the crusts cut off, which made John smile. His Mum always said if he wanted curly hair he had to eat his crusts. There was an array of sandwiches and a pot of tea with china cups and sauces. The maid had also brought a bottle of Tattinger, she poured the champagne into flutes and added a curl of gold leaf and a single raspberry. This lady sure knew how to live.

"I hope I am not boring you John" she asked. "Not in the least Maggie" replied John politely. Maggie went on, "My film career did well, I made it as a Bond girl which was quite an accolade. Raquel Welch, Liz Taylor, Frank Sinatra and the rat pack were all frequent visitors to my house. The films dried up in the mid-seventies, so my manager got me on to TV, you know like Family Fortunes. I hosted that for a short time and then the Wheel of Fortune, and I was also on The Golden Shot for a short time. My career seemed to die at that point. I was living back in England when Graham found me this place. He said I could live here rent free. I hit the hard times and when I said, I hit hard times, I meant I hit them hard, the fame and adulation had gone".

"The next part of my story is the reason I asked you to come and see me. Graham had called one night rather upset and he told me about your Mum and him. He really loved your Mum, but he was a gentleman John, and he knew he had done wrong by his brother. We sat drinking red wine until the early hours and for the one and only time Graham and I made love in front of the log fire. It was so very romantic for me, I idolised Graham and to have spent those few hours in his arms was something I would never forget"

John spoke gently to her, "Maggie you don't have to tell me all this". "John I do", replied Maggie, "after that night I found out I was pregnant. I never told Graham. I went to stay with my sister in France until the baby was born and then I gave up the baby for adoption. I wasn't a stable enough person to be a mother John" "So are you telling me I have a half sister or brother?" asked John. "You have a half-sister, John" said Maggie. "Have you had any contact with her?" "No I haven't John, all I know is that she was raised in Alsace, on the French German border, by a French couple. That is pretty much my story John, it is up to you if you want to try and find her, but I am too old now for any upheaval in my life. So I would appreciate it, if you kept me out of this, if you decide to try and make contact".

John was confused, "I don't know what to say Maggie and seeing that it is a day of surprises, you need to know Cotton House was left to me in Uncle Graham's will. I have signed the papers drawn up at the solicitors and I want to hand the house over to you". Maggie looked at him, "You are so like your Uncle Graham, handsome, suave, humble and so very kind. Like you John, I don't know what to say".

She hugged him and asked him if he would come and see her again "Of course I will Maggie, I have enjoyed your story and I am sure you have many more. Just one thing though, why is this house called Cotton House?" "it has a bit of dark history John, it was originally owned and built by Sir Dudley Markham-Duberry. Dudley had made his money in the slave trade and when it was built all the locals it Cotton House because of its roots in the Slave trade. When your Uncle Graham brought it, he knew it as a child, so he had it renamed Cotton House". "Maggie, I have so enjoyed today, thank you so much" "It has been my pleasure John. Molly will show you out".

John left Cotton House more confused than when he arrived. On arrival he had been a man without any family and now he finds out, somewhere, and if she is still alive, there is a half-sister. He also thought about his Uncle Graham not only had he a son that didn't recognise him until he was ready to die, but he also had a daughter he didn't even know about. Life can take some cruel twists sometimes. 'I wonder if Kev knew about this?' he thought. John decided to call for a quick drink at the Spinning Jenny. The pub was very busy for a Saturday night Joni was working the bar and luckily Kev was having a night off. His beloved Sheffield Wednesday had beaten Cardiff to go top of the Championship League so he was celebrating. At the same time he was giving Bob and Jack some stick about the fortunes of Derby County, who were eight places below them.

John got a drink and saw his chance to speak to Kev. "Have you got a minute Kev?" he asked. "What's up lad?" asked Kev. "I have been for afternoon tea to Cotton House this afternoon". Kev interrupted quickly, "John, please don't ask me anything, I promised Graham I would never say a word and I want to keep my promise to him" "Uncle Graham is dead and he never knew he had a daughter Kev". Reluctantly Kev continued, "Ok I'll tell you what I know. He did tell me he had spent the night with Maggie Else, I remember saying at the time 'you lucky sod'. He never said he regretted it, but he did say it was a one off. Some two months later Maggie told him she was going to stay with her sister in France and could he just check on the house because she wasn't sure how long she would be away for".

"Graham and I went down to the house about three weeks later, we were going to play snooker at Hittington Working Men's Club, so it was handy to pop in. We entered the beautiful house and just checked everything was ok. It was then that Graham saw a letter on Maggie's bedside table, he read it and in it Maggie said, *'You know I asked you if I could come over to stay until things are sorted well I would like to come now. I know time is of the essence I am beginning...........'* The letter stopped there. Graham surmised that Maggie had fallen pregnant from that one night of passion. He told me he did ask Maggie, but she denied, it so Graham took her word. She said she hadn't finished the letter because she was telling her sister that she was beginning to feel depressed, but realised her sister was poorly and didn't want to burden her with her troubles".

Kev looked at John, "John, are you going to tell me something different?" "Swear you won't tell a soul Kev?. Kev nodded "You know me son" "Yes, Maggie was pregnant but she had the baby girl adopted. She will be about thirty six or thirty seven now Kev" said John. "Did she say she had any contact?" asked Kev. "No, and she told me it was up to me if I wanted to try and find her in France but I wasn't to involve her". "So are you going too?" "I really don't know Kev. I just wonder if I should make some provisions for her, from Uncle Graham's money. I mean he was her dad" "Only you can decide that, John lad" "Thanks Kev, you get back with the lads, I am going to shoot off, it's Annie Tanney's funeral tomorrow"

"Ok lad, see you in the week" and with that John was gone.

John got home poured himself a glass of Jameson's and took it to bed. He slept surprisingly well, considering everything that was going round in his head.

John spent the morning looking at websites in France where you could obtain adoption information. He still wasn't sure what to do, but thought he would see if he could find her before making the final decision.

He left the cottage at 2.15pm to ensure he got to Pritwich Church. The church sat snugly near the village green it was built in 1873 much of the original building prior to this date had been destroyed. There were a few people in the Church and by the time they brought Annie into Church there were only about twenty odd people, which wasn't a bad turn out, considering that she wasn't that well known. Carol Lestar was there, she would go to most funerals, if she only knew the people slightly. As they say in Derbyshire 'She would have been present at a dog hanging!!'.

The vicar stood in the pulpit, "Ladies and Gentlemen thank you for being here today, to pray for Annie, as she leaves this life to carry on her journey. As you all of you here today, knew Annie was a lady with a gift. She had helped many souls during her life. I believe one of those chosen people are here today and wishes to give a reading. John would you like to come up please?". John made his way to the pulpit.

He cleared his throat; there was a quiver in his voice. "I have come here today, like all of you, to give thanks to a very special lad. This lady touched so many lives during her time on this earth. I am saddened to say that I never got to know this special lady well enough. I would not have been here today without the love and kindness this lady gave to me through our God".

"Annie sat with me, never leaving my side, she prayed for me, held my hand and whilst the doctors had done everything humanly possible to save my life, Annie never gave up even though they thought it was over for me and for that I will be forever eternally thankful".

"I would like to read a passage from the bible Mathew 16:20".

"When Jesus showed himself to the disciples on the evening of the day of his rising from the dead, only ten of the disciples saw him, for Judas was no longer among them, and Thomas the twin (which is the meaning of his other name, Didymus) was absent. The other disciples said to Thomas, "We have seen the Lord!"

But Thomas said, "I will not believe that he has risen, unless I can see in his hands the marks of the nails on the cross. I must see them with my own eyes, and put my hand into the wound in his side, before I will believe."

A week passed away, and on the next Sunday evening the disciples were together again, and at this time Thomas was with them. The doors were shut but suddenly Jesus was seen again standing in the middle of the room. He said, as before, "Peace be with you."

Then he turned to Thomas, and said to him, "Thomas, come here, and touch my hands with your finger, and put your hand into my side; and no longer refuse to believe that I am living, but have faith in me!" And Thomas answered him, "My Lord and my God"

John then looked over at Annie's coffin, it was draped in white lilies. "Farewell beautiful Annie and thank you for everything you did for this world" John stepped down from the pulpit. Saron was crying and he could see a couple of other people crying. Carl Milton was in the congregation which John thought was nice.

The vicar asked the congregation to stand for the first hymn 'There is a Green Hill Far Away'. The hymn was well received the congregation were singing loudly. The hymn ended and everyone sat down and the vicar delivered his bible reading before one more hymn. 'Abide with Me' was sung as Annie's coffin was carried out of the church. John, Saron and Saron's mother went to the graveside. The vicar did a small speech and a handful of soil was thrown on the coffin.

Most of the congregation were present at the Tow'd Man. John felt a little awkward with Saron, but this was Annie's day and he owed Annie so much. Saron pulled John on one side, "Look John, I tried to explain to you on the phone, but it's always better to speak face to face. I am sorry for behaving like I have. It's just that the pub takes so much out of me, I never realised what hard work it is. Clara and Denis made it look so easy. Anyway I don't know if you want us to see each other anymore". John thought a lot of Saron but he did think it was over and now he was seeing Sandra. "Saron please don't take this the wrong way, I thought we were finished, but I would like to still be friends". The emotions of the day had clearly got to Saron and she ran into the back room crying and in quite a state. Carol Lestar leaned forward "Now what have you done now, pretty boy?" "Oh, Saron is just very upset about Annie, it's understandable" replied John. "You see young Mr Gammon, I know you and from where I'm stood that's another broken heart!".

Luckily for John his phone rang. "Sorry Carol, I need to take this" "Sorry to bother you Sir, but we have another murder on our hands a body has been found murdered at Cowdale Church" "Not again Yap, male or female?" "Female Sir, very badly beaten and the left ear had been removed. Forensics are there now with Inspector Smarty and

Inspector Lee" "Ok I'll call them" said John. "Sorry about the ringing Sir, with you being at a funeral and all that" "Don't worry Ian, it comes with the territory" and Gammon cancelled the call. He immediately called Dave Smarty. "What have we got Dave?" "Pretty much the same sort of markings as the other murders, Sir. Female, I would say about twenty five years old red hair, slim build. Whoever is doing this, is one sick person Sir" "Listen Dave see if you can get forensics to rush this through for us. I will come back this afternoon" said John. "We can handle it Sir" offered Yap. "I would prefer to come back Dave" "Ok Sir, I will see you in a bit".

John stayed at Annie's wake for another hour, then made his excuses and left for Bixton Police Station. Whilst he was driving to Bixton, he put the local radio station on. To his horror the news had got hold of the murder and were running it.

"Good morning listeners, yet a again we have a murder in Cowdale. I asked earlier for our listeners to phone in with their thoughts on this subject. I have a Mrs Deliah Heaton on the line from Micklock. Good morning Deliah, what are your thoughts?" asked the presenter. "I am shocked that yet another poor, tragic girl has been found. What are the Police Force doing about it? It's been going on for months, people are getting scared to go out" "Good point Deliah. Just what is our inept force doing about it? If Chief Inspector John Gammon would like to reassure the public, he is very welcome to call me and we will get him live on air".

Gammon thought about calling, but he had no facts about this murder and they just wanted cheap air time, it wouldn't serve any purpose just yet.

By the time Gammon got to the station he was livid because now they had the press against them. Gammon knew he was running out of time fast. He pulled into the car park and there was another call, this time it was the Home Office. "Chief

Inspector Gammon?" asked the voice. "Yes" answered John. "This is Humphrey Smart. You are probably aware that we have massive concerns about these murders on your patch and the latest one that the press boys have got hold of, and are running with, is quite a damning article on the abilities of Bixton Police Force. We need to sort this mess out. We have to do something, so I am sending Detective Inspector Sandra Pond and Detective Inspector Andrew Hodgson from The National Crime Agency. It will do two things, hopefully it will speed up the arrest of whoever is doing this and it will keep the press boys of our backs. The Home Secretary has been asked to be kept up to speed on developments. The two officers I am sending are experts in the field of serial killers and will be a major asset to your team Gammon. They will be with you first thing in the morning". Gammon was fuming that was all he needed.

Gammon entered the station and told Yap to get everyone in the incident room. Once they were all there it was plain to see from his body language that he was about to blow. "Smarty, Lee, how the hell did the press boys get hold of this?" John snapped. "I think they were tipped off Sir. They were there at the scene when we arrived" "Any stick men found?" "Yes Sir, one with the body and one on the door to the church". "The press lads have got hold of this and are running quite a nasty article on us in tomorrow's tabloids. To add to that, I have just had the Home Office call me and they are sending two new officers to help. Apparently they are 'experts' in the field of Serial Killers".

John continued, "Let's get a head start shall we, have we a name for the girl?" "Dental records show her to be one Candice Logan. She worked at Pippa's frozen foods on the packing line and her last known address is Bunts Hall, Cowdale" "Not another one that worked there with Denis Clark, there's a picture emerging here again" said John "Inspector Smarty, come with me, let's go to Pippa's frozen foods and get some details on Candice from their HR people".

It was a beautiful afternoon, Dave Smarty was driving, so Gammon had time to admire the beautiful view and to think about his day so far. Annie was now at rest and poor Candice Logan would be joining Annie, but in much worse circumstances. The winding hill up to Pippa's Frozen Foods took in some of the most spectacular scenery imaginable.

Gammon and Smarty arrived and headed for the reception. The young girl on reception was busy on her mobile phone. Gammon was guessing by the tone of the conversation that she was having a argument with her boyfriend. After a few minutes and no sign of her attending to them, Gammon spoke up and showed her his badge. The girl immediately apologised, but then started to tell Gammon and Smarty what an arsehole her boyfriend was. Gammon said, "Can I stop you there, we would like to see somebody from HR please".

The receptionist seemed a bit miffed and she put a call out for Jenny Fenney to come to reception. "Take a seat, she will be along shortly". Fenney arrived, she was a lady in her mid-fifties, very smart and appeared very professional. "Can I help you?" she asked. Gammon and Smarty showed their warrant cards. "Please follow me" she took them into a small side office. "What is this about Chief Inspector?" "You had a Candice Logan working for you?" said Smarty. "Yes, nice girl Candice" "I'm sorry to tell you, she was found murdered this morning". Jenny was clearly upset, "Oh no, not another one" "Yes, I am afraid so. What I would like from you, is some information. I believe she lived at Bunts Hall in Cowdale is that correct?" "Yes, she lived with her mother, apparently she lost her father in a shooting accident when she was a young girl" "What else can you tell me about Candice? Had she any friends at work" asked John. "She pretty much kept herself to herself, although there were rumours she had met somebody" "Do you have a name for this somebody?" "Sorry know I don't Sir". "Ok, well thank you for your time Jenny, I would appreciate if you kept this quiet today as we need to inform her mother" "Of course Mr Gammon" she promised. As Gammon and Smarty left the reception area Denis Clark was coming down the side of the building on a fork truck. He nodded sheepishly to them. "There's my prime suspect Sir" said Smarty. "It all seems too easy for me Dave, so I'm not so sure". Lingcliffe to Cowdale was another lovely run, but Gammon couldn't enjoy it knowing what he had to do next.

Bunts Hall was just a small cottage on the village green not the place of grandeur your mind conjured up. Gammon knocked on the door of the little cottage, it had mullion windows and ivy with beautiful purple and blue clematis intertwined over the porch. After a few moments a lady in her early fifties answered the door. "Mrs Logan?" asked Gammon. "If you are selling for a charity or Jehovah witnesses I am ok" and she attempted to close the door. Smarty put his foot in the way and showed his warrant card.

Mrs Logan quickly opened the door and apologised. "May we come in?" asked Gammon, "Are you on your own Mrs Logan?" "No Sir, Nancy from over the road is here, why?" "Please sit down Mrs Logan". She sat down and Nancy came through. "What's going on Bernice?" "I don't know" she replied.

John spoke clearly, "We have the sad task of informing you that at some point during last night and the early hours of this morning, your daughter has been murdered". Mrs Logan fainted. Nancy grabbed her and Smarty went into the kitchen to get a glass of water. She started to come round, Nancy was telling Gammon how Mr and Mrs Logan had tried for many years to have children and had almost given up, when Candice made an appearance. Mrs Logan was crying hysterically. Nancy made everyone a drink and after five minutes, she was starting to calm down. "Mrs Logan" John began again. "Please call me Bernice Sir". "Bernice did you not wonder where Candice was last night and why she didn't come home last night?" "She had got herself a boyfriend, I'd never met him, but I know he had a big car and she had started stopping over at his house. She was twenty six Mr Gammon and a good girl, never gave me and her father an ounce of trouble and I was pleased she had met someone" "Did she tell you his name?" "All she told me was that he was a lot older than her". "What colour was the car Bernice?" "It was like a minty green, not a nice colour". Nancy chimed in. "It was an old Rover I saw it. Bernice isn't into cars, but my Bob liked his cars when he was alive and we had one like that but in blue".

"I am sorry to say Bernice, I will have to ask you to formally identify your daughter's body. Would you like me to send round the grief councillor?". Bernice shook her head and Nancy said she would go with her. "If there is nothing else I can help you at his very sad time Bernice". She grabbed Gammon's arm, "Just get the person that did this to my Candice" "I will Bernice, I promise you". Gammon and Smarty left and once in the car Gammon turned to Smarty "That's another parent's life ruined Dave" "Doesn't get any easier Sir". Gammon got on the radio to Sergeant Milton "Milton see if you can find anybody in the area that drives a minty green coloured Rover, there can't be many of them about" "Ok Sir" "Oh and arrange to pick up a Mrs Bernice Logan and her friend in the morning and take them to identify her daughter please Sergeant" "Will do Sir".

It was almost five o clock when Gammon and Smarty got back to Bixton they were met by an excited Milton. "Sir, I can only find one minty green colured Rover and guess who owns it?" "Who?" asked John "Denis Clark" replied Milton. "Get him over here" spat Gammon. "Inspector Lee is on the way back with him and his solicitor is waiting in the interview room" "Well done Carl, good shout" said john and he turned to Smarty, "Maybe your hunch is right Dave".

Gammon grabbed a coffee and as he sat in his office waiting for Denis Clarke to arrive, his phone rang, it was the Micklock Globe. "Chief Inspector, do you have any comments about the article we and the National's are running tomorrow?" "Yeah, I have actually. Get stuffed" and John ended the call. Sergeant Yap informed Gammon that Denis Clark was in interview room one with his solicitor and Milton and Smarty. "Ok I am on my way down, thank you Ian".

Milton went through the procedure for the tape. "Well we meet again Denis" "What do you want Mr Gammon?" "Do you own a Rover car?" "Yes I do Mr Gammon" "Is it a minty green colour?" "Yes it is. What is this?" "Do you know a Candice Logan" asked Gammon. Clark suddenly became agitated. "Yes she works with me at Pippa's frozen Foods". "Were you seeing her?" Clark whispered to his solicitor. "Sort of" he replied. "Now Denis, I am not here to play games. Candice Logan was murdered last night". Gammon watched for some kind of expression. Clark seemed in a daze. "Did you understand what I just told you Denis?" Clark hesitated. In a quiet voice he answered, yes. "So where were you last night between the hours 2.00am and 5.00am?" asked John "At home in bed" replied Clark. "Had you seen Candice last night?" "Yes Mr Gammon, she came to my house, we had a take away and a couple of lagers and then she said she was walking home. The clutch had gone on my car and she said she couldn't afford a taxi" "I thought you were married Denis?" "I was, but she left me" "Why did she leave you Denis?" "She said I was a womaniser" "And are you Denis?" "No Sir I am not. Anyway the silly cow took her things and I have never seen or heard from her since. She was always nagging that she didn't like it in Cowdale. She said everybody knew everybody else's business. I am best shut of her" "So you don't know where she has gone then" "Don't know and don't care".

Gammon thought this a little odd but carried on with the questioning. "You see Denis, what I am struggling with here is, the fact two of the murders have been in Cowdale. where you live. You have a history of violence. One of the murdered girls you found and the one last night you were seeing and had seen her last night. Now you have to admit this is more than a coincidence. I am going to hold you for forty eight hours and I will be getting a search warrant for your property" "You people never give in do you? I came here to change my life. I'm not a killer Mr Gammon" "At the moment Mr Clark, we only have your word for that, take him to the cells" John instructed.

Clarke's solicitor turned to Gammon and said that he would be back after forty eight hours and if Clark was gling to be charged, he expected him to be released. "Good day Mr Hammond" said Gammon and showed him the door. Gammon came out of the incident room. "Milton we desperately need to find Chan Chi" "Sir I have a man on the phone who say's he needs to talk to you urgently" "Ok Sergeant, put him through to my office". John picked up the phone, "Hello" "Mr Gammon? It's me, Billy" "You have until tomorrow Billy" said Gammon. "I need to see you today, can I meet you somewhere?" "Right, head for Dilley Dale go into the churchyard, then round the back, past the old oak tree you will see a bench in memory of a Michael Holmes, I will meet you there". The phone went dead. Gammon grabbed his coat and skipped downstairs. "I will be out for a while Sergeant Yap, call me on the mobile if you need me" "Ok Sir".

Gammon jumped in his car and headed for Dilley Dale, he cut through the winding roads of Swinster, over the small bridge separating the two villages arriving at the Church. The church was a sight to behold, parts of it dated back to Norman times. The old oak tree is reputedly the oldest in England at over 2000 years old. Gammon walked passed the big stained glass window, then passed Sir Joseph Stinton's family burial plot. Stinton was a local benefactor, his forefathers built Stinton-in-the- Peak and Sir Joseph lived most of his life in Dilley Hall on the hillside overlooking Dilley Dale. John arrived at the seat to find Billy with two massive men either side of him. "Who are you?" asked John. "We are friends of Billy's, aren't we Billy? We were out walking and Billy said he had arranged to meet you here for a chat, so don't mind us". "Come over here Billy", said John. "He's fine here, aren't you Billy?" "Look you two clowns, I think you should leave". Billy, at this point was shaking so much he almost wet himself.

"Listen you two dog dancers, you tell your boss Chan, that John Gammon is coming for him, and he would be better finding me, than the other way round".

The guy on the right of Billy stood and bent over Gammon, his face up close to Gammon's and his breath was dreadful. Gammon reeled away. "Gammon, Chan Chi doesn't answer to you, and trust me you really don't want to cross him" "Are you threatening me scum bag?" and Gammon took a pace forward. "Just letting you know the situation. Come on Billy let's finish our walk ay? I think the nice policeman is finished here". Billy and the two bruisers walked away. Billy turned to look at Gammon his face was filled with fear. Gammon knew he could do nothing, they hadn't committed a crime. He walked back to the car hoping to see them drive off, hoping he could trace the number plate. He waited almost half an hour but there was no sign.

Gammon decided to make his way back to Bixton. Feeling a little annoyed that they had got to Billy. He arrived at Bixton and was greeted by DI Sandra Pond and DI Andy Hodgson. "Good morning Sir" and they introduced themselves. Gammon asked Yap to show them to his office and he collared Smarty and Lee. "Get Denis Clark's car checked out and I want his house searching. We have twenty fours left before I have to release Clark and we now have the added pressure of Pond and Hodgson, who I will introduce to the team in about half an hour" "Ok Sir I will arrange for the car to get towed back here for Forensics. Inspector Lee and I will get the house searched".

Gammon started to climb the stairs when Yap said he had somebody on the phone wanting to speak with him. Gammon took the call. "Mr Gammon, I am a dead man walking, they have told me Chan has ordered me dead but they are playing with me and have let me go. Chan is staying at a house in Ackbourne, 14, Frogmarch View. It's the only house standing since the rest were knocked down in the fifties". "Billy come into the station and we will protect you". The phone went dead. Gammon ran up the stairs told Pond and Hodgson to come with him and he would explain in the car.

On the way Gammon explained what had happened with Billy Holland. Inspector Pond seemed to question Gammon's methods.

John held his tongue and realised that these two were going to cause him problems.

They arrived at Frogmarch View, a former terraced house which had seen better days. Hodgson went round the back and Gammon kicked in the front door. Inspector Pond started to vomit when she saw the scene in the living room. Holland had been tied to a chair it looked like his neck had been broken. His tongue had been cut out but then stuffed back in his mouth. Hung round his neck was a cardboard sign, it simply said 'dead men don't talk'. Just then hearing the commotion Andy Hodgson appeared at the door and immediately threw up at the sight of poor Billy.

Gammon called the station and told Yap to sort Forensics etc. "Right don't touch anything". When everyone arrived John said, "Wally I need something from this" "I will do my best John. The writing on the cardboard sign had been done in what looks like Holland's blood".

"Right Pond, let's get back and introduce you to the team. "Before you go John" said Wally, "We are pretty stretched at the minute. Is the Rover a priority over this here today?" "If you can work on both Wally, I'd appreciate it. I have the guy whose car it is, in custody until tomorrow, unless I apply for an extension" "I've got Gilkin and three others at the house, I will pull back Stoppard to do the car then John, and we will crack on with this" "I appreciate that mate" "Come on Hodgson you as well, let's go and introduce you two to the team now you have met the Forensic boys".

They arrived back at Bixton Gammon called a meeting in the incident room to get Pond and Hodgson up to speed.

Back at Bixton, Yap showed Gammon the Micklock Globe front page, also the Bixton News. Both headlines were embarrassing. It showed Gammon at the races, glass in hand, with a headline in the Globe which said "That's it Chief Inspector you enjoy yourself while the Peak District lives in fear". The Bixton News ran the headline "Time for Gammon to go back to London and let somebody who can catch a serial killer come and save or community". "Not good reading Sir", Inspector Pond said sarcastically. "It will give you something to report back to Hammond then, wont it Inspector?. Take these two down to the incident room and get the rest of the team there as well please Ian".

The incident room was full. Gammon walked in and it went quiet. "Ok listen up everybody, what I want to say first is newspaper reports don't bother me. What would bother me is if I didn't have my team's full backing". Quite a few hands went up. "Yes, Inspector Lee?" "Just want to say, you are the best man for the job and today's news is tomorrow's chip paper Sir". "Thanks for that Lee". A loud cheer of agreement went up. Inspector Hodgson put his hand up. Gammon spoke "This is Inspector Andy Hodgson and next to him is Inspector Sandra Pond they are both here to help catch whoever is doing these horrific things. Hodgson what would you like to say?" "Well first of all Sir, can I just say that you clearly have the backing of your team. We are not here as any kind of slight on you or your team. Our expertise is in the field of Serial Killers and like you, all we want to get this put to bed". Gammon was a little surprised at Hodgson's statement although he didn't get the same feeling with Inspector Pond.

"I will run through the unsolved murders thus far and if Inspector Lee wouldn't mind bringing you fully up to speed on where we are so that we can all get back to work" "No problem Sir".

"Murder victim one, Maria Dooley, Victim two, Poppy Chi, Victim three, Alice Beadman and Victim four, Candice Logan. They are the victims of a perceived serial killer. We have also had killings of the following people who may or may not be related to the cases, Billy Steele, Billy Holland and Sergeant Wisey".

"We have the following suspects which Inspector Lee will go into further detail about straight after this meeting. Andrew Bilkin, Tony Lacey, Rupert Bare, Denis Clark and Chan Chi. Most of the other suspects are now ruled out. Ok everyone back to work. Sergeant Milton case notes from Forensics on Candice Logan, Clark's Rover car and findings from the house search, please. Thanks" and Gammon left the incident room.

"Sir, a Mr Beeching is online one" "Did he say where he was from?" "No Sir" "Ok put him through to my office". "Hello, Chief Inspector John Gammon here, can I help you?" "I'm not sure that you are capable of being a Chief Inspector Gammon" said the voice. John asked "I'm sorry who is this?". The voice replied, "I am Lord Beeching, Head of Serious Crimes UK and your boss, although you probably haven't heard of me". "Actually Sir, I haven't" "I am assuming DI Pond and DI Hodgson have arrived? I was the man that instructed Hammond to sort this mess out. Have you seen the papers Gammon?" "I have seen the local headlines, yes" "The bloody nationals are running with this. What the hell is happening up there?" "We have suspects Sir, but nothing concrete". "Right, I want Pond and Hodgson to head up the case and to report directly to me". John was annoyed, "With all due respect Sir, I hardly think this is fair" "I don't care if you think this bloody fair Gammon. What I do care about, is the good name of this force. I want a meeting with you in London tomorrow. I will see you at my club, it's the Havant in Kensington Square be there at 2.00pm. Tell the door man you are meeting Lord Beeching" with that the phone went dead. Gammon was fizzing "Who the hell did he think he was? I will bloody well give him my warrant card and he can stick the job" he thought.

It was 4.30pm when Gammon left the station still very annoyed. John's defence mechanism kicked in and he did what he always did when things were going wrong, he headed straight for the pub. In this case

Up The Steps Maggie's. He pulled into the car park and could see it wasn't very busy. "Double Brandy and a pint of Doogle Dog please". The young girl behind the bar duly served him. After an hour John had sunk four double Brandy's. After all he had given up down in London, the Peak District seemed to constantly kicking him in the teeth. The bar slowly filled up with early door's drinkers. It was 6.30pm when he heard a friendly voice, it was Jayne Thornley-Coil. "Are you celebrating John?" "Hardly Jayne sit down" "I don't want to intrude" she said. "You are not intruding. I am on my own".

John told her what had happened. "I saw the Micklock Globe John, that is bang out of order" "Probably true though Jayne, I think I have outstayed my welcome in the Peak District" said John. "Stop talking soft you, have loads of friends John" "Aye and a few enemies by the look of things. Let me get you a drink" "I'll have a Drambuie over ice please John". John went to the bar and ordered the drink for Jayne and just a pint for himself, he thought he best slow down.

"Are you not buying me one handsome?" "Hey Sheba, sorry didn't see you there, what would you like?" "That's a leading question Mr Gammon" and she laughed, "Just a half of lager will be fine" "Are you going to join us?". Sheba looked across to where John was sat, "No best not, two's company and all that" "Give over. Jayne just came talking to me because I was sat on my own" "Well if you are sure I'm not being a nuisance John". Sheba gave John a hand with the drinks and they sat down. "I heard about you making the front page of the Daily Mail John, what a load of tosh, hey Jayne?" "I have just been telling him that" "Just bloody ignore them, you are a great copper and will sort this. I know you will" "Well thanks for the vote of confidence ladies".

It got to 9.30pm and Jayne said she had to leave she had a site meeting at 7.30am on Micklock Moor. "How are you getting home

John?" asked Jayne "I'll take him Jayne" said Sheba, "I have only had two halves of lager" "Ok well chin up Mr Gammon, don't let the buggers grind you down, that's what my old dad would say".

At around 11.00pm they called last orders. "Come on John let me get you home" "Have you got a spare room Sheba?" "Why?" "I just don't fancy going back to an empty house. I'll just hit the Jameson's then I won't be able to function tomorrow" "Come on then Gammon, at least you'll be able to climb the stairs, instead of sleeping on the settee like last time. This is becoming a habit what would Saron say?" "We're not together anymore, Sheba" "Really?" Sheba said, scarcely able to hold the excitement in her voice.

They arrived at Sheba's cottage. "Would you like a drink John? Get down Bones". Bones was Sheba's working dog, which was a very excitable sheep dog. "I'll have a black coffee please Sheba". John watched Sheba walk towards the sink to fill up the kettle her dark hair flowing behind her she was a stunning girl with mischievous blue eyes, perfectly formed white teeth that appeared to light up her whole face when she smiled.

"Do you want sugar John, or are you sweet enough? Sorry daft question" and she laughed. John stood up to take the coffee from her and by accident brushed against her. They both stopped and looked deep into each other's eyes. John kissed her longingly. After what seemed like eternity Sheba pulled away. "John we are not sleeping together, I have had a nice night, but I am not being another notch on your bed post".

"You're not being" "Thanks John, I like you, but you carry too much baggage about and I don't want to be used. Look I am sorry if I read the situation wrong" "You didn't read it wrong John, you just need to decide what you want. Anyway I'm off to bed, your room is the one opposite. I will see you in the morning John" "Will you take me for my car first thing please Sheba?" "Of course, night, night" "Yes, goodnight".

John sat for a minute and thought about what Sheba had said and he knew she was right. He also thought about tomorrow and the meeting with Beeching. Should he call it a day? He didn't need the job, he was financially very secure, but what would he do? He did love the job, other than at times likes these. John went up to his room and was soon asleep. He woke with a bit of a start, he could hear Sheba calling him.

"John, John, breakfast is ready" Sheba had made him a bacon and egg sandwich, it smelt gorgeous. "I hope you like your bacon crispy, tough if you don't" and she laughed. "Thanks Sheba, this is lovely bacon" "All killed on the farm, my uncle keeps pigs and supplies bacon and sausage to Chatsworth, the local shops and the pubs" "It really is good. What's your Uncle's name?" "Ron Fry" said Sheba. "I know him, I'm sure he was a mate of my Mum and Dad's. Is his wife's name, Dolly?" "It was, she died about two years back" "Oh sorry" "No problem, but he has never really got over it, he just lives for his pigs now".

With breakfast finished Sheba gave John a lift to pick his car up from UP The Steps Maggie's, she gave him a little peck on the cheek as he got out of the car. John smiled and thanked her for her honesty. "See you around Mr G" and she drove off.

John drove into work. He had decided to keep Denis Clark in custody for a further seventy two hours. So he informed Yap and explained he had to go to London on urgent business, so would not be in until tomorrow.

Gammon decided to drive down to London and pick up the train at Stanmore. Gammon arrived at the Havant Club spot on 2.00pm. He had decided, if there was a hint from Beeching that he wasn't doing his job properly, then he would tell him to stick it.

The Havant was a grand building with a canopy over the door displaying the name, The Havant Gentleman's Club. John approached the door and was stopped by the doorman, he was wearing a full length black coat, white shirt, black tie and a top hat with gold braid and the Havant club crest emblazoned at the front of the hat. "Sorry Sir, members only". John showed his warrant card and said he had a meeting with Lord Beeching. "I'm sorry Sir, there is no Lord Beeching registered as a member of this club. I have worked here thirty years and I know all forty four members of this club. I also know who is here today and there is no Lord Beeching, and never has been Sir. So if you would kindly step away from the front of the building" "Are you sure?" "Sir I am not in the habit of lying" "I didn't say you were, but you could be mistaken" said John. "No Sir, I am not mistaken".

John was livid this appeared to have been a wild goose chase. He headed back to Stanmore. As he approached his car there was a note on the windscreen. "Enjoyed your trip thick copper?" John could not believe he had wasted a day, he should have checked, but he had been that annoyed he just didn't think. Somebody was playing games with him. John decided to call an old friend he had worked with in London. "Jeremy?" "Is that you John?" "Yes mate, how are you?" "I'm good John thanks. What are you doing? This is a nice surprise" "Been let down at a meeting and wondered if you wanted a quick beer before I leave London?" "Mate, I would've loved to, but I am in Holland on one of these 'information swap things' that they dream up" "No problem Jeremy, another time then" "Yeah, just give me a call, come and stop for the weekend and we can have a catch up" "Will do Jeremy, enjoy Holland".

John headed back to Derbyshire. Halfway up the motorway his phone rang. "John Wally here, we have some DNA from the cardboard that was around Holland's neck. We also have a very sharp knife that we have found in Denis Clark's car, it was taped under the spare wheel, we nearly missed it "Have you got any DNA off that?" "The good news is, yes, it's Candice Logan's" said

Wally. "Right I am on my way back should be at Bixton around 7.00pm. Wally, will you hang on for me?" "I will still be here, we are working our way through everything else John" "Top man Wally, see you in a bit". Gammon was feeling good, after a crap day, things were looking up.

John's timing wasn't far out it was 7.10 pm when he pulled into the car park at Bixton. Gammon felt full of anticipation. "Evening Sergeant Trimble" he said "Evening Sir, on the late shift?" "Something like that Di" and he headed down to Forensics.

"Wally mate, thanks for this" "Anytime John. Right come into my office let me tell you what we have found. The knife has DNA on it from Denis Clark and Candice Logan. We found hairs samples from Poppy Chi also, on the back seat. In the house we found an envelope and inside there was a letter. It had letters cut out from a newspaper, like a blackmail letter. It said "You will never catch me, thick copper. I have all the ears so I know when you are coming Gammon"

"Bang tidy Wally, that's brilliant" replied Gammon. "I have more John" continued Wally, "Police at Dover picked up Chan Chi tonight and he is on his way back here". "Bloody hell Wally, I think all my birthdays have come at once. When he gets here, take a swab from him and let's see if it matches any DNA samples we have from Billy Holland, Sergeant Wisey or Billy Steele". "Fingers crossed hey John" "You bet Wally" replied John.

It was almost 10.00pm when Kent police arrived with Chan Chi, he was taken straight to interview room one. Gammon had spoken to Inspector Lee, he was working late and he agreed to wait with Gammon to interview Chan Chi.

With the interview tape running, Gammon opened the interview. Chi had already arranged for his solicitor to be present while he was being escorted to Bixton. "Can you confirm your name?" asked John "Chan Chi" was the reply. "Mr Chi, are you aware the police have been looking for you for some weeks" "No comment" he said. "What was the relationship with your sister?" "No comment" he said again. Gammon turned to Chi's solicitor. "Please express to your client that not cooperating will not help his cause in the long run" "Chief Inspector Gammon, my client has the right to answer your questions with no comment" "Ok Mr Chi, this can wait until morning, you will be taken to a holding cell where I can keep you for forty eight hours. You will be swabbed for DNA and dependent on the result, the interview tomorrow may take a different course. I would suggest you sleep on your thoughts and possibly co-operate tomorrow. Interview terminated".

"Thanks for staying Inspector Lee" said John. "No problem Sir, looking forward to nailing him tomorrow" "Let's hope so" replied John. John left for the night but called into see Kev at the Spinning Jenny.

"Evening lad, you are late tonight" "It's been a long one, give me a pint of your very best Pedigree Kev" "Have you eaten yet John?" enquired Doreen. "Not yet, Doreen" "Right give me a minute and I will knock you a plate of food up. It's been quiz night and Kev always goes over the top with food for the quiz team". Doreen returned with a bowl of chips, a bowl of Chilli and some rice, three sausages on sticks with little pineapples squares on them and a small bowl of shepherd's pie. "Enjoy that lad, I can't have Emily looking down on me knowing her lad is hungry" "That's very good of you what do I owe you" asked John. "Nothing you daft sod, just get it eaten before it goes cold".

John had another two pints, thanked Kev and Doreen and drove back to the cottage. 'What a day' he thought, as he climbed under the fluffy duvet. John was soon fast asleep. The light woke John, he hadn't quite shut his curtains last night. He looked at the clock 6.10am. "Well I'm awake now, I might as well get up" he said to himself. He showered and got changed for work. It was a beautiful morning as he set of for Bixton.

When he arrived, it was just 8.10am. Word had got out about the DNA results, and all the team were in early. John was so impressed with his team, their commitment was second to none. "Thanks team, we started together we will finish together" said John "We anticipated you would be in early, so took the liberty of phoning Clarks solicitor, he's in interview room one with Milton and Clark Sir" "Great, well done Sergeant Yap".

"Good Morning Denis, I think it's time you came clean about these murders" "What are you on about Mr Gammon?" "We have searched your house and your car and what we have found is enough to charge you". "Mr Gammon I really don't know what you are talking about". Gammon showed Denis Clark the fish knife that was found taped to the underside of the spare wheel in the boot of the car. "Do you recognise this knife Denis?" "No" "Really? Can you explain how it might have your DNA and that of Candice Logan on it?" "Mr Gammon, I don't know. I am telling you the truth". John continued,

"Ok what about a hair that was found on the back seat of your car, which came from Poppy Chi?" "Mr Gammon, Poppy Chi has never been in my car. I only knew her because she worked at the Chinese where I buy my take aways from".

Gammon's experience was telling him something was wrong and this had always been the case with Denis Clark. Deep down Clark really did think he was trying to make a new start in life. "Denis we also found this. Exhibit three for the tape. We are showing Mr Clark a letter found at his house" "This is wrong Mr Gammon, I haven't seen these things" "Denis I am going to ask you one more time, this evidence is damning" "I am being set up Mr Gammon" said Clark.

Just then Sergeant Yap entered the room, he whispered in Gammon's ear. "I'm suspending the interview" and he left the room. Yap had told him Tony Lacey's wife was in interview room two. She was crying and saying she needed to see Chief

Inspector Gammon. "Inspector Gammon. Mrs Lacey how can I help you?" "You interviewed my husband about the Maria Dooley case, he is a violent man Mr Gammon. Last night we had been to the club and as usual Tony was round every bit of skirt he could find. When we got home we had a massive row. I threatened to leave and that's when he said 'leave if you want, there is a killer out there and I know who he is'" Gammon asked her, "Did he say who?" "I goaded him to tell me and he said it was him, but if I told anyone they couldn't prove it and that he had covered his tracks and he had fit somebody up for the murders. I haven't slept all night, I don't know if it was bravado or he was just trying to scare me, but I do know he is capable of these things Mr Gammon" "How do you know that, Mrs Lacey?" "He was head gardener in Oxford when I met him. Tony is a good looking man and in those days he was full of fun. I fell for him, I got pregnant but I lost the baby and our relationship never really recovered from that. It was twenty years ago and I remember a couple of girls being murdered and the killer taking body parts as trophies as the police said. It came on the news one night that they believed the killer worked in either the landscape or farming community. I never thought anything about it at the time, but within days Tony said we were moving to Derbyshire, he'd got work at Chatsworth".

"Well that hardly puts Mr Lacey in the frame, does it Mrs Lacey?" stated John. "When I went to do the banking with Tony's first wage, it was about fifty pounds less than where he worked before and when I told him about it he said he wasn't head gardener at Chatsworth, but he thought it was a good career move. Again I was annoyed because I gave up a good job, so we were quite a lot of money down. About eight months ago I found a letter from somebody called Maria. It basically said he was to stop bothering her, she had a boyfriend and she wasn't interested and if he carried on she would tell his wife. I was furious Mr Gammon, I thought it was starting all over again. Tony tried to deny it saying it was daft Andrew who she was talking about and that she had got mixed up, because I think Andrew Birkin or Bilkin something like that was besotted with her and Tony worked with him"

Mrs Lacey continued, "Again I dismissed it, but all this came together when we had the row last night. I think he has killed these girls, Mr Gammon". "Ok, calm down, Mrs Lacey. I will get somebody to get you a drink. Where is Mr Lacey now?" asked John "He went out after the argument and didn't come back. I am guessing he is at work" "Ok I will get him brought in". Mrs Lacey panicked, "He won't see Mr Gammon will he?" John assured her, "No, I will make sure of that". "I could not live with myself if he is the killer and I didn't say something" she said. "You have done the right thing, Mrs Lacey. Stay in here and I will sort you a drink out".

Gammon went out and told Sergeant Yap what had happened and instructed him to get Mrs Lacey a coffee. Gammon then sent

Inspector Lee to pick up Tony Lacey and get him back to the station urgently.

Next Gammon went back into the interview room with Clark. The tape was started again. "Denis do you know a Tony Lacey?" "Yes, I know Tony why?" "How do you know him?" asked Gammon "He quite often does the church flowers. Once the flower arrangements are slightly losing their freshness, the Duke gives new ones to the church, so Tony brings them up for us. He's a nice guy, we have become good friends". "Have you ever discussed why you moved down here at any time, with Tony Lacey, Denis?" "I don't drink, hardly at all since I got into the church, but one night Tony brought a bottle of whisky that the Duke had given him at Christmas. He said he wanted to share it with me, I didn't want to offend him, so we sat up all night drinking. I did tell him about myself and he listened, but he didn't judge me, Mr Gammon". "Ok, well I intend to hold you for a while longer Denis. Interview suspended". They took Clark back to the holding cell. "What is going on Chief Inspector?" asked Clarks solicitor. "Let's just say I will be in touch" and Gammon left him to make his own way out of the building.

Once the solicitor had left Sergeant Milton questioned "Why with all this damning evidence, why haven't you charged Clark, Mr Gammon" "Watch and learn Carl, watch and learn" said John.

Lacey arrived at the station. Inspector Lee had already told him to call his solicitor and for him to meet him at Bixton. Both solicitor and Lacey arrived at the same time and were shown immediately into Interview room one. Milton started the tape running. "Mr Lacey, thank you for coming here today" "I didn't get given a choice, what is this all about?". "How well did you know Maria Dooley?" asked Gammon, "Oh not that old chestnut again" "Answer the question Mr Lacey" "I didn't know her. A lad I work with Andrew Bilkin, was always banging on about her, but I didn't know her" "Ok, how well did you know Poppy

Chi?" asked Gammon. "Got me there Gammon never heard of her" "What about Alice Beadman and Candice Logan?" Lacey leaned across the table, "I get where this is going, these are the girls that have been murdered correct?" "Yes that is correct. I believe you used to live in Oxford correct?" "Yes, but what has that got to do with anything?" "Well you see Tony, we have been in touch with Oxford Police and at about the time you left Oxford, two girls had been raped and murdered and certain parts of their body, namely their left ears, had been removed as a trophy". "And your point is?". "I am getting to it, Tony. So you left Oxford and why was that?" Lacey replied "The wife didn't particularly like it down there and I fancied bettering myself, so I applied for a job at Chatsworth House, it was better money, so I took it".

John started to put things together, "So let me get this straight. The Oxford Police had narrowed the killer down to either an Agricultural worker or a Landscape gardener, somebody that had contact with soil and fertilizer. And you suddenly decide, to up sticks and come to Derbyshire? It appears the same killer followed you" "Oh piss off Gammon, this is bollocks. Where has this all come from?". Lacey suddenly realised why he was in custody. "This is my barmy wife's doing isn't it?" "Why would you think that, Tony?" "We had a big argument last night and she is paranoid about me and other women".

John questioned him further, "So going back to Maria Dooley, Poppy Chi, Alice Beadman and Candice Logan, are you still saying you didn't know them?" "Yes I bloody am" snapped Lacey. "And you had no involvement with these killings or the killing of two girls in Oxford? Do you know Denis Clark?". Gammon could see the concern showing on Lacey's face. "Denis Clark, I don't think so?" replied Lacey "So you have never delivered flowers to Cowdale church?".

Realising he was getting in deep, Lacey's persona changed. "Oh that Denis, of course, he's a nice bloke, a bit odd. I don't know him very well" "So have you ever been to his house" asked Gammon. "No, why would I?".

Just then Sergeant Yap came in and whispered in Gammons ear. "Just suspend the interview please, while I speak with Sergeant Yap". They left the room. "So what are you telling me Sergeant" "I've just taken a call from Oxford constabulary. They said don't let Lacey go. They have a witness, some girl had been sexually violated before the two girls in Oxford were killed, but the perpetrator had been disturbed and ran off but they have DNA and they would like a sample for matching from Lacey" "This gets better Ian, thanks".

Gammon went back into the interview room. "I am further suspending the interview while we take a DNA sample from Mr Lacey. This could take a couple of hours while we get the results back, so put Mr Lacey in a holding cell" and he turned to Lacey's solicitor "If you wish to get a drink and something to eat the canteen is still open because this could be a long night". With that Gammon went to his office and waited for Oxford Police to arrive.

They arrived along with a lady in her mid-thirties. "Good evening Chief Inspector, I am DI Brand and this DI Mackay. This, Sir, is Jaycee Ricnor, the lady we were telling you about and this is the DNA sample we would like you to compare to see if we have a match". Gammon sent Di Trimble off with the sample. "Take Jaycee to the canteen and sort out a drink for her please DI Lee". Gammon then turned to Brand and Mackay "Ok, come up to my office, Forensics won't take long with the DNA and I can run through what I have gleaned from Lacey and his wife".

Once in Gammons office, Brand turned to Gammon, "What is Mrs Lacey's name Sir?" "Sandra, why?" "Oh it's just I have something in the back of my mind. I arrested a Laureen Lacy quite a few years ago when I was a Bobby on the beat. This woman had severely beaten this guy up in a club. She was very lucky for some reason the man didn't want to press charges. Anyway not our Lacey so let's move on".

After an hour John Walvin knocked on Gammons door, He went in and he nodded to the Oxford DI's and turned to Gammon. "No match Sir. We checked our data base and no match there either, sorry. Tony Lacey isn't your man" "Bugger! but thank you John".

John spoke to the two detectives. "Well gents, sorry for the wasted journey" "No problem Sir, we might have struck lucky. Good luck with your cases". The officers and Jaycee Ricnor left Bixton for the journey to Oxford.

Gammon grabbed Lee, "Come on, enough mucking about. I am going to charge Denis Clark, we have enough on him". They reconvened the interview with Clark and his solicitor. "Denis Clark after much deliberation, we have decided to charge you with the murders of Maria Dooley, Poppy Chi, Alice Beadman and Candice Logan. You do not have to say anything, but what you do say, will be taken down and maybe used against you in a court of law. Take him away Inspector Lee".

Clark kept protesting his innocence, "It isn't me Mr Gammon" and he said this over and over again as he was led away. Gammon left the interview room. "Sir just heard from Kent Police, not good I am afraid. The vehicle carrying Chan Chi had an accident on the way here and the two officers were killed. Chan is nowhere to be seen" "Shit, we get one result and then another one slips through our fingers. I am going to release Lacey, I don't like the guy, but everything he has lied about doesn't stack up to murder, unlike Clark".

They informed Lacey that he was free to go, but Gammon did say "Next time, if there is one, don't lie about things, because most of the things you have told me have been un-true" "Mr Gammon, I know I lied to you but it looked bad for me. I'm not a killer honestly". "Release Mr Lacey Sergeant, you are free to go Mr Lacey".

Gammon then went to see Sandra Lacey. "Sandra, I am very sorry but it isn't your husband that was doing these things, so we have had to release him" "You are wrong Mr Gammon, he is very violent, he will kill me" "If you need an officer to escort you home, we can talk to Mr Lacey that would not be a problem". At this point Sandra Lacey became aggressive "You bloody idiots, the lot of you and she stormed out". DI Lee turned to Gammon "She wasn't a happy bunny Sir" Gammon just shook his head. "Right that's me done for the night, let me know if they get Chan Chi, Sergeant Trimble". "I will Sir".

Gammon locked his office and thanked everyone for their hard work "We will have a tidy up meeting in the morning" he said as he was leaving.

Once home, John was so tired he climbed straight into bed and was soon fast asleep. He didn't wake until 8.00am, so he quickly showered and grabbed a strong coffee and left for another day at the Station.

"Morning Sergeant" "Morning Sir" "Any news from Kent?" "Nothing Sir". Gammon went to his office and told Trimble to organise a 9.00am meeting in the incident room, I want everyone to attend.

The room was full by 9.00am when Gammon strode in. "Ok, cut the noise. Last night I took the step of charging Denis Clark with the murder of the four girls, based on evidence found by Forensics. Tony Lacey was also interviewed based on evidence given by his wife, but was released without charge. Chan Chi was arrested by Kent Police he was last believed to be heading for France. Kent Police were escorting him back to Derbyshire, when it is believed an accident occurred. The two officers lost their lives and there is no sign of Chan Chi" "Sir?" "Yes, DI Pond" "Should there not be a press release about Denis Clark and Chan Chi?" "All in good time DI Pond". "Right thank you everyone for your efforts, we just need Chan Chi now". Gammon left the room.

DI Scooper followed him. "You ignoring me?" she asked. "Sorry Sandra, a lots happened over the last twenty four hours" "What like Sheba Filey and you at Up The Steps Maggie's?" "Look Sandra, I'm not prepared to discuss this at work and he marched off".

"Sir, just received a call form a neighbour of Tony Lacey's, she says he is dead!" "Get your coat Scooper" he said to Sandra and rushed out. Gammon drove like the wind to Cowdale and to the home of the Lacey's. They rented a cottage on the road to Cowdale. As Gammon and Scooper approached, they could see a crowd standing outside the cottage. They got out of the car and were met by a lady "I'm Mrs Ada Allsop, neighbour of Sandra's" "What do you know Mrs Allsop?" "Early hours of this morning Tony and Sandra had been arguing, which wasn't uncommon, poor Tony would often have a black eye on a Saturday night at the Legion" "Really?" said Gammon. "Oh yes, very violent women is Sandra and as strong as an ox. Don't let her appearance fool you. Nobody in this village would say anything to Sandra. Tony on the other hand was a bit of a joker, always winding folk up and telling jokes. Think he has had a few affairs to be honest, but I don't blame him with how Sandra is". Gammon looked at Scooper. Can this really be the same timid women he had met only last night?

"I haven't finished yet" said Mrs Allsop. "Sorry Mrs Allsop" said John. "Call me Ada" "Sorry, Ada". "Well it was about 6.00am, I knew it was that time because my Fred cycles to work at the same time every day. He works at the chicken factory, been there almost forty years, you know" "Can we just stick to the Lacey's please Ada" said john impatiently. "Well, I was only saying. Anyway Fred had just left and I always go down to the gate and wave him off, I always have done all our married life. That's the problem with young one's today" "Ada, just tell me about the Lacey's please!". "Well, I heard Tony scream, so I ran next door and knocked on the door and asked if everything was ok. I didn't get an answer, so I looked through the curtains and I could see Tony in a pool of blood, with Sandra stood over him with the knife. I called you and then went and got my best friend, Lily Stones. She is a lovely lady, I will have to introduce you". "Ok thanks Ada, now please everyone go home there is nothing to see".

Gammon knocked on the door. "Sandra, it's John Gammon, let me in please". She shouted back, "He attacked me, Mr Gammon!!" "Open the door Sandra, or I will be forced to force it open". Sandra Lacey appeared at the door covered in blood, with the knife still in her hand. "Put the knife down Sandra". Sandra dropped the knife, it bounced on the kitchen tiles just missing Scoopers foot. Scooper radioed for an ambulance and Forensics.

"Just sit down Sandra while I look at Tony". Gammon closed Tony's eyes, he was dead. "Did you kill Tony, Sandra?" She nodded. "Is that yes?" She nodded again. "Sandra Lacey, I am arresting you for the murder of Tony Lacey" and he read Sandra her rights. By now John Walvin had arrived with the Forensic team, Scooper took Lacey to the car. "Keeping us busy John" said Walvin. "You like it really, Wally" and they both laughed.

Gammon, Scooper and Sandra Lacey headed back to Bixton, there was an eerie silence to the drive back. Gammon could not stop thinking about what Ada Allsop had said about Sandra and Tony Lacey. There was this quiet woman, making out her husband was violent and all the time it was her. Something wasn't ringing true.

Gammon then remembered the name, Laureen Lacey, the one the Oxford Police had mentioned. Once in the interview room, Sandra Lacey had the duty solicitor sit in on the interview. "Sandra Lacey, is that your correct and full name?" "Yes" she replied. "Did you, in the early hours of this morning, kill your husband with a carving knife?" "Yes" "Why Sandra?" asked Gammon. "I feared for my life. I told you that when I spoke with you last night, but you still released Tony".

"Well you see Sandra, I am getting a different picture from the villagers of Cowdale" "What do you mean?" "People say that you are the violent person in the relationship". Suddenly Sandra lost it, she jumped up shouting "they are lying bastards". Scooper and Smarty restrained Lacey. Seeing a different side of Sandra now, John instructed Scooper. "Scooper, I want Mrs Lacey's DNA taking and a full medical. We will reconvene once this is done". Scooper took Lacey to the doctor to perform the medical and take the DNA. Gammon grabbed a coffee and waited. They eventually returned. Lacey sat down with her solicitor and Scooper asked Gammon to step outside the room. "Sandra Lacey's DNA matches the DNA from the girl in Oxford that was sexually violated. Not being ignorant here, but I keep hearing 'sexually violated' what exactly does that mean?" "It can mean many things Sir, but mainly it means it was a human body used on the victim" "Wow, this changes things. Sergeant Yap, inform Oxford Police what we have on Sandra Lacey".

"Sandra what sort of job did you have in Oxford?" asked John. "What has this got to do with me defending myself against Tony?" "Just answer the question?" "I worked at B&Q" "Whereabouts in B&Q?" "I was in the garden centre, I used to plant all the seedlings" she said. "Right, so going back to Tony, what happened?" "When I got back from the station, he was saying that I had dropped him in it with you people and that I was a liar, all these nasty things. It went on for hours then he suddenly flipped and said he was going to kill me. He lunged at me and knocked me to the floor. I had been making a cheese sandwich so I had the knife in my hand, he jumped on top of me and the knife penetrated his heart. Yes, I said I killed him, but his action of falling on top of me meant he fell onto the knife, so technically he killed himself" "I will be the judge of that Sandra. I intend to charge you with the murder of Tony Lacey".

"Last night we were contacted by Oxford Police, who have DNA from a young girl who was violently and sexually violated and guess what? the DNA matches yours. Would you like to comment on that?". Lacey went quiet. "You have gone by a different name in the past haven't you Sandra?" Lacey would not look up. "Sandra the game is up, I want answers and trust me it's better that you co-operate". Lacey looked up and it was like she had a split personality. She growled at Gammon "Yes I did that to the bitch and all those others that my scumbag husband had flirted round" "Hold it there Sandra, by others, who do you mean?" "Those two in Oxford, I killed them and attacked that girl but I was bloody disturbed before I could kill her, so tell her she is a lucky bitch".

Gammon continued, "What about the four girls here in the Peak District?" "That bloody Maria Dooley, he was besotted with her, but she thought she was too good for my Tony". Gammon was starting to see Lacey's twisted mind coming out. "What about Poppy Chi" "Oh yeah the druggy girl, she was just a slapper. I straightened her up" and she laughed. "Alice Beadman?" "Actually she was ok I thought, but she came in the Legion on her hen night and was playing up to Tony so she had to have it as well" said Lacey. "Why Candice Logan?" asked John. "I didn't like her, she was up her own arse, she looked down at me and my Tony" "So why did you set Denis Clark up then?" "Tony told me all about him. I thought he had been out with some girl but he told me about Clark and how he had reformed his life and that they had sat drinking whisky all night. I knew he was easy to set up, the dumb ass, so I broke into his house and car and I knew you plod's would eventually search the house and car" and she laughed. "Why did you take a trophy like their ears?" "I was fair, I always did it just as they were dying to see the look on their faces?" "Where are they now?" "I never kept them, I just threw them away". "What about the stick men drawings found with the bodies and at the churches?" She laughed, "Just my bit of fun, kept you lot guessing" and she laughed again. This woman was criminally insane. Gammon charged her with all the murders and told Smarty to put her in the holding cells ready to be transferred to Oxford for their investigations.

"Release Denis Clark please Milton. All charges against him are dropped. Arrange a press conference for 2.00pm this afternoon please." "Where Sir?" "Get a conference room set up at Bixton Spa Hotel". Gammon felt elated in one sense, but relieved that he hadn't told the world that Clark had been charged earlier.

"Sandra arrange for a buffet for all the team up at the Tow'd Man" ordered John. "Is that a good idea John" "Yes Angelina and Saron were involved in the case, it's only correct we celebrate together" "Ok, I hope you know what you are doing" she said.

Gammon arrived at Bixton Spa Hotel at 1.45pm, the press boys and TV cameras were already waiting. He chose Dave Smarty to sit alongside him. "Ladies and gentleman, we have today, charged a forty six year old women from Cowdale with the murders of Tony Lacey, Maria Dooley, Poppy Chi, Alice Beadman and Candice Logan". A voice spoke up. "Roy Parkington, Daily Mail. Mr Gammon have you got a name?" "Yes, she is Mr Tony Lacey's wife, Sandra Lacey". "Mick Trott, Sky News. Mr Gammon how did you figure out she was the killer?" "I was contacted by Oxford Police, we received DNA from a previous crime in Oxford of a similar nature and the DNA matched. Mrs Lacey then confessed to the killings and is now in a holding cell waiting to be transferred to Oxford for that force to carry out their own investigations". "James Crowfoot, Micklock Globe, I would imagine you are relieved Mr Gammon after the adverse publicity". This man really rankled Gammon. "Mr Crowfoot the adverse publicity, whilst it may sell papers, does not help the investigations or team moral. My officers have spent an enormous amount of time away from their families and I would like to thank them personally for their efforts. That's your lot gents". Someone shouted, "Is it true you arrested and charged another man Gammon? What about the other murders Billy Holland, Billy Steele and one of your officers Wisey?" Gammon responded, "They are on-going investigations, thank you, no more questions".

Gammon and Smarty left by the side door and headed back to Bixton. "Well done Sir you handled that really well". "I'm not too pleased with myself, I was taken in with that women and charged the wrong person initially. I would like to know how that got out Dave". "You can't keep secrets in these small towns Sir. Let's be pleased with what we have achieved and have a few beers to celebrate tonight".

ANNIE TANNEY

John left the station and drove down to Hittington, he had informed the landlord that he would be leaving in a month now that Jayne Thornley- Coil had finished the holiday cottages. He had to sort out the paperwork for the houses he had been left. The money in the bank, he wanted to give to Dilley Dale Cottage Hospital on the understanding that it was renamed Annie Tanney Cottage Hospital in memory of Annie. He thought he would also take a couple of weeks off, once Chi was found and that was sorted, he would then to try and find his half-sister in France.

John showered put on his light blue Paul Smith shirt with a pair of brown trousers and his light tan shoes and headed for the Tow'd Man. He arrived and to his surprise almost everyone was there. He opened the latched door and was greeted by Saron who was holding a big cake which simply said "Well done Bixton Nick". They all sang 'for he's a jolly good fellow". John told Angelina the bar was on him, not just for the police, but for anyone in the pub. She smiled and informed the bar staff. Saron had arranged Tony Baloney to do the disco so this had turned into a proper party. At one point in the evening John looked across the room at Angelina, Saron and Sheba all talking and Sandra and Joni who had come with Carl. Both surprisingly, were talking to each other.

Time was moving on for John Gammon and this case had been tough for him and his relationships, he wasn't sure if he could continue doing the job he once loved. Maybe Annie dying had affected him more than he thought.........

ANNIE TANNEY

Annie Tanney is book five in the series about John Gammon a Peak District Detective. We have seen much turmoil in John's life in his career and private life.

I hope you have had chance to view some of the fictitious places on my Facebook page Colin Joseph Galtrey (Author). There are quite a few photographs depicting the places I write about. You may know them as somewhere else in the Peak District. Hope you find the time to visit the pubs John Gammon frequents and have as much enjoyment trying to work out the characters.

To everyone that has kindly taken the time to read and review the John Gammon series may I offer a very big thank you to you all for your support and for sharing in the trials' and tribulations of John Gammon.

ANNIE TANNEY

When I meet people that have read the books, I am often asked who is this character based on and where is this or that place. My answer is always; the books are based on fiction and are written purely from my imagination. But I am sure as you read them you will assume and that's half the fun of the books.

My latest book which should be on Amazon at the end of July 2016 is called **"Looking for Shona"** This book is mainly set in London, Ireland and the Caribbean it is my first historical love story so quite exciting for me personally. The John Gammon books will start again hopefully Christmas 2016.

Thanks again for all your continued support.

CJ Galtrey

ANNIE TANNEY

Printed in Great Britain
by Amazon